STILL WAITING IN THE DARK

CM Thompson

For the K Thompsons

Nothing says I love you quite like having three books that are all about violence, murder and hate, dedicated to you.

For Ashley

Thank you for all your help in making this book a book, Without you, this book would have been burnt on a pyre many months ago.

FOREWORD

This book refers to events that happened in the author's previous two books "What Lies in the Dark" and "Who Killed Anne-Marie?"

Reading those books won't answer any questions you might have. Except for maybe two.

CHAPTER ONE

Some people live very boring lives, others are a little more exciting. Some people are never quite aware of what is really going on around them, just how often they walk so close to something wicked. Other people realise seconds too late, where the real darkness lies.

It is amazing just how often people look in the wrong direction when they are scared. They turn towards the obvious danger, leaving their backs exposed. What's also amazing is how connected everything is, how lives overlap with each other, but at the same time, everyone is so disconnected and alone. The same thing that brings people together can be the same thing that tears them apart.

A certain serial killer is a great example of this, one lamely named "The Numbers Killer" by an unimaginative media. Years ago, this killer mercilessly struck the city over and over, leaving each of his victims branded with a number on her hand. The killings have stopped now but no one was ever brought to justice for these murders. One of his victims was called Joanna Reagan. Joanna still lies buried in the forest, the number eight engraved in her hand, her skin, her pain all long disintegrated.

The closest anyone ever came to finding Joanna was when eight-year-old Anita Gardner, fell down hard, in a dark corner of a forest, onto Joanna's shallow grave. Perhaps if Anita had looked down, perhaps if she'd realised what was under her hand, perhaps Joanna would have been found. Perhaps Anita would have spent a few years in therapy. Perhaps she might even have lived past sixteen, having already been taught a valuable lesson about looking closely in the right direction. But now, like Joanna, she is still missing, never far from people's minds but never found. Only her mother still believes that one day, she might come home.

Not that she has a home to come back to. The remaining Gardners were all but forced out of the city, driven out partly by the fall-out from a well-intended but misguided media campaign, partly by the stares and hushed whispers. Not forgetting of course those triggering, echoing, memories. On her bad days, Anita's mother could not even enter a room without being painfully reminded of Anita. Here is where Anita drew over the walls, here is where she played with her toys. Here is where she was very much alive. She couldn't bear watching her daughter's friends grow older, leaving for new adventures without Anita.

Her mother still calls the old home from time to time, just to make sure that the new occupants definitely have their address in a safe place, are they sure? Are they sure they haven't seen anything? Sorry to keep checking like this, it's just …

Alexandra lives in that house now, but it's not her home either. Alexandra listens, confused, to those calls, listening to her father comforting in a tone she doesn't recognise, assuring this stranger that yes he understands. No, he would feel the same way. Yes he definitely still has their new address and number, no, honest to god, no, he swears he won't let anyone else have it, no matter who they claim to be. Alexandra knows when her father has hung up the phone because the tone of his voice instantly goes from compassionate to condemning. She doesn't know what he means when he says that the bitch deserved it, what kind of parent lets their sixteen-year-old go out, UNSUPERVISED, drinking with strangers UNDERAGE, and if Alexandra even so much as looks at a pub... Alexandra doesn't understand why she can't look at a pub, but obediently averts her eyes when passing one. Not that her father notices.

Her stepmother makes appropriate agreeing noises, whilst continuing to paint or file her nails. Alexandra is scared of her stepmother's long nails, they remind her of talons, ready to seize and scratch. She is scared of her stepmother's new things, which she has been intently warned not to touch, she knows that anything that might even look like it belongs to her step-mother is off limits.

Alexandra would like very much to go back to her old home. She doesn't understand this new life. She doesn't under-stand the phone calls and her father's personality changes. She doesn't understand why they moved here or why her mother went away and this new woman has taken her place. Why the other children laugh at her and won't let her play with them. Why people think they have to talk to her LOUDLY and sssll-looooowwllyy.

One thing she does understand, with childish certainty, is that the house at the bottom of her street is a bad house. She doesn't have to be warned about it, she just knows. If Alexandra has to walk anywhere near it, when she is being hurried along and she can't possibly avoid it, she takes a deep breath and runs past it, as fast as she can. Always holding her breath for as long as possible, as if the mere matter of inhaling near this house will bring on a certain death. It is only a matter of time before some monster bursts out of those rotting windows, its fangs drooling in it's desperation to feast on flesh, it's claws bared and ready to dig deep. Alexandra intends not to be within dragging distance, when it finally does.

Everyone knows, without being told, that monsters live in houses like this one. People have been whispering about this one for years. They call it the Krill's house, she doesn't know who the Krill is or was, or why he has such a funny name, but it doesn't matter because the Krill was taken away to prison and is never ever coming back. What matters is that a new monster lives there now, an even worse monster. Sure, the house looks empty, but it's not.

Her father has a lot to say about this house too, lots of

scathing words and angry hand gestures. He uses words like "eye sore" "should be condemned." He has plans for that house, plans he won't share. Alexandra hopes that soon, a hero will appear, ready to take the monster away to monster prison or wherever the bad monsters go. Then someone nice will move in, someone who will fix the roof, plant roses, maybe even someone willing to be her friend. But in the meantime, she can never take her eyes off that house. Never. Which means she will never notice who else is watching her, waiting for the right moment. You see, what Alexandra doesn't understand is that monsters don't live in ruined houses, they don't live anywhere that might draw attention to themselves. They live in normal houses, they try to appear normal, as normal as possible, encouraging people to like them, to trust them. They wait and wait for that one single opportunity to welcome you inside their normal houses, waiting for that one special moment.

Like the dead, the real monsters are very good at waiting.

CHAPTER TWO

Nobody else knows this yet, but tonight, tonight is the last night of happiness. The last night of raising glasses with unguarded smiles, with the ease of those who think that their worst days are far far behind them. It is a Friday night, the middle of October and people are out, enjoying those last nights before Christmas obligations snatch away their precious time and money. A night to let loose and laugh. No one is paying much attention to the two girls in the corner. Some are purposely going out of their way not to see them. Others send drinks their way, still without openly acknowledging the girls and their knowing smiles. If people knew, that within months, those girls who walked like they owned the world, would both be dead, they might have paid even less attention.

Jenna had noticed one of the girls early on in the evening, noticed her ruby red stilettos with pure admiration and with the jealously of someone who is ten years older, who knows she can never again wear a heel that high. Jenna had watched those shoes strut to the bar, before she looked around and noticed several others, also watching the shoes, or watching something else slightly higher. Now, she sees flashes of red, hears the unmistakable clop and knows those shoes are on the move again. She is no longer watching them, instead she is only taking long gulps of regrets and cocktail, her attention on her friends. They are talking about future plans, a little holiday is on the cards and they are trying to agree on a place to go. Jenna personally doesn't care where she goes, she just wants to feel warm again. When she is warm, she feels calmer, more secure. Tonight, she is mostly drinking to forget that it is still only October and the nights are only going to get colder and darker.

It is a clear night, that last peaceful night, and she watches the stars through dead eyes, long past feeling the cold or the pain. Unaware, the city around her, sleeps on. Those who thought they were safe now, those who swore that they would never again be afraid of a monster, are still blissfully unaware that they about to break their promise.

The sun rises on Saturday morning, bringing with it dog walkers and joggers, all hurrying quickly through the Park, adverting their eyes from the used condoms, litter and torn strands of hair. Dogs whine and pull on their leads but their owners keep walking, eyes firmly fixed ahead. Past experience has taught them the importance of looking away. They keep their gaze upwards, pretending to admire the fine blue skies, the first fall of leaves, anything and everything but they always resist the urge to look down. But there is always someone, some-one who just has to look and scream. Raising the alarm just so everyone knows who is back.

If someone were to describe DCI Samantha Colvin, the politest explanation would involve the words pain in the backside. Even the nicer words like dedicated and hardworking would be ac-companied by dramatic eye rolls. Her partner, Nicolas A. Grimm is mostly noted for his dad jokes and considered just about as useful as damp toilet paper. He is still considered to be the per-sonable and more tolerable of the two.

Here is another interesting fact about Sam Colvin, she will never ever truly forgive herself for how she reacted to the news of a new victim, no one should ever react to the news of murder with "Oh, thank fuck!" Thank fuck for a distraction from the horrible case she was already working, 'working' really meaning going nowhere fast with.

She is still stuck with that case, the one concerning the demise of Anne-Marie Mills. Still being harangued with phone calls from Anne-Marie's bitch of a mother, still haunted by that clinging smell of despair. That case will never truly go away, every time she sniffs a scent of alcohol, dust or misery, which is often, she will be reminded. But at least she has something new to think about, something new to torture herself at night with. This new victim has become every surviving officers new top priority. The Numbers Killer is back.

The sense of relief Colvin had felt, dissipated with the first of the crime scene photos, shuddering out of her with a quiet gasp. Just when she thought she was used to the worst of humanity, someone had to go one step further. She could handle seeing pictures of bruises and blood splatter, pictures of personal hell, they were all she had been staring at hourly on the Anne-Marie Mills case. She can study crime scene pictures professionally and assess them, analyse them without a problem. She can handle the eyes, the age of the victim, the blood but not those pictures of torn tufts of hair. Something inside Colvin whimpered at the sight of those long blonde strands, damp with blood.

The victim's name was Ruby Williams and someone had hated her so much, that day on Friday 19th October, some time between 11pm and midnight, they had beaten her, torn out her hair, strangled her, then cut open her throat. Then just to finish the job, they had carved a deep number one into her left hand. Then they left her, her body crushed against dying plants, in a flower bed at Kings Park, without a second thought.

That's what really has everyone's attention. That number one. No one on the police force likes numbers, those little everywhere reminders of some very bad years. No one in the city is particularly fond of numbers either, especially not when they are carved into the hand of a young victim.

Not since The Numbers Killer, not since that utter bastard struck the city, showering blood and fear everywhere he went. They thought a lot about him but knew next to nothing about him. That was the worst part, not knowing what was really lying in the dark. He struck the city for years, killing at least eleven women, maybe twelve, thirteen, twenty or thirty-one, depending on who you asked, where you looked and what you believed. Some of his victims were killed brutally, some more quickly, but all were left dead or dying with a number on their hands. It has been three years and they still haven't found all of his victims. The killings abruptly stopped with the death of one Joseph Walker and the cases were considered to be closed. But, if you gave anyone in the city half a chance, or even some police officers half a minute, they will tell you all about the cover ups, that the true number of his victims has been suppressed (so that the police don't look bad ... so the police don't look worse.) There are over a hundred websites dedicated to him, five published books on him, three more works in progress, rumours of a movie and one small plaque dedicated to the female police officer who died stopping him. Victoria Bulrush, who has left behind one devoted husband and two sons, who now have some serious issues. What people won't tell you, is what they did, the mistakes they made, trying to protect themselves from what was in the dark.

They don't speak much about those eleven women. They speak even less of the missing women. The first known victim they can't say much about, of her they only found a few scattered bones, a facial reconstruction and a polaroid. It is only from the polaroid that they know that this still-a-Jane-Doe was branded with a number two.

There were others, they know that, Jane Doe died somewhere between two and five years before the next known victim, Fran Lizzie Taylor. Everyone knows about the twenty-two branded on her right hand. Everyone knows what her mother did. What the husband of the next victim, Adelina Sasha (26) did. Many a scathing news article or think piece has been written about what they did. The police remain tight lipped about their own fallen Shannon Leona (30) and Victoria Bulrush (no number) still trying to protect their officers and their families. Robert "Robbie Bobbie" Leona is still their friend after all. The others,

8

Stella McQam (28), Isobel Hilarie (34), Madison Albrook (36), Kim Donaghue (38), "Rosie" (40) Brandi Parr (42) and Ebony Jackson (44) have just been quietly buried in people's minds, not considered interesting or scandalous enough to be anything more than a chapter or in some cases, a footnote.

Colvin can remember following the media reports of The Numbers Killer, with interest, feeling safe only because she was miles away from the chaos. She transferred to the city months after his death, or alleged death, depending on who you spoke to. She can still remember her own relief that she would never have to work on a case as bad as that one. (But still wanting to, just to prove she could.) When she first got here, everyone talked about him, everywhere she went. Hairdressers, taxi drivers, store assistants, everyone had their own theory about who he really was, what the police should have done, about what was now being covered up. It was all anyone would talk about, to the point she stopped telling people she was a police officer.

Sam Colvin shudders again, with the memories of hundreds of paranoia-fuelled "discussions." She tries to turn her attention back to the briefing, which has now turned into a rather animated argument about whether this really is The Numbers Killer back again or not. One officer is already listing the old suspects he wants questioning, a satisfied gleam in his eye. They are losing sight of the victim in the sea of accusations and I-told-you-sos! Funny enough, it is the officers who were known friends of Walker, who are bleating the loudest. Maybe Colvin needs to have a quiet word with someone higher up, about checking their alibis, just in case.

No one has noticed so far that she hasn't said anything. She is trying to form her own, more rational, arguments for why this couldn't possibly be the same killer, based on a few crime scene photos, reports and her already frazzled memory. Really, she needs them to stop talking for five minutes so she can think. Annoyed, she pulls out a spare piece of paper, clearly heading the page, "To Do." She writes:

'Find Ruby William's mobile.'

Then she underlines it twice. Colvin thinks that will provide the answer to her biggest question: What was Ruby Williams doing, out alone at Kings Park? Given that Ruby was a seventeen-year-old girl, her phone was likely to have been her main source of communication, so why hasn't anyone mentioned it so far? She expects that Ruby's phone will be able to tell them a lot about her last movements. It might even tell them what Ruby was doing in the park, dressed in a leather jacket, short leather skirt and big red heels.

'Set up surveillance'

They need to set up some kind of surveillance on the park, in case the killer comes back to the area. Also try to obtain as much CCTV footage as they can. Maybe have an officer there to interview any regulars, who may have noticed something out of the ordinary.

'Research'

Research The Numbers Killer is an obvious one, maybe too obvious. But also any information she can find on copycat killers, maybe do a refresher on organised serial killers.

It is a pretty pathetic list, she admits to herself, knowing she can do better, but is unable to think straight. So many thoughts running through her overloaded mind, so many phone calls to make. Why are they wasting time arguing? They know they need to act fast, regardless of whether this is The Numbers Killer or not, so why are they wasting time?

Time for a second list, since she can't get a word in edgeways, between the officers with old grievances and the officers with new grievances. This sheet she headers with "Reasons why this couldn't be The Numbers Killer." Taking the time to print the words neatly and clearly. Next to her, Grimm reads over her shoulder, rolls his eyes and goes back to his own sheet of paper, which comprises mostly of doodles.

Colvin stares hard at the picture still on screen, that hand, that cut. Some officers have already pointed out that it might not be a number one at all. But they don't think it was a defence wound, Ruby had no real defence wounds, no chance to think about fighting back. That cut on her hand, you could argue it was purposely cut, the mark of a practiced killer. But you could also argue, given the severity of her other injuries, that it was the result of a frenzied attack.

She makes a note on the To Do list, to compare this number against the other numbers, the numbers imprinted on the other Number Killers victims, As she sits, contemplating comparing mutilations like some weird kind of handwriting/ number analysis, it slowly dawns on her just how fucked up her job can be sometimes.

If you take away the number, what would you think this is? She asks herself silently. Her first thoughts are: Rape attack, gone wrong. (Another item for the To Do list, no one has mentioned any signs of sexual assault, double check.) But then, would there not be more signs of disturbances in her clothes? More defence wounds? More lower body injuries?

Maybe it was a personal attack of a different nature? There was a lot of rage in the attack, that suggests a personal kill, or, also as someone else has already argued, it could just be the result of The Numbers Killer releasing three years of pent up rage.

She also couldn't argue that the killer didn't know what he was doing and it is rare to see that with crimes of passion or first kills. This attack appears to have been fairly well planned and practised, score one for those insisting that this is the work of The Numbers Killer.

But then, if this isn't the work of The Numbers Killer and it was someone new, someone's first attack, first time criminals, they usually commit their first offence close to somewhere they are familiar with. Somewhere close to where they live, work, or visit very frequently. There are always exceptions to this, as with anything really but generally they pick a place where they feel confident, a place they know the screams won't be heard. All the more reason to go back to Kings Park, find out who the regular visitors are.

But if this really was The Numbers Killer, where has he been these last few years, why start again now? Is this the start of a new code or the continuation of an old one?

She looks down at her clearly headed, but otherwise blank paper, if she can't come up with a clear argument, they will keep ignoring her. This is maddening! No, the Anne-Marie Mills case is maddening, this is confusing, deliberately misleading. It is hair pulling, eye twisting, pure vexation!

Over three hundred contacts.
Thirty four missed calls.
14 from "Dad"
4 from "Daddy P"
1 from "Daddy S"
3 from "BF name"
2 from "Your Bitch"
2 from Unknown
1 from "F.C."
One text from "Carl-E" saying "U home?" followed by eight calls, one every ten minutes.

Grimm sighs, staring at a screen that makes no sense. He continues, not for the first time, to quietly curse Colvin under his breath. She just had to ask, "Where is Ruby Williams' mobile?" and you just know, someone was just waiting for some gullible officer to ask that, that someone else had already taken a look at it and said "Oh no, not it!" and then waited innocently, for some-one else to ask. So they could say "oh yes, here it is, you deal with it."

So that became their assignment, look at Ruby Williams' mobile and it soon became apparent that Ruby spent a lot of time arranging meetings with older men, who were keen to demonstrate their desire for a discreet but fun time. She had been exceedingly popular on several sugardaddy websites, those annoying websites that really value anonymity and discretion. Which made finding any of her rejected 'Daddies' or even some of her current 'Daddies' extremely difficult. Especially since several members on these sites, went inactive within minutes of Ruby's photo being shown on the news. "Daddy P" and "Daddy S" have permanently disconnected their mobiles and Grimm thinks those mobiles have probably been carefully wiped, then broken and carefully disposed of, with sweaty shaking hands.

Grimm doesn't suspect any of these men. Sure he would like to have stern talks with some of them, but he doesn't suspect any of them to be linked to Ruby's murder. If this was a personal attack, given how careful the assailant had been, he would have destroyed Ruby's mobile too. Grimm is sure of it. This phone is nothing but three hundred plus false leads, he thinks, leads he has to investigate just in case.

"Dad" who called fourteen times, has been confirmed to be Ruby's actual father, Barry Williams. An intimidating man, who Grimm thought might explode when he found out about Ruby's "other" Daddies. Instead he laid his head in his hands, taking long slow breaths, answering their further questions through gritted teeth.

His daughter had told him that she was going to meet her best friend Carly Ellis (Carl-E on her contact list.) telling him that they were going to see a movie, that his daughter had kissed him goodbye, promising to text him to let him know if she was coming home or staying the night with Carly. When she didn't text, he kept trying to call her and Carly over and over, until he got THE call.

When she left, she was wearing black tracksuit bottoms and her favourite black hoodie, the one with "Cute Stuff" emblazoned on the front of it. He would never let her wear those other kinds of clothes, the ones she had been found wearing, he doesn't even know where or when she got them. He had been lenient with her, ever since her mother died from a drug overdose, three years ago. But he wasn't that lenient. He didn't know that she had been going to pubs… or those other things. He had trusted her, she was his only child…he…he can't…

Grimm had tried to comfort him, one father to another, had agreed to do whatever he could to catch this son of a bitch, though he can't keep his promise to allow Mr Williams ten minutes alone, in a secluded room with the aforementioned son of a bitch. There are rules after all.

One contact down, still over three hundred left to go.

CHAPTER THREE

Let us talk calmly and quietly, like civilised people do. Let's talk about betrayal, about the punishment for betrayal. The true cost of not doing what is expected of you.

The smile is what they really remember. Later on, when they dream again of the blood, it is the smile that still lingers in their minds long after waking. It has become a symbol of everything yet to come, that smile cracked beyond all realms of insanity.

Officer Vogel was supposed to be the lead that night, he was supposed to be helping patrol Kings Park, bravely waiting to scare the monsters who only come out at night, well those and the invincible teenagers who only wanted an unseen smoke somewhere quiet. It has been nearly a month since Ruby Williams' death, every patrol so far has reported back no sightings. It has gotten a lot colder and perhaps, under a different circumstance, Vogel could be forgiven for stepping away for a brief time, to warm up. So could the other officers, the gates to the park were locked after all, though the fences were easily climbable, but really, who would want to, in this weather?

The finer details at this point, are still unclear, no one really wants to tell the truth, about how long they were away, unofficially off duty, not wanting a harsher suspension or even a dismissal. But it is obvious that Vogel was the first one to come back, must have seen something or someone moving inside the park, close to the gates, leading him to climb the fence and investigate.

His smile was the first hint that something was really wrong. The other officers approached carefully, stomachs churning in dread, that Oh Shit! Feeling rising like bile. Then they saw what Vogel was smiling at, and the bile rose higher, choking through throats, burning away any remaining hope. Vogel smiled on, far gone away to a happier place and not coming back any time soon.

Colvin, after fifteen phone calls and five attempts at a home interview, is finally standing face to face with Carly Ellis. Carly is dressed similarly to Ruby Williams, short dark skirt, even shorter sparkly top. The kind of outfit that would make someone purse their lips and say 'she must be cold, wearing that.' Carly's skin even has a similar mottled look. But this is not the meeting Colvin had been hoping for. She had hoped to meet Carly whilst she was still alive for starters. She also had hoped not to be one of the officers who had to attend the autopsy.

Carly had been found sometime around 3 a.m on Friday 9th November, in Kings Park, by the unfortunate Officer Vogel, her body rapidly cooling in the cold November air. Thankfully not as badly beaten as Ruby Williams but that still seems like only a small mercy. The cynics amongst them are in full overdrive now, whispering things like 'If only that pussy Vogel had raised the alarm sooner, they might have caught this guy!' (instead of, you know, having a full mental breakdown, the kind linked with a very early retirement.) It was more than harsh but still true. The assailant must have still been at work on Carly when Vogel climbed into the park, moving fast in the darkness to escape, whilst Carly bled and Vogel smiled. That lead to other darker questions, how did the assailant know the park would be empty at that time? Did they know that the other officers had left? Had they watched and waited for that perfect moment? Had an officer willingly or unknowingly told them that they were leaving? Was it another officer? What about Carly? How did the assailant even get her in the park without anyone noticing? Did she agree to meet someone? In that park, at that time of night, that place where her friend had died less than a month ago? Carly must have known her killer to be willing to meet them here, or did she just not care that much about Ruby?

Perhaps that is the question that everyone should really be asking, Colvin thinks. They need to focus more on finding out where Carly was last seen, what might have brought her to the park. There were no signs of drag marks or anything more than a brief struggle, nothing to suggest that she did not go to the park willingly. But no, officers were wasting time instead muttering amongst themselves about the death of another young woman, a slightly older student called Madison Albrook. a victim of The Numbers Killer, who died, throat cut, just like Carly and who was unceremoniously dumped on a bed of poppies in a park (but not the same park), just like Carly. Madison had a number 36 on her right hand. Carly had a number 2 cut into her left hand. Admittedly, Madison's number had been drawn on with a felt tip and she had been brazenly attacked in the middle of the day, in a crowded park, unlike Carly. But the officers are ignoring those little details, in their 'this must be the work of The Numbers Killer theories.'

Colvin tries not to stare at the table, her job only being to collect evidence, she instead wonders just how much visibility the assailant actually had at three a.m. She tries to remember the park, she can't remember it being that light, no floodlights or streetlights. Could the assailant see that well or was that the reason why that number 2 looks slightly wobbly? Did the assailant attack by moonlight? Streetlight? Torch light? Or even just by the light of a mobile phone? In which case, could the assailant even see where the body fell? To Colvin, it sounded like Carly was dumped by a killer who didn't care where she fell, admittedly similar to Madison Albrook, almost as if he had been planning to do something else with her body, but had found out first-hand what the term dead weight really means. Even skinny nineteen-year-olds are heavier than they look. Colvin is still willing to bet serious money that this killer had started to carry her, then decided fuck it, she is not worth this and dropped her, an easily discarded play toy.

Only an hour ago, she was sat at her desk, trying to find some missed clue on the Anne-Marie Mills case, when Grimm told her that they had to go, her heart sinking with dread as he said the words "Female found dead in a flower bed. Throat slit, she has a number two." Now she is standing here, closer than she wants to be, to a dead girl, watching as others work, documenting the damage, thoughts of Anne-Marie Mills far from her mind. Her thoughts concentrating on holding this without shaking and trying not to inhale.

Jenna keeps trying to pretend that she knows nothing. It is partially true, she is not gifted with overwhelming intellect, but she is smarter than she is pretending to be. Jenna's friends are playing the same game. Yes, they were in the same bar as Ruby Williams and Carly Ellis on that night, but they don't know anything and they certainly didn't see anything. They have discussed not seeing anything over and over, murmuring and reassuring each other over wine. Yes, they saw the girls, but they didn't really see them. Jenna honestly only remembers Ruby's stilettos, everything else that night is nothing more than a blur of alcohol and regrets. Nothing worth bothering the police with, despite the appeals for information. They saw nothing helpful, couldn't even describe the other people in the bar that night.

Later, when the second bottle had been drained, but the mood was still sober, when they talked about The Numbers Killer and how close they had been before, all of them have a story about that time, their own rumours, still mutating with misinformation after all these years. They talked about those times of carefully watching the streets, the neighbours, the boyfriends, just to be sure. Of never quite being sure of some people. When they finally left that night, each made sure that no one followed them home, reassured themselves again that they definitely hadn't seen something that they weren't supposed to see. That there was really no reason for them to be targeted too, because they definitely hadn't seen anything and there was no reason for them to be next. No reason at all.

Not that a serial killer really needs a reason.

Days later, in yet another briefing, Grimm talks about the three hundred plus contacts on Ruby Williams' phone, most of whom won't have anything to do with the police. A large majority of those contacts are no longer active. Carly Ellis' phone has not yet been found. Colvin tries to talk neutrally about lighting conditions in Kings Park, accompanied with appropriate time related pictures, about the degree of familiarity that the assailant must have with the park, to work in that level of darkness. Then she moves on to talking about the visual similarities between Ruby and Carly, that there is a possibility that the assailant is targeting a specific type rather than specific people. She even goes as far as to suggest that maybe the assailant didn't even know Carly and Ruby were friends (she doesn't really believe that, but someone had to say it.) Another officer present at the autopsy talks about Carly's numerous wounds, similar to Ruby's, again the lack of defence wounds, the blow to the head that first stunned her before the attack. The number that might not be a number cut into her hand.

Another officer reports back that Carly and Ruby were active users on the same SugarDaddy websites and maybe a link can be found there, a suggestion as well, for how the assailant managed to lure Carly to the park, but it still didn't really make sense. The officer also put forward the suggestion that maybe Ruby and Carly had attempted to blackmail a client and the numbers were a misdirection. Or perhaps this was the revenge of a very upset wife?

Officer Dalbiac, who had been given the job of going through Carly's rented room, reports that amongst the mess, they had found clothes similar to those Ruby had last been seen wearing by her father. The track suit bottoms and black hoodie emblazoned with the slogan "Cute Stuff" had been found in a bag, kicked out of sight, under the sofa.

More worryingly, some officers are asking for certain other officers to be put under surveillance. Micheals, Tichan, Seasions and Juda, all those officers who had worked on previous

The Numbers Killer case, even the retired officers like Fletcher, Hendy and Leona, not forgetting the soon to be retired Vogel. Also those officers responsible for that slip up at the park. The slip up shouldn't have happened, perhaps someone dropped the ball on purpose. Someone who knew this much about how The Numbers Killer operated had to have been involved with the police somehow. Someone who had been in the right position, someone who could have planted evidence indicting Walker. These requests are being met with fairly explosive outrage.

Colvin is quiet, for once she isn't trying to argue against her fellow officers, isn't protesting (out loud at least) against their (stupid) plans involving old suspects from The Numbers Killer case. She really doesn't want to call any attention to herself, doesn't want someone to turn around and say "Weren't you supposed to find Carly Ellis? Take her into protective custody?" Doesn't want someone to ask why Carly might willingly (arguably) meet up with a serial killer, but refuse to speak to a police officer. Doesn't want to think about it.

The officers talk and shout and argue but no one really listens. They are all waiting for the real updates, the new theories on the number sequences, updates on the suspects interviews, any updates from the forensic teams, any information that might actually lead them to a satisfying result.

CHAPTER FOUR

I am planning on a beautiful Christmas present, specially picked just for you. It is not returnable. No refund can be given for fear. I hope you like it. I plan to make it a reoccurring gift. A little someone just for you every week. I hope you like her, maybe just for you, I will even put a ribbon on her.

They say that you can see ghosts in Kings Park now, two similar looking girls, wandering around, still looking for their heads.

Some say a monster, created and enraged in a laboratory, roams the park at night, looking for fresh meat. They say a police officer went insane just looking at it.

Some say The Numbers Killer never left, never died, that he is working now with the police, in exchange for his own pick of victims.

Some say the serial killer is a widespread myth, invented to stop women from becoming too independent, forcing them to rely on male pack protection.

Some say the serial killer is not human, that no human could be capable of such mutilations, a monster, an alien, an animal.

But they all agree, it is not safe to walk alone at night.

It's Friday 21st December, the night of Lucy Swann's work Christmas party. Lucy wasn't supposed to be going alone to-night, she was supposed to be picked up by work friends. They were supposed to all go together, gossip together and share a least two bottles of Prosecco between them. But at the last minute, Steve accidentally insulted Monika, who upset Kayla, who told Sabrina, who promptly refused to be in the same room as Steve, and wouldn't change her mind about not coming to the party, no matter what was said and who apologised. Mike, the driver, caught a cold from his three-year-old daughter and couldn't drive under that strong influence of cold medicine. Every taxi company Lucy rang, was already fully booked for the evening and no one else lived on her side of the city, so Lucy is left with three choices.

Stay home, alone, as she has done for the last two weeks, since breaking up with her boyfriend. Staying home would mean she misses the chance to flirt with Tom from IT.

Go, but drive herself, meaning she couldn't drink, which would also mean she will probably lose her nerve and not flirt with the aforementioned Tom, who really does have the most gorgeous brown eyes.

Go and have a great time, then walk back alone, that same ten minute walk home that she has walked for years. Sure it goes near Kings Park but it wasn't like she was going to be coming back at stupid o clock in the morning, she would be home by eleven, at the very latest and there would be plenty of other people around, also walking home from their various Christmas commitments. Maybe, if she was lucky, Tom might even offer to drive her home.

She will be fine, she decides, she will be fine.

Nicholas Grimm leans back in his armchair, enjoying the warmth and the satisfaction of a job nearly well done. If he closes his eyes, he can picture a fireplace, fire blazing, stockings neatly hung, loving children playing quietly in front of a tree, loving wife about to bring him a nice drink.

If he opens his eyes, he will probably see something that needs fixing, damp washing drying on a radiator, a daughter having a temper tantrum and Mrs Grimm with that look in her eye. He is keeping his eyes closed for as long as possible, to try and enjoy this brief break from work. Take a break from thinking about all the things he needs to go out and buy tomorrow, for his last minute Christmas shopping. Maybe some flowers for Mrs Grimm, who is still upset by the news he will be working Christmas Day, that he will be missing dinner with her family. Her family being two sisters, (one in the middle of a bitter divorce) their five hyperactive children, her one how-can-he-always-be-this-drunk uncle and her eagle eyed parents. Such a shame. He will only have time to watch his daughters open their presents, then he will have to go, such a shame.

Idly, he wonders what he is going to get for Christmas this year. Last year it was seven ties, so this year will probably be a sock year. Lots and lots of socks. He opens his eyes expectantly as his wife clears her throat, he still smiles at her, waiting for her command, no matter what awful festive job she has in mind for him, it is still better than going to work.

Colvin is technically off duty too, though there are doubts that she understands what that means. She is a contradiction of feelings right now, they have finally made an arrest on the Anne-Marie Mills case, they had a very strong case for the court although the suspect is still making her nervous. That sly smile every time she was interviewed, Colvin knows the suspect is going to do something but what? But still, it looks like the trial is going to be a success, a testament to her skills and fortitude. It means that she will no longer spend her office time in dread of yet another phone call from that formidable mother! No more pressure to just close the case and focus on Ruby Williams and Carly Ellis. She should be happy about that and she is, but, she is still stinging with the feeling of failure, from not finding Carly Ellis in time. That feeling is what keeps her looking in her free time, searching various sugar daddy websites, looking for other possible victims, by not strictly approved methods. Catching so many glimpses of a world that she didn't even know existed in this city. So far, everything has been a bust, but that only means she needs to look closer, try harder. If she can solve the Anne-

Marie Mills case, she can solve this one.

Plus, it's a Friday night and she is in that same panicky mode, that she has been for every Friday, since the 9th of November. The assailant appears to only be active on Fridays, very early Friday mornings and very late Friday nights. She spends her Fridays now, holding one long breath, unable to do anything, unable to relax or exhale until Saturday afternoon. Maybe she needs to go for a nice long walk tonight, double check that certain officers are actually patrolling where they need to patrol, check that people aren't being too stupid, check certain pubs, to make sure they are no longer serving underaged girls. Check to make sure that there are no teenage girls with long blonde hair, standing alone in dark places.

Why waste time worrying about things that might happen, when you can actively work to prevent them from happening?

Lucy Swann is not having a great night. Her three attempts to flirt with Tom have been met with indifference, as the normally friendly Tom is more occupied with angrily tapping on his phone, giving off the impression he was fighting a virtual war against someone and they had him by the gigabytes. Lucy then tried to find someone else to flirt with, or at least talk to, but no one is talkative tonight, there is a dark mood in the room, one that can't be brightened by tinsel. Rumours are circling about layoffs, those poor girls and nepotism.

Then, to make it worse, that bitch from PR had to go and spill a large glass of red wine all over her golden dress! Oh sure, there were apologises, promises to pay for dry cleaning, all said with that falsetto tone of voice. She knew that Lucy had no choice but to accept her trite apologises, knowing that her boss and her boss's boss were standing close by, listening intently.

At ten o'clock, she decides she has had enough, it is time to slip away quietly, time to go home for a hot chocolate with a large splash of condolence brandy, time to go.

Officer McGallan is not having a merry evening either. It is cold and drizzling. He is stuck listening to a city, that he feels worlds away from, as buzzes of laughter and excited chatter pass him by, encircling him as he walks the same streets over and over.

A command comes in over his walkie talkie, it's his turn to go through Kings Park again. Sighing as he replies, he grips his torch tight in one hand, readying his other hand on his panic button, as he strolls through the unlocked gates.

The flowers creep him out, every time he comes through, those vibrant happy colours don't belong in a place of winter and death. Not that he can do anything about them, as he walks past, shining his torch into every shadow. If they really wanted to cut down the amount of crime in this park, they should install more lights, he grumbles to himself again, stomping down a random path. He exchanges nods with another patrolling officer and walks another circuit before reporting back that all is well.

Lucy shrieks with disgust as her heel splashes down in an unseen puddle. She is cold, soggy and cursing every factor that led to her walking home alone tonight. She had spent days searching for the perfect pair of gold shoes, to match her dress and now they are ruined! Her dress is ruined! Her hair feels like a damp mop! And for what? Ten minutes of awkward chat with a guy who was more interested in his phone, a lacklustre dinner and some how-come-this-is-so-expensive-yet-so-disgusting wine! She stumbles slightly, these are not shoes that were made for walking home in the rain. She would be better to walk home barefoot, but she can't face the thought of putting her bare feet onto that cold muddy pavement, treading in who knows what. Maybe even treading in dried blood, a forbidden thought whispers, as she gets closer to Kings Park, it can't all have been washed away.

She glances around, suddenly nervous, suddenly aware of how alone she is. She is so close to home now, she just needs to keep moving, she just needs to make it past the park. She can't stop here, anywhere but here.

Officer McGallan can't help but notice the amount of hostility in the air tonight. For every look of gratitude, he gets from certain passers-by, there is another person looking at him with ... anger? Resentment? Are they angry at him? The uniform he wears? Or just the fact that it has come to this? McGallan doesn't want to find out. He is just hoping he can get to the end of his shift before someone starts to 'express' themselves. He has never known a night like this before.

A twinkle of glitter and gold catches his eye, ahead a dark haired girl in a gold dress, moves to cross the road. Then she is gone. He is about to follow, wanting to make sure she gets home safe, when another order comes through on his walkie-talkie. Its time for another patrol of the park.

Colvin is on the wrong side of the park. She can't see anything beyond the flashing blue lights and the crowds. She is too late. She can't hear anything useful, only the unguarded mutterings of the public, speculating about the girl who lies dead on the other side of the park. She can't feel anything except another flare up of failure. She can't do anything now except move amongst the masses, try to memorise faces and descriptions but she can't see much beyond the darkness.

She just can't understand where they went wrong. Everywhere she looked tonight, she saw uniformed officers, patrolling on a regular basis but with random sequences. They were doing everything right! How could they fail again so badly?

Now Steve, who accidentally insulted Monika, can't sleep because of regrets and the feeling that everyone is talking about him at work. Monika, who upset Kayla, is on stress leave. Kayla, who told Sabrina, is insisting she did nothing wrong, it wasn't her fault. Sabrina can't even look at a bottle of Prosecco without feeling sick and guilty. Mike who was too sick too drive, knows he shouldn't blame himself, but still does. But that bitch from PR is secretly thrilled that she is no longer obligated to pay for any dry cleaning on that expensive gold dress.

Jenna has brought five newspapers today, just for the front page, for the five different perspectives and pictures of the untimely deceased Lucy Swann.

She stares hard, trying to remember, has she seen this girl before? In better times? Namely did she see her that night in October, in that pub? Jenna has spent so long trying to repress all memories of that night, so long refusing to remember anything, now she can't be sure. She doesn't think so, Lucy looks like the type of girl who goes out to cocktail bars, for one quick drink before leaving early, because she has yoga in the morning. A healthy girl, not like Jenna or her friends.

But the five newspapers alone aren't enough, she needs more, more information, more details, better pictures. She needs to know everything.

They know who she was, where she had been, where she was going, they know so much and yet so little.

McGallen reports seeing Lucy Swann walking away from Kings park at around 10.30pm on Friday 21st December. He was the last witness to see her alive. Somewhere within a twenty minute time frame, someone else caught up with her, either chased her or carried her back to Kings Park, depositing her body in front of the main gates.

They can guess where the assailant first encountered Lucy, the spot being marked with one golden shoe. Scientists are still arguing over the stains on the back of her feet, disagreeing on whether she was dragged, or if these are stains from walking / running, the mud and rain has distorted everything.

They know how she died. She had only two wounds on her body, only one was fatal. A cut throat and a marked hand. a half-hearted kill, with none of the brutality of the first kills. Perhaps she wasn't who he thought she was, a mistaken identity realised too late, perhaps he lost the taste or perhaps he was interrupted.

They don't know why the assailant took the time to take her back to the park, (if he did) or if she was being chased, why there were no cries for help, they don't know why no one else saw or heard anything when there were so many people around.

They don't know why they believed Colvin, when she previously suggested that the assailant chose his victims because of specific physical attributes, instead of targeting specific women, since Lucy was completely different to the first two victims, different hair colour, skin colour, dress sense and so forth.

They don't know what the mark on her right hand means. Some are bravely suggesting that maybe they were wrong, maybe the markings on all the victims, are not numbers, but a different kind of code, a more complex code, what some think is a one could be an I or a slash. The two could even be a J or a Z or even a different symbol entirely. Others are still insisting that the markings are numbers, still insisting that this is the work of The Numbers Killer, returning with a different code or even that this is still part of the original code, meaning this new sequence goes 1 – 2 – 1. What that means, only time and more victims will reveal.

Some of those believers are also making comparisons between this death and another victim of The Numbers Killer, victim '38' Kim Donaghue, who was also killed, coming from a Christmas party. They are suggesting that maybe the assailant was on the hunt in the restaurant areas, purposely looking to target a victim leaving alone. They want to look more closely at the CCTV in those areas.

Somewhere, at some point, in all the chaos, Christmas quietly passed by, so did a very subdue New Year, then the first week of January. Colvin just put her head down and worked. And worked yet still getting nowhere. Tempers at the station are at an all time high and officers just can't stop themselves from majorly fucking up, one officer after another, turning each day into a full frontal assault from the press.

First came the harassment complaint from a certain Mr Fitzherbert Charington the third, also known as Fat Crack, a former drug dealer who had been a suspect in the original Number Killer investigation. He lodged an official harassment complaint and then took the time to talk loudly and extensively to anyone who would listen, namely the press and certain channels popular on social media. Colvin can't really blame him, certain officers had been overeager in their finger pointing, but now several other 'old' suspects have also stepped forward to complain, loudly. There was no Christmas goodwill extended to the police this year, and the public fall out is still echoing.

Also damaging their enquiries is a similar complaint from a new suspect; the ex-boyfriend of Lucy Swann. He hadn't taken the break up well, shouting several regrettable and hostile comments at Lucy at the time of dumping. This, in turn, led to Officer Seasons fixating on the idea of him as a suspect in the investigation. Seasons proclaimed that Lucy wasn't killed by the same person who killed Carly and Ruby and that the 'number' on Lucy was nothing but classic misdirection. He ignored all evidence that didn't quite fit into this theory, and tried to arrest the nineteen-year-old boy despite his solid alibi and the lack of any solid evidence. His parents are still outraged and are also now making themselves known to the media.

Colvin herself, admittedly, also made some mistakes here. She had been trying to find a link between Ruby, Carly and Lucy. She had been trying to covertly find out if Lucy had also signed up to a certain sugardaddy website. She had not been as subtle as she thought and it took quite a few apologises to Lucy's family to smooth things down. While they are, thankfully, not complaining as loudly as some, all further interactions have been extremely strained and Colvin can't help but feel they might be holding information back.

But at least she hadn't fucked up as badly as Grimm, who has now been suspended for allegedly kissing someone, someone about to be convicted of murder. Despite the fact it happened before the arrest and, as Grimm insists, they kissed him, catching him off-guard, he is still in trouble for not reporting it at the time. An incident which led to people questioning what else had not been reported?

Colvin is mostly annoyed that, not only has he compromised one of her cases, but he has also dragged her down with him. She has now been 'temporarily' bumped down to desk work whilst they "look for a new partner" for her. Within hours she went from being a high flyer to someone who couldn't be trusted alone with the photocopier. She might be here for a while since certain officers are unwilling to work with her due to some stepped on toes, jealously issues and how vocal she was in protesting against the arrest of the ex-boyfriend.

It is giving her a little breathing space, time to sit back and think about some of the more confusing aspects of these cases. She is still trying to decide if Ruby, Carly or Lucy actually knew their attacker? At one point Colvin would have willingly put money on them not knowing their attacker, that it wasn't a personal attack. Not personal, as in the mere act of taking someone else's life is not personal, just a thing to satisfy a desire and nothing more. But then, why was Ruby so severely beaten? That surely suggested something more? But it could just be mindless violence, a killer showing what he can do when he knows he has time. They all thought at first that Carly knew her attacker. The only reason anyone would meet that late, in that park would be for personal reasons. But they can't find anything on Carly's phone that proves she had arranged to meet anyone. She, as far as they could tell from her phone, she before her death, had been refusing to meet with anyone, no matter what or how much they had been willing to offer.

As far as she could tell, Ruby Williams had been lured to her death, probably through that website, Carly Ellis was a puzzle and Lucy Swann was an opportunist kill. Perhaps the killer had changed his tactics, knowing his original bait was now wary or perhaps he was trying something new? Perhaps he has the confidence now to pick and choose his prey, now he knows how easy it is? Perhaps he had planned this for years? One argument where those other officers do have a point, is how fast this killer is striking, she has never known a new serial killer to keep attacking again and again so quickly. This one had barely any cooling off time before attacking again, almost as if this all had been carefully planned in advance.

She can't stop thinking about what else the assailant has planned. The original Numbers Killer actively worked to upset and provoke the public as well as his victims. If this is The Numbers Killer returned or even a copycat, some kind of mental explosives were being primed, ready for unleashing. It just needs one small flame of idiocy. She needs to be out there working and not sitting here, cursing the fact her partner, in a time of high tempers and dangerously short fuses, just had to slap a big bullseye on his own backside.

CHAPTER FIVE

Good things come to those who wait.

"Please! No more!"

On Wednesday 17th February, Ziva left the house around 6.30pm, stepping out into the darkness, fully absorbed in her own little world, blocking out the sounds of the evening with her favourite podcast. Over a thousand times now, she has gone over this in her mind, tried to remember just something, other than the ordinary. Cursing herself for not checking, not looking around to see who might be watching. Sometimes she tries to make excuses to herself, it was cold and raining that evening, she was already running late, what happened wasn't her fault. But she just can't shake that feeling, things would be different if she had only looked around, if she could just remember seeing someone. Or, if she had chosen not to go, but she always looked forward to Open Mike night. They had pre-banned everyone from murder, as a topic, that night. There had been too many gloomy memorials and tributes already. That night was about celebrating the goodness in the world, about escaping from reality, about trying to be happy and positive, just for a few hours.

No words will ever take Ziva out of this reality again, no poem will ever ignite flames in her soul, no speech will ever arouse her heart. Words mean nothing to her now.

"Then what happened? What time did you leave?" The voice is sympathetic but impatient. It is trying to be kind, trying to understand, but Ziva is tired of voices like these. Ziva listens to the tick of clock, that constant irritating reminder that the world keeps turning, no matter how much she screams at it to stop.

"Around ten."

Maybe she shouldn't have walked home alone, but it wasn't like it was a Friday night. And, as she used to say with a self-depreciating laugh, no killer ever attacked a fat girl. Perhaps she had been a little scared when she left, maybe, but she knew she would be fine.

She left Open Mike on a high because they had liked her poem. Even Mardy Mim had said something vaguely positive about it, Ziva is even considering the idea of submitting it somewhere.

Ziva can still remember wasting precious minutes just staring up at the full moon; her mind buzzing with new ideas for new poems, not caring about the rain hitting her face. That feeling of cold shock, even the water was urging her to get home.

She didn't listen to anything on the way home, no podcast, no music. Just the hum of the city and the soft patter of rain. She'd paid no notice to the world around her, not wanting anything to destroy her euphoria.

"Please, no more." She doesn't want to remember any more, doesn't want to go back to that place again. But they are persistent, they need answers.

She can't remember if the door was locked or unlocked and she can't remember if she locked it behind her. She probably didn't. Leena would be home from work soon and she never remembered her key. It didn't matter because their other housemate was home anyway. Ziva can remember putting her bag down, relieved to be home safe. She knows she called out to Priya, excited to tell her all about her night. She bustled noisily, shredding her wet coat and shoes before moving into the kitchen for a nice, warming drink.

Then she can remember staring. Staring and staring but not comprehending. Maybe she screamed, but she never stopped staring at that thing, that inhuman mess, wearing Priya's pyjamas and her favourite slippers. That thing that couldn't be Priya. Not her best friend.

Then there were arms, arms pulling at her, shaking her, before clasping her tight and half dragging, half carrying her out of the room, finally silencing those screams she didn't even realise were still escaping from something primeval, deep inside of her. Arms that continued to hold her, tried to comfort her, tried to reach her. Eventually those arms admitted failure. There must have been a human attached to those arms but Ziva can't remember anything else, couldn't say if it was male or female, friend or stranger, all she can remember is seeing that unrecognisable mess of human on her kitchen floor.

Things get blurry after that. The only way she can describe it is that she floated somewhere, somewhere where sirens wailed and there were electronic beeps and constant noise when she needed silence. Somewhere where a thousand different unrecognisable voices asked her the same questions over and over. Always asking questions she couldn't answer. So much time spent in a timeless place that, even now, she couldn't tell how long she'd been there. It could have been hours or it could have been weeks, she can't recall any more.

Even when she realised where she was, what they had done, she still clung to the fog, not wanting to face anything, not wanting to accept that Priya was gone.

"Please, no more." They want to go over it again, Ziva pleads the same thing over and over, no more, please, no more. But no one listens. Not the nurses, not the police, not Priya's family. Everyone keeps insisting she must have seen something. They swarmed her at the funeral, all demanding answers. They insist she must have seen something; a face at a window, someone staring. She must have sensed something was off with someone, just give them a description, it doesn't matter how vague, a name, something, Priya must have mentioned someone! Just try to remember something, something more. They all want revenge. Ziva just wants there to be no more.

CHAPTER SIX

Living alone means lying to yourself sometimes. Harmless lies like 'if I buy that cake, I won't eat it all in one go' or 'I will definitely vacuum tomorrow' or, my personal favourite, 'that thumping sound came from the neighbour's house, it's just them moving around, like they do every day. There is nothing to fear. There is no one else in my home.' I like noisy neighbours, so useful to disguise certain thumps.

Having reassured themselves with these lies, the lone little lamb will close its eyes and go back to sleep, all happy in their safe little house, in their safe little neighbourhood, where it is has always been safe to leave a window open downstairs. Everything is just so happy and safe, it's the lullaby they sing themselves to sleep with; you are safe here, my dear, you are safe here, nothing to fear.

They look so happy when they are sleeping, this one hasn't stirred once. I have brushed the hair away from her face, breathed gently against her and not even a flutter of eyelids. I am curious to see what it will take to wake her, how far I can go.

She needs to wake up soon. I can't have her missing all the fun.

Nicholas A. Grimm (formerly a DCI, now a disgrace) would have kissed his wife goodbye this morning but she turned her face away at the last moment. He tried not to dwell on it too much and kissed his daughter instead. She didn't care; she was too busy scooping and squashing her half eaten soggy cereal, laughing at the sounds it made.

"I'll be back at six." He says unnecessarily, knowing she no longer cares what time he comes home and, even if she did, that he hasn't been home on time in years but he still needed to say something, something to prove nothing. He walks out alone, head down, heart cold, into the March drizzle.

Grimm tries to remain upbeat as he walks into work, conscious of the pointing and unwelcoming stares. He is not surprised, he knew it would be like this but it's amazing just how much it hurts. He did nothing wrong! He can't let anything show right now though, no emotions, no weaknesses, not if he wants to keep his job. Just put one foot in front of the other and keep walking, clench everything that can be clenched and don't think of her. Think of your family, think of your pension, today is going to be the worst day and when it is over, nothing will be as bad as this again, just don't think about her and you will be fine, he tries to order himself, concentrating instead on moving forward. He walks the familiar route to his desk, everything and nothing has changed here. Unsurprisingly no one greets him or acknowledges he exists. He has worked here for nearly three years but it's his first day all over again. There are words they use for police officers like him, bad words.

Grimm never thought he would be seen as a bad guy. He has always thought of himself as a good cop, a loving husband and a devoted father, not necessarily in that order. Well, maybe in that order. But now, now all that has been swirled into the toilet bowl because of one uninitiated kiss.

And of course, not forgetting one lying manipulating bitch, who also turned out to be a murdering manipulating bitch. Oh damn it, don't start thinking about her.

Now, one twelve week suspension, a misconduct hearing, and a written warning later, he is haunted by the feeling he will never be praised or promoted again, there are people who will make sure of that, just like they will make sure he knows he is not welcome back. All because he brushed something off, laughed it off instead of reporting it to a superior officer. He had not followed protocol and she made sure she dragged him down.

The fuc-- no he can't waste any more time with anger. He has had over twelve weeks of stewing. He sits down slowly at his desk, starting the slow arduous task of catching up. He wonders where Colvin is, what she has been doing without him. He almost dreads seeing her. Unlike everyone else, she is not going to hate him, she is just going to be disappointed.

Yet they need him and Colvin. Okay, maybe they need Colvin more than him, but he has his uses and that's really the only reason he hasn't already been demoted. They need all the officers with experience of investigating murders they can get, and more. He has been keeping up with the news reports, he knows the sense of fear and panic is thick in the air. Everyone in the city knows who is back and they are shitting themselves.

Colvin is tired, you can tell by the size of the chip on her shoulder. She has spent too many hours thinking and she is slowly burning out. Too many unfollowed leads, too many stupid men interfering, too many dead ends and that never ending nagging feeling she is missing something vital.

Around two years ago she was a rising star at her old station then she made the decision, or the mistake, to transfer here. Now she feels like a meteorite, crashing down. Oh she has had some successes. She is Sam Colvin after all. The Irene Jones case, the James Perkins case and, most notably, the Anne-Marie Mills case. That case is why she has been put back on this task force now. She was right and she kept working when everyone else had given up. And this is either a reward or a punishment for her tenacity. Given how some officers hate a know-it-all and how some want the young upstart to fall hard and fast, she will either succeed and do all the hard work for them or she will fail into silence and an office corner. Perhaps her superiors consider it a win-win situation either way. Perhaps that's a little harsh and perhaps she is willing to admit that she is a little bitter but she can't shake that feeling that they are waiting for her to crack, they have their knowing smiles ready, they are waiting for her to complain about there not being enough help or enough hours.

Waiting for her to break down and she is determined not to give them the satisfaction.

She thinks she knows how to handle herself now, she has learnt to look closely at the little details, the important little details like sleeves. She thinks she knows how to recognise the over eagerness of a liar, pleading to be believed. She won't be fooled again by how normal a killer can look, talk or act. She knows how to handle herself amongst all the toadying and the back-stabbing. But the stupidity is another story.

They should be closer to catching this guy by now but, instead, they are still at square one. Eight weeks! She has had to listen to eight weeks of stupidity! Eight weeks of desk work, of hearing the idiocy evolve around her. It still stings that she wasn't even notified about Priya Smythes death and, when she was finally allowed back into the case meetings, her suggestions were met with accusations of stalling! Officers refusing to listen to how stupid they had been, too quick to point out her previous failed ideas, her failed attempts to reach Carly Ellis, her little mess up with Lucy Swann's family. Like her mistakes were worse than arresting a teenager, worse than making them a laughing stock in the eyes of the public and the press, worse than alienating themselves from an entire community?

Speaking of stupid men she sees Grimm slumped over his desk, mouth moving as he reads through his many emails. She is relieved he is back as she needs someone to help with the grunt work and the reports reading. She needs a fresh pair of eyes and a different perspective. But she is still annoyed, this investigation is being run by stupid idiots and the last thing she needs is another stupid idiot joining the team. He didn't just jeopardise his own career but hers too and this golden girl can't risk another tarnish to her reputation.

She notices he has brought her a fresh coffee and wonders if it's an attempt at an apology? An ice-breaker? Or just an acknowledgement that they have a fuck ton of work to do? She sips it either way. At this point, it could be laced with cyanide and she would still drink it. He will need to be updated, which would require talking to him, but thankfully it should only take about ten minutes to bring him up to speed.

She needs to tell him that they have finally finished the job he started, contacting all Ruby William's "friends". The three hundred plus contacts on her phone, her school friends, every boy who was known to have even looked in her direction (including the creepy ones her father mentioned). Nothing useful had come out of it though. Another officer is still valiantly trying to track the Sugar Daddies but they aren't holding out much hope.

She doesn't have much to update him with in regards to Carly Ellis. She was barely home from the age of fourteen onwards, completely leaving the day she turned eighteen and had no contact with her mother for the last two years. Rumour is that Carly's mother had to be shown quite a few photos before she even remembered Carly and she didn't remember her fondly. Oh, also the tox report had finally come back, again. Apparently Seasons didn't believe the first set of results and had sent off another sample to be tested, he is still refusing to believe that Carly had been completely sober and drug free when she died.

There aren't any updates regarding Lucy Swann. They are still trying desperately to undo the media damage but Colvin fears that it will be a long time before the police are seen as anything more than bumbling idiots in the eyes of the public.

That just leaves Priya Smythe and her death has changed everything. To start with they had been expecting the assailant to strike again quickly, within a few weeks of Lucy's death, on a Friday night, but when no one had been killed and marked in January, they started to relax, thinking perhaps the half-hearted killing of Lucy, signified that the assailant lost their nerve. But then Priya was killed two months later, on the 17th February, a Wednesday night, in her own home.

Now, female residents of the city are afraid to go out on Fridays but also afraid of staying home on Wednesdays. They are lucky they don't know all the details. Colvin has heard them all second hand, has seen the ashen faces of her colleagues and the photos, she will need to warn Grimm carefully about those before showing him. At least he won't have the traumatised screams of Priya's housemate, Ziva, constantly echoing in his mind.

They know that some time between 6.45pm and 9pm, Priya had sat in her pyjamas in her shared kitchen, eating cereal and watching a film on her iPad. They had found the blood splattered bowl, still half full, and Priya's autopsy had confirmed that she had been the one eating. They don't know if she let the assailant into her house or if he let himself in through the unlocked door. What Colvin really wants to know is whether the film had been paused? If it was paused it suggests that maybe she got up to let someone in. If not, it suggests that maybe she had been caught unaware. No one can give her an answer and it is too late to check.

The fact that Priya was in her pyjamas suggests that maybe she wasn't expecting anyone, but then some have suggested that it meant she was and that maybe it was someone from a certain Sugar Daddy website, but they can't produce any evidence to back this up.

The switch to home invasion felt odd to Colvin. It suggested to her that the killer had been watching the house for a long time and knew what days Priya was home alone, which seemed odd for a killer who lured and killed opportunistically. Maybe something made him realise that she was alone in the house and he took a chance?

What was also odd was that, for the first time, the assailant had used a knife as well as fists to inflict pain. Priya's cause of death had been exsanguination and they had counted nearly forty cuts on her body, a mixture of deep and lighter cuts. Possibly the lighter cuts were hesitation marks. If that was true, then it could be the first time that the assailant has shown hesitation or possible insecurity. Perhaps it was outside of their comfort zone, the first attack inside someone's home? Perhaps they had more time with Priya and were unsure how to use it or perhaps it was something stupid like they were using an unfamiliar blade? Colvin hopes that maybe the killer is losing confidence and maybe it's another sign that the assailant is slowing down.

Priya's death had however ended the code argument as there was a clearly defined number cut into each hand. A three cut into her left hand and a two cut into her right. The officers were all in agreement that they were definitely numbers but now they are arguing if this makes her code a three and a two, two separate numbers or a thirty two or a twenty three. Some are even arguing that maybe she is not connected to the other victims and that this is a separate number, cut by someone else trying to mislead them.

They did find a partial footprint on the kitchen floor, a match to one found at Kings Park, suggesting there could be a link but the bad news is it's a size nine, one of the most common male shoe sizes and the shoe itself was just as common.

Priya's death had hit the national papers. She had belonged to many online and offline strong communities and they weren't staying quiet about her death. Priya had been training to become a lawyer. One of her housemates had described her as outspoken, well liked and not afraid of anything. Her favourite hobby apparently was arguing with strangers on the internet. She had been a member of nine online global discussions groups and had a large range of interests from gardening, recipes, murder and law. She was a very valued member of these communities and rumours of her death have been greatly exaggerated across their forums. As a result the online sleuths are now swarming. Some are already outraged that their "helpful" suggestions are being ignored. The relentless onslaught of questions and demands from the public had been part of her responsibility, when she was on desk duty and they had been unbelievably exhausting.

On second thoughts, it might take more than ten minutes to explain all that to Grimm.

Two weeks later and Grimm still doesn't quite know what the hell is going on. Things haven't gotten any better. In fact, things are getting much, much worse and that's not just because of the vapour rub he is smearing under his nose. He can still remember when he first started investigating serious crimes, being given that age old advice to always put vapour rub underneath his nose for those particularly nasty cases (and so many of them were particularly nasty). Something menthol to block out the smell of the dead. Surprisingly, it works. Not brilliantly as it was never intended for such a market but it works.

What they never told him was what to do when your young children catch colds, when your wife insists on using vapour rubs to help them breathe through the snotty congestion. What do you do then? When those loving, adoring, mentholated children lean in for a goodnight kiss and you have to clench every muscle in your body to stop yourself from recoiling in disgust, as that smell is now permanently associated with over a thousand and one nights of terror, a bedtime story you can't even hint at to those sweet innocent children. They don't understand how much you hate that smell now.

He is rubbing the wretched stuff under his nose right now, trying to keep the memories from twisting in his head. They have been warned that this is a particularly bad one. Which is probably why he has been sent to investigate, dragging Colvin down with him.

"We were asked to do a wellness check by her family, apparently she missed her grandmother's birthday party on Sunday, and they panicked when she didn't answer her phone after two days."

Another home invasion, another innocent woman attacked in what should have been a safe place. "Victim has not yet been identified but suspected to be thirty-one-year-old Mary Angus." Their oldest victim so far, but still so young.

She had a nice house, before, Grimm can see that she had

put a lot of effort into matching her soft pinks, greys and occasional blues. He can see it used to have a nice little charm to it. He is more of a grey fan himself, hides the dirt, not too clinical and doesn't remind him of blood, that's all he wants these days. He doesn't really care that much about interior design, he is just trying to distract himself from the brutality. The downstairs furniture was disturbed, someone had been rummaging.

"No cause of death yet or estimation for time of death, all they could tell us is that she has been dead for several days. She lived alone."

Grimm doesn't like it when people live alone, especially young people. He has urged Colvin in what he thinks is a subtle manner, to get a housemate, boyfriend, live-in butler etc. There is a certain vulnerability that comes with living alone, an unnecessary vulnerability, people should not be easy pickings. Colvin, so far, just ignores his subtle hints.

He stares hard around the room, scrutinising the weaknesses of the house, looking for anything to indicate how the assailant broke in. What led to this attack? Why this target? Grimm has spent a lot of time staring at people's homes, thinking about how to break in. It is all too easy to find people's weak points, even now, when everyone thinks that they are taking extra special precautions. His wife always laughs at him when he says they need more security measures, theirs is the safest house on the street and they still need more?

"Front door was locked, we forced entry. No other sign of forced entry anywhere else." Grimm looks at the old sash windows, easy enough to open and close. The forensic officer examining it for fingerprints and tool marks thinks the same thing.

"They are finishing upstairs if you want to take a look before they move her." Colvin finishes her briefing clinically. She has already been upstairs, already seen enough, already shutting down all emotions so she can do her job. Grimm knows by the way she is acting that this is going to be bad. Trying not to show fear or reluctance he starts to climb the stairs taking deep, slow menthol breaths and making sure not to touch certain smears.

Colvin, not really wanting to look again, but not knowing what else to do, follows.

On her first visit to the room the fifth thing Colvin noticed was the victim's (presumably) expensive-looking mobile still sat untouched on her bedside table. Its battery, much like its owner, was long deceased. A blood splatter, long dried, ran across its screen.

The fourth thing Colvin noticed was that the cloth that had been used to gag the victim, it was the same colour and pattern as the victim's bed sheets.

The third thing Colvin noticed was the smell. It took a few minutes to notice but, when she inhaled deeply, trying to choke back down the bile, it hit her.

The second thing Colvin noticed, with disbelief, was the pink needle-nose pliers and matching hammer laying discarded close by, both covered in drops of blood and clumps of skin. An open miniature pink toolbox was at the foot of the bed. Colvin suspects it belongs to the victim rather than the killer. She could be wrong, but if it did belong to the killer, why didn't they take it away with them? Why did a killer seemingly come prepared but still wandered around Mary Angus's house, grabbing random items (a tool box, scissors, kitchen knife) with a "What is this? What can I do with it? What kind of pain can I inflict with this" mentality.

That didn't make sense, well none of this made sense, murders never make sense, but it made even less sense. The killer took the time to search the house but only for possible weapons, taking nothing of value (as far as she can tell.) While the victim just lay there, her phone in reach. Possibly she was unconscious but, if so, the killer was taking a risk that she wouldn't regain consciousness any time soon. The bruises on her wrists indicated at some point she was held down but not permanently restrained.

The first thing Colvin noticed was the barely recognisable face of the victim. Everyone who entered the room stood shocked for a few moments, hit by the long dead screams of pain, feeling nothing but anger for what had been done, grief because it had been done and horror because it had been done so brutally.

Re-entering the room whilst waiting for Grimm to recover from that first initial shock, Colvin tries to numb herself to her feelings. She still can't understand why someone had to be so cruel, what kind of sadistic monster would do something like this? What he did to Ruby was horrific, Priya had been even worse and now this? Colvin looks down again at the hammer, the tiny piece of scalp still clinging on and shudders. A cruel sadistic killer, growing in confidence, what could be worse?

CHAPTER SEVEN

Driving helps me to think. I like to think about them. What fun I had with them, how good that last one smelt. Her car smells just like her, reminding me of her each time I breathe in. I can't stop thinking about her, about how good she was... yes. She had good taste in cars too. She wasn't worthy to drive this beauty.

I think about other things too, not just about how long it will take for them to discover her, but how long it will take for them to realise her car is missing too. Should be a while, I have time to enjoy this for a little longer. You taught me not to underestimate them, they are idiots yes, but experienced idiots and even idiots get lucky sometimes. Never make it easy for them by doing something stupid.

I think about the other things you have taught me too. About how hard it is to keep a body hidden, how hard it is to protect myself from them. But I have thought a lot about this and the bodies. They are nothing, why waste time trying to hide them? Why not display one's work with pride? Let them fear, these women, they regard themselves too highly, they need to be taught their place again and fear is the best teacher. Fear makes them stupider too. We shouldn't fear them, they should fear us.

Driving around makes it easier to find the easy pickings. I try to do a full circuit every day now, every street, every cul-de-sac, get to know the rough areas, the quiet areas, which neighbourhoods won't even bother calling the police, and which ones are too scared to even peek through their curtains. The neighbourhoods with the faulty street lights. The busy houses, the houses with only ever one light on at night, the empty houses. They make it all so easy.

They don't know that I am watching them, that I am just

waiting for one of the dumb cows to separate out from the herd. It's the perfect hunting weather, everyone is walking past, heads down, not looking at anyone, just rushing to get out of the rain. Someone is going to be so grateful when I offer them a lift, promising to get them home safe.

It rains and rains, the women they go by, walking fast, no one noticing anyone or anything in their desperation to get out of the cold clinging rain. They don't look where they are going either. It rains and rains but he doesn't mind, it's only water, he will be home safe soon.

She won't be.

Colvin and Grimm don't say anything as the presumed Mary Angus is taken away. They stay out of the way of the forensic team, as the team swab, photograph, poke and prod around. They should be talking about the victim's hands, a starkly cut 4 on her left hand and a softer scratch of a 3 on her right. Priya Smythe was killed less than three weeks ago, similarly cut with the numbers 3 and 2. They were missing something, something obvious. The code has changed again. They are going to have to rethink their theories.

Officers Tichan and Juda are dispatched with a unit to conduct neighbourhood interviews, Officers Patel, Anderson and Bolz to talk to family and friends. Officers Grimm and Colvin are instructed to stay in the house (this order sends an unwanted shiver down both officers spines) to search for anything that might indicate that Mary Angus had been expecting someone or that she had a secret life like Ruby and Lucy, (a special punishment just for Colvin, if she is going to criticise officers for missing details, then she can be the one next in the firing line.) Most importantly, they are to look for the victim's purse and her keys.

It's not like they were alone in the house, there are still a small number of the forensic team wandering around, checking, packing up. Colvin can tell by their faces that they haven't found anything that important. Maybe a swab will come back with something, maybe. There are still tests to run, an autopsy to complete but she is not hopeful. Still, they got lucky with the Anne-Marie Mills case, a tiny shred of evidence was all they had needed. They will get lucky again. They have to.

"Let's take this room by room." Grimm quietly says, breathing hard through his nose, still trying to use the vapour rub as a shield. He needs to add a thicker layer. Colvin thinks he is talking to her but the suggestion was aimed at the oversized pink teddy bear to her left. She wonders idly what will happen to the bear now, would it be kept? Donated? Thrown away? Discarded as quickly as its former owner? Would it ever be hugged again? She would like very much to hug the bear herself right now, to assure it that the monster it had seen would be caught and punished for what it did. She doesn't say this out loud to Grimm and will never know that he is currently feeling the same way.

Grimm starts to mentally grid and check list the house; four rooms plus a bathroom and small outside back garden. They need to check for any other signs of entry, any signs that someone had been waiting in the garden, watching. Kitchen, living room, they suspect the killer had been rummaging for something, check for anything to indicate what could be missing, what might have been taken. Follow the blood splatter trail.

They follow the forensic markers into the kitchen, intending to start there. There are no blood marks or smears around the back door; it is firmly locked, no signs of forced entry and, without Mary Angus' keys, they can't get into the small garden without leaving the house. There is a member of the forensic team out there performing a perfunctory search. Colvin watches them for a moment then looks at the garden. It's very neat and pretty, a small piece of Astroturf, bordered with tubs of flowers. Colvin photographs what she can then turns her attention back to the kitchen. There is a smear of blood on the knife block, the largest knife missing. Colvin can remember seeing it upstairs.

"One set of dinner plates and cutlery on the drainer." Grimm narrates into a voice recorder, either she ate alone or they had a very polite killer. "So far it appears the only thing missing from the kitchen is a kitchen knife." Grimm looks inside the cupboards, inside the drawers. "Blood on the knife block and on the floor suggests the assailant began the attack on the victim upstairs first, then came downstairs again, possibly in search of weaponry. No fingerprints so far, likely to have worn gloves." Maybe they will get lucky and find the gloves discarded somewhere close by, better yet, in a suspect's home, irrefutable evidence, and they might get their budget unexpectedly quadrupled and a pig might even fly.

It could have been the victim, bleeding only slightly, coming downstairs, grabbing a knife, rummaging for another weapon then going back upstairs, to be finished off. Or was knocked out and carried upstairs. Maybe she did fight back, maybe they will find traces of someone else's blood for once. It just didn't seem likely.

Grimm opens the plain blue fridge slowly. He looks carefully at the leftovers for one, the now mouldy salads and vegetables. A small freezer compartment at the top of the fridge with nothing but ice-cream inside. He also notes that there are no signs of alcohol anywhere in the house, Mary Angus didn't have so much as one wine glass. So far, no hidden drugs, mobiles, money or porn. Nothing to indicate that Mary Angus was not as neat and pretty as her house suggests. But then they have only covered the kitchen so far.

Back into the living room Colvin checks out the bookcase in the corner, it has on it more photographs and candles than books. Colvin carefully photographs the photos, wanting an idea of who Mary Angus had been close to, then she carefully checks for anything that might be hidden in the frames. Grimm looks through the chest of drawers and notes that only the bottom drawer had been left open, usually the mark of an amateur burglar; they always start with the top drawer and work their way down, having to open and close each one. The pros save themselves valuable time by starting with the bottom drawer and working their way up. There is nothing exciting in the drawers; one was filled with scarves, another small pieces of costume jewellery, another was lots and lots of romantic comedy DVDs, with the legitimate DVDs inside and nothing else. Nothing taped underneath the drawers either.

Two hours of carefully checking everything downstairs and 200 pictures later, Colvin finds herself peering into Mary Angus's bathroom. There are no smears or blood drops in here, no obvious signs of misplacement. All perfectly normal as well; two tiny cacti on the windowsill, medicine cabinet full of make-up, make-up removal supplies and basic medication, nothing to suggest that Mary had any problems or even an indication that Mary had a love life. Colvin is beginning to suspect that Mary's only downfall in life was a lack of investment in basic security measures.

Grimm came out of the spare bedroom startling her. He is struggling still with the smell of decomposition which is following them both like a shadow. Unenthusiastically they both turn to the main bedroom. The forensic team have taken away most of it, gone of course is the victim, the blood soaked sheets, the weapons, the misused tools and the mobile phone. They haven't taken the blood splatters or the feeling of fear and desperation and the smell of death. Those things can never really be taken away. Colvin pities the next person who will sleep in this room.

It is a small room, dominated mostly by the bed. A wardrobe in the corner with some sensible clothes inside and another teddy bear. Grimm squeezes it carefully checking for something inside and ends up with more dried blood on his gloves.

Nothing, just like Priya Smythe. Colvin thinks over the similarities; both women were attacked in their home when they were presumably alone. Priya had been attacked in the kitchen. Mary had the contents of the kitchen brought to her. How did the attacker know that both women were alone in the house? Was the attacker known to both victims? Had he stalked both of them? Did they have something in common? Why the toolbox?

How could someone spend so much time stalking and yet come so ill-prepared? Or was that part of the fun? Hurting a victim with her own property? As well as using victims as a personal punching bag? And why had no one in the neighbourhoods reported any screaming? Why was the assailant so confident? How did he know he had time enough to both torture and search the house? Why search Mary Angus's house but not Priyas? What made him so certain that no one would hear the screams? That no one would come to the victims aid?

Why take Mary Angus's purse and house keys? Was he planning on coming back? Colvin tries to remember if anyone else's purse or house keys were missing. Did they take Mary's car? If so, why? Did the assailant need to transport something? Or was he too tired from physically abusing Mary Angus to walk home? Does that indicate that maybe all the previous places were within walking distance of the assailant's house?

"We need to know when Mary Angus's credit cards were last used." She says out loud to Grimm who nods, already having made a note of it. They have nothing left to search, they have found nothing. Colvin knows that there will be jeers from the other officers about how even Little Miss Perfect can't find a clue. Heaven help her if one of the others had actually managed to find something useful.

He slowly pulls the car to a stop, turning off the engine and lights but leaving the radio on quietly. A love song starts, its tenderness contrasting against the heavy rain beating against the windscreen, causing her to shiver slightly. They are both smiling with anticipation as he runs a hand down her soft coconut scented hair. Then he leans in for a long kiss and she answers with another eager kiss of her own, trailing her hands eagerly down his warm skin. One kiss follows another and soon their seatbelts are off. She feels so good but the handbrake doesn't. He doesn't want to stop kissing, stop touching but he also wants more, wants to be able to reach more. Huskily he suggests, quite daringly for him, that they move to the back seats. She surprises herself with a sultry yes.

They both get out of the car and he intends to move slowly to the back car doors, wanting to use the rain as an excuse to get out of wet clothes. He takes a slow deep breath, inhaling the intoxicating aroma of rain, grass … and smoke? She screams and points to another car on the other side of the field.

"Get in the car and call the police." He yells, all thoughts of romance gone. He watches helplessly as the flames grow, he intended to run over there, make sure no one was inside but the sound and sight of the tyres exploding, paralyses him. He can only watch, open-mouthed, soaked to the skin, not even hearing her pleading calls.

Rain pours down into every crevice soaking her filthy clothes against her bruised skin, firmly plastering her long hair into the mud and leaking down into the holes of her once expensive boots. The fire burns close by, too fiercely to be extinguished by mere rain. She doesn't feel the heat, the smack of the burning rubber as the tyres explode. She doesn't even feel the crunch as a clumsy boot treads over her already broken fingers. They didn't need to check for vital signs when they finally notice her, she was long gone.

Sam Colvin is aware of a change in the atmosphere as she enters the station the next morning. There are whispers and more frantic than usual phone calls. She is, at least, informed that the eleven o'clock briefing has been brought forward to right now, if she would kindly move into the conference room, yes bring your notes.

They all sit, divided in their groups; the officers who were here when The Numbers Killer was last assaulting the city vs the outsiders. Grimm comes in last, taking one of the many spare seats next to Colvin. She would have preferred to sit alone this morning. They start by talking about the Mary Angus case, each summarising what they have found so far. There are many pointed looks and quiet sniggers, when Colvin is forced to admit that they found nothing searching her house. They are confident that the assailant broke in via the window, carefully closing it as they left and that it was not a burglary gone wrong as the assailant's focus was on mutilating Mary Angus and nothing appeared to be missing except for her purse and house keys.

Equally Patel and Boltz gained very little from speaking to her family; Mary had been a very private person and told her family minimal personal information. Her mother had been hopeful that she had been seeing someone but Mary never confirmed or denied it. Her father was estranged from the rest of the family and no one could even confirm he was still in the country.

Anderson and another officer repeated similar information from her workplace; that she had been fairly well liked but she was described as aloof, private and distant. Her co-workers had last seen her on Tuesday 9th April and they had been worried about her, especially when she didn't answer the phone. They had been expecting her to return any day now, if only to claim the purse she had left on her desk. Then a ten-minute diversion as they speculate on why the assailant had searched the house so thoroughly, what he could have been looking for? Weapons had been their original guess, given the grievous misuse of Mary's toolkit but that didn't really make sense, given that she had already been injured at the time of the search. But, if it wasn't weapons, then what else could the assailant have been looking for? Drugs? Trophies? Just because they could? The general agreement was that there must have been something else in the house, Seasions, with a nasty gleam in his eye, volunteers to return to double-check the house. Finally Anderson is allowed to finish his part of the briefing; they are still interviewing, they still have Mary Angus's friends to talk to, they are working their way through the contact list on her phone. But so far nothing.

Her phone was the one found on her bedside table, which had seen all but recorded nothing. From what they can tell she had last accessed her phone around 10pm on Tuesday 9th, playing one of the many games on it, then the battery slowly drained away as the phone calls, voicemails and texts started trickling in. They think that the assailant had surprised her in bed, probably whilst she was asleep.

She never stood a chance, Colvin thinks sadly. She notices that Grimm is not contributing to anything and even looks slightly bored as Anderson talks on. He isn't even taking notes! Colvin herself is momentarily distracted as she tries to remember the last time Grimm was actually helpful. She is not missing much as Tichan and Juda recount what they have learnt so far by interviewing the neighbourhood. Which is nothing. Despite the assailant leaving Mary Angus's house, presumably covered in her blood, no-one noticed or heard anything unusual. The only interesting thing to note is that her next door neighbour, who knew her vaguely by sight, had thought she was away because her car, a noticeable shiny blue muscle car had been gone all week.

"Has an APB out on the car?" Colvin quietly asks.

"Oh haven't you heard? The car was found last night." No one dares to snicker as Chief Morkam speaks but Colvin caught a few more of their mocking looks. Lights are quickly dimmed and the projector is warming up as Morkam continues to talk about what happened last night. They hadn't even finished Mary Angus's autopsy when the call about a car fire came in. The body of an unnamed woman, with a number cut in her hand, lying close by.

Grimm's heart sunk deep in his chest, when the picture finally came on screen and he recognised the woman. She had been the Queen of the World once and she knew it. A fighter who would do anything to defend her title, young, beautiful, untouchable except for a high fee. She had everything and needed nothing except another hit. How quietly she fell, they all do, the clients suddenly get rougher as the fee gets cheaper and the drugs harder to find. Confidence abdicating its place to its favourite cousin, Desperation.

Her parents had once called her Wendy, Wendy Michealson. She was "twenty" the last time Grimm had seen her, back in

55

her better days, when, in reality, she was still sixteen or seventeen. They all stare at him when he tells them her name, even Morkam looks faintly surprised until he tells them that he has twice arrested her and has the scar to prove it.

The door slams loudly, signalling his brother is home. Adrian can hear, even from here, the tinny noise of angry music blaring through his brother's headphones. Stamp stamp stamp to the fridge, stamp stamp to his room, slam. DO. NOT. DISTURB.

Adrian almost misses the younger version of his brother, back in his whiny days and the fake fights they used to have. Now his brother is just angry all the time, angry at anyone who even breathes in his direction, lashing out with the merest provocation, to the point Adrian doesn't even try to talk to him any more. Then they fight because Adrian is "ignoring" him.

Music begins to blast from his brothers room, vibrating through the ceiling with loud angry thuds, his brother daring him to start another fight. Adrian grits his teeth and refuses to take the bait, packing up his maths homework to take to the library while mentally apologising to the neighbours.

They were divided up again after the meeting had finally concluded with some officers continuing their investigation into Mary Angus and their interviews. Those who had found nothing useful and had nothing else to do started on the Wendy Michealson case. Colvin and Grimm are assigned to "assist" the forensic examination at the site where Wendy Michealson had been found. Which basically means standing around in the cold, wet muddy field while trying not to get in the way of the forensic team but also not allowing anyone else on the scene. A fairly easy job for once as no-one except a traumatised teenage couple knew that they were out here. Grimm was happy to leave the station, knowing that the other officers would be openly speculating about how well he knew Wendy Michealson, Colvin was less happy, feeling that she is still being kept on the side-lines.

She is determined to use her time at this field wisely, to discover all she can. Right now she is scrutinising the multiple tyre marks in the mud. She would confide her thoughts in Grimm but he has taken up an "observation" position at the other side of the field. Which is fine, she doesn't need his help anyway. From what she can tell, it appears that the assailant drove the car here, probably with Wendy Michealson sitting in the front seat, killed her, drove away and then drove back. Possibly to get an accelerant, possibly to try his luck at seizing another potential victim. It is hard to tell now; they could be the same tyre tracks or they could be the tracks of the emergency response teams. They have no easy way of distinguishing each tread pattern, each footprint in the soft gooey mud. Did the assailant walk to Mary Angus's house then drive her car here? How did the assailant get home? They were estimating that Wendy has been dead for at least two days and Mary Angus around seven days, so what did the assailant do with her car in the meantime? Was the car torched last night because the assailant knew that they had finally found Mary Angus? How did the assailant know she had been found? The information had been kept out of the news so was the assailant watching the house? Watching the whole time they were there yesterday? A cold shiver shakes through Colvin's body, so many maddening questions and all the answers seem out of reach.

Focus on what's here, she tells herself, starting with what little remains of what was once Mary Angus's pride and joy. A burnt out shell of a car that will never be driven again. Any possible DNA evidence from the assailant would have been burnt away, which is probably why the flame was lit, but then why take the victim out of the car? Was she killed here? In this isolated field where no-one could hear her screaming? Did the assailant see the other car was on the field but still chose to set fire to the car, knowing no-one would see them in the heavy rain and darkness? Was the fire set purposely to draw them in? A special message of "Look upon my work and fear me! I am untouchable"

A long time ago Colvin once thought herself to be untouchable. Unstoppable. Now, out here in the field, she is not so sure. You can't doubt yourself when you are an officer of the law, you should never have time to doubt yourself. But they are just going round in circles again with this case and now they are back to the beginning again. They are back to: a high risk woman, brought to a secluded area, violently attacked and killed. They wouldn't have linked Wendy Michealson to Priya Smythe or Mary Angus if Mary Angus's car hadn't been here. That and of course the number, a deep number 5 in Wendy's broken left hand.

The rain starts again, falling heavily from the sky, washing away any remaining minuscules of precious evidence. Colvin starts to noticeably shiver as she thinks to herself what might happen if they don't stop this killer soon.

A certain dread comes with spring. A special dread. Spring is the time of planting, of clearing away the winter rot. People start to open their eyes again, they start walking out into the countryside for a nice bit of fresh air, they start exploring again and start finding things that have been hidden for years. Things like mouldy old sticks that look like bones, animal bones, or sometimes human bones with shoes still attached. Some panic, some search the internet "I have found a bone, what do I do?" and some call the police straight away. Others convince themselves that it is not human and rebury it, deep in their garden, then, for some inexplicable reason, they put their house on the market. Spring is the estate agent's busy season for a reason. Then spring becomes summer and not all the skeletons of the past stay silent.

A certain dread comes with spring. A special dread. Spring is the time of planting, of clearing away the winter rot. People start to open their eyes again, they start walking out into the countryside for a nice bit of fresh air, they start exploring again, start finding things that have been hidden for years. Things like mouldy old sticks, mouldy old sticks that look like bones, animal bones, human bones, shoes still attached. Some panic, some search the internet "I have found a bone, what do I do?" some call the police straight away. Others convince themselves that it is not human and rebury it again, deep in their garden, then for some inexplicable reason, they put their house on the market, spring is the estate agent's busy season for a reason. Some even load the bones into a bin bag and take them to the dump along with the rest of the garden rubbish. spring becomes summer and the skeletons of the past stay silent.

CHAPTER EIGHT

There is a different element to home invasion. Out there on the streets everyone knows it's not safe. It's your fault for wearing the wrong things, saying the wrong thing or even just having the wrong type of voice or appearance. It's your fault, you shouldn't have been born looking like that, you shouldn't have been out at this time of night, you shouldn't have fallen for the oldest trick in the book, whatever, it's your fault.

But home is different; you are supposed to be safe in your own home, unless you did something stupid like date or marry the wrong person or leave your door unlocked, then it's back to being your fault again. But home is meant to be the place where you can hide from the rest of the world. Safely.

When you are afraid, in your home they say it's really just a dread of being alone. It's not because you fear an intruder in the house, but because you fear the silence, the loneliness. You don't really fear that tell-tale creak of the stairs, shrieking under the weight of someone else's foot because you know you are alone. It's bollocks that the fear of the dark is just the survival instinct kicking in. You shouldn't ignore it.

You are meant to be safe when you are at home. You are meant to be safe when you are young and protected by Mummy and Daddy. So invincible. That's another lesson that needs teaching; no one is invincible except me.

Saturday 8th June and it's too damn hot. Day four of a relentless heatwave sees the city reluctantly waking up after a long night of wrestling with duvets, exhausted and already irritated. A perfect mix for a bad day. Most police officers know from first-hand experience that today is going to be a very bad day as tired, sweaty people brush against other tired sweaty people, as day drinkers stand up too fast from unshaded tables, knocking over drinks and goodwill. All it takes is one person not saying excuse me or sorry, for a push to become a punch, all because tired hot people don't back down, no matter how petty the issue.

Let's not forget that the city is already sinking deep into a sharp knifes edge, too many rumours of an overstated death, whispers and recounted memories of how bad it was, during that first round with The Numbers Killer. Now its round two and too many people have already been knocked out, before they even knew that they were fighting. When hot, angry people live in fear they need something to release their pent up frustrations on, a well-rested face or a police officer or maybe just someone who looks like they won't fight back. So many sitting ducks out there today. So many easy shots.

This is just the beginning, the start of what could be a long hot summer. Some officers really hate a hot summer as people go outside more, start taking more stupid risks and start doing stupid things like hiking with barely any water or drinking alcohol in a hot sun, slowly dehydrating with every sip or not wearing enough sunscreen and screaming murder when someone gently accidentally brushes on burnt skin. All these things draw attention away from the important issues like finding a serial killer, dividing their forces and leaving an easy opening for that certain someone to strike.

To make it even worse it is that kind of humid heat, the one that makes you conscious of every sensation, the constant warmth, the itching, the slow trickle of sweat running down your back, the tickle of a fly landing on your arm. Insects are everywhere, swarming around houses and workplaces with their constant irritating buzz, it is a chore to keep them away from faces, fruit and other food.

Some flies have found a delicious snack out on the park this morning,

The two girls lay side by side, their t-shirts and shorts folded into a neat pile beside them. They have lain back in their swim wear, on their towels, bathing in a pool of their own blood. That poor dog walker is going to need more than just a sympathetic ear. Her Labrador pulled her over, eager to lick at the meat and she pulled him back without looking, muttering an apology to those girls. A sad whine stopped her, forcing her to look. She sees the blood, the flies and the numbers. There is no mistaking them. By sunset, the whole hot, overstimulated city will know.

Everyone around Jenna is talking about the murdered women, all six, no seven of them. Seven? No mate, it's at least fifteen, at least! The same conversation and theories repeated day in, day out for months now. All people can talk about are those poor women, the ones the police are denying have a connection. The police are trying to hide the truth from them, that he is back and no one is to be trusted. The last known kill was back in April but they all know there have been more and the police aren't telling them everything they should be. Jenna shifts uncomfortably in her seat, feeling stuck in a haze of heat, sweat and death.

"If the first killings took place over a span of at least four years and he is back three years later, then he must be between the ages of thirty and sixty, most likely mid-late forties." A voice asserts confidently.

"He must have spent time in prison, how else would he have stayed out of sight for so long?"

"God it's so hot today"

"He could have been in the army, practising his killing in another country."

"Seriously, does that window open?"

"Is there a way of finding out who has been released from prison in the last few months?"

"I am sure there must be."

There are always ways of finding things out on the internet. They just might not always be true. Jenna inwardly chides, deciding to close out the conversations around her with an earbud and some soothing music, trying to imagine herself alone on a breezy tropical island. She pretends to focus on her phone but her eyes dart around her, is anyone watching her? It's always so hard to tell. She tries to memorise some of the more suspicious faces, repeating their descriptions in her mind, ready to describe them to the police.

"He wore a dirty white t-shirt and torn jeans. An earring in one ear and has blonde highlights in his short dark spikes. I noticed him because he wouldn't sit still."

"Male, about six foot, muscular, looks like he could take out a woman in one blow." And he was sitting across from her… oh god, oh god. Jenna tries to calm her breathing, he looks familiar? Had he been in the pub that night? Was he watching her? Jenna tries to pretend that this is her stop and gets off the bus two stops early, anxious to get away from Ben the beloved primary school teacher.

The "game" doesn't stop when she gets off the bus. She is noticing everyone now, the pack of mean looking teenagers, all ready to follow and pounce. The elderly man with a cane, who could just be wearing a wig and make up, all ready to follow and knock her out with his heavy stick. She walks quickly, trying not to run, she can't run in these shoes anyway and it's too hot to run, damn it! She is never wearing these shoes again! Is anyone following her? Is anyone watching to see where she lives? She walks down the wrong street on purpose, ducking into a corner shop, pretending to be interested in the window display, all the while peeking out to see if anyone is following her, to the slight amusement of the shop owner.

Did they strip off to sunbathe? Or were they forced to? Did the killer pick them because they were there? Or did they provoke him with their skimpy swimsuits? (You can guess which angle some will take tonight) There is no downplaying this one, no attempt to keep the city calm. Not that Colvin can even try to do that.

This raises another important question, how did the killer manage to take out both of them? Without the other screaming, without no one else seeing anything? Here in this busy park? This had been a fast kill, no beatings this time, just a cut to the throat. Maybe the second girl didn't have time to react, maybe they were both asleep when it happened, maybe they were drunk? They were not old enough to be drunk though, especially not that early in the morning.

Colvin mulls this over as she watches from afar, needing to witness but not get in the way of the forensics team. Already there are irritations, the weather being the source of them all by causing the rates of decomposition to speed up, making body temperatures unreliable for determining time of death. Sweat cascades down her own face, ruining her own professional look with flustered skin. She sips carefully at her water, it won't do to faint here, where everyone can see.

Around her Colvin can hear murmurings, whilst the general public were secured away, out of sight, they won't go away either. They stood around, trying to zoom in with their cameras, one guy even tried to launch a drone but was quickly stopped. They are all looking for an opportunity to see … something. They are talking amongst themselves, a steady hum of rumours, fears and outrageous speculations. Not realising that they themselves are being watched, photographed and observed by several discreet officers. Colvin starts giving orders quickly and quietly, spare officers are dispatched to seize any available CCTV footage from the surrounding areas, potential witnesses carefully herded away for questioning.

They are lifting the girls up now, hosting them respectably into body bags, anger and pain radiating out from underneath their protective gear. More photographs and swabs then the towels and clothes can be removed too. Colvin can see from her vantage point that the crushed grass that was underneath the girls is only slightly lighter than the grass around it. This indicates that the girls had not lain here for a long time.

Colvin can guess what happened; they lay here, on their towels, probably chatting happily when a shadow loomed above them. All they could see was the knife, which ordered them to strip off their clothes, then fold them neatly in a pile, no, that wasn't right. A killer willing to leave them exposed like this, on full display to the world, wouldn't care about folding clothes and they wouldn't be wearing swimwear.

They must have taken off their clothes themselves, maybe laid down to sunbathe and then the knife struck. But why hadn't either of them made a sound? Why had no one else noticed? Colvin looks around again. Perhaps, for modesty purposes, the girls had picked a slightly more secluded spot thinking they would be safe there together, away from leering eyes?

People will be blaming them for this, saying what do you expect? Flaunting themselves publicly, that wasn't right. Only middle aged men were allowed to strip down and enjoy the feeling of sun on their skin. They will blame the girls, their parents, their friends, everyone except the killer.

"Don't just stand there, do something!" a female voice yells at Colvin, cutting deep into her thoughts. The crowd falls silent, waiting to see how she will react. She can feel every eye watching her, silently challenging her, here she is, a police officer, something to channel their anger and fear on.

"Well, do something!" the voice demands again. "We are dying out here and YOU DON'T EVEN CARE!" Another voice close by shushes and soothes, urging the first voice away. They are all still waiting for a reaction, waiting for her to do or say something, preferably something stupid, something to give them all an excuse.

It's Saturday and Adrian would like to spend the day not existing. He would like not to exist for a long time, only coming back into being again when the whispers have stopped at school, when he is old enough to move out, when the good times can finally begin. He really doesn't want to be anywhere. Not at school, where he is constantly being pointed out by not so subtle pointers. Not at home, where his brother is ruling through fear. Not at his grandfather's house, where his deceased mother still dominates every conversation.

It didn't used to be like this, Adrian used to be one of the good guys, the one they could trust to walk them home from school in those times when no one walked home alone. He was the World's Best Big Brother, despite the fights. He was the brave one, the good boy. The worst of it is, he did nothing wrong. This is all his brother's doing, he doesn't even know exactly what his brother did, but it was bad, everyone said it was. So bad it couldn't be talked about. All they could do was whisper and mutter about how the apple doesn't fall far from the tree and the rotten apple, well that just stinks up the whole garden, spreading its rot through all its nearest and dearest. Adrian is not like his brother or his mother, nothing like them at all, no matter what they say.

He wanted to spend his summer somewhere far, far away from his brother and their whispers. Somewhere where his name wasn't met with suspicion or those knowing looks. But his father said no, he needed someone home to watch his brother, while he is at work. Someone to keep an eye on the unwatchable. He'll even pay Adrian to do so and followed this with a "please son, I can't do this without you". His father knows what kind of summer he is condemning Adrian to, that it is a cost higher than he can afford to pay, but Adrian just can't say no.

There was a time Grimm might have defended Colvin and stood by her side as she helplessly stood alone, bearing the brunt of the public hostility, but he didn't want to bring any attention to himself, didn't want his face on the news again, didn't want to remind the world that he still existed.

The incident is still bugging her even though she handled

it well enough in the end. He can tell by how subdue she is now, not contributing anything as they meet with the others to discuss Victimology. Juda is currently comparing bank statements, which sounded weird when he first suggested it, but kind of makes sense. It would have been a great idea if it had worked, but they can all plainly see that all eight of the women had nothing in common. If they used a gym, it wasn't the same one, they shopped in different places, led very different lives, four of them appeared not to even know each other.

The last two. Grimm wishes they were the last, but no, the latest two, they have now been formally identified as sixteen-year-old Claire Atkins and seventeen-year-old Nikki Woods, best friends since early childhood. Claire's devastated mother had confirmed that the girls had left together at 10am, planning to spend the hot day sunbathing and maybe a little swimming afterwards. Grimm unconsciously brushes his arm, still feeling the buzz of the flies. They had been found around noon by the dog walker. No one else they spoke to remembered seeing them or anything useful in the meantime. Grimm mechanically balls his hands into angry fists. Those girls were too young to be spending the day alone, someone should have watched out for them… why didn't they… Grimm swallows hard, knowing he is blaming the wrong people but… He glares down at his notebook

- Ruby Williams, 17 years old, full time student and sugar girl. Killed on Friday 19th October, found at Kings Park Saturday 20th. Badly beaten, strangled, throat cut, number one on hand.
- Carly Williams, 19, full time sugar girl. Killed and found Friday 9th November, Kings Park. Beaten, throat cut, number two.
- Lucy Swann, 21, Financial Advisor. Killed Friday 21st December, Kings Park. Beaten, throat cut, number one
- Priya Smythe, 22, University Student (Law.) Killed Wednesday 17th February in own home. Badly beaten, throat cut, either number thirty-two or twenty-three.

- Mary Angus 27, Auditor. Likely to have been killed on Tuesday 9th April or Wednesday 10th in own home, discovered 16th April. Badly beaten, suffocated, throat cut, either number forty-three or thirty-four. Only victim to have car stolen.
- Wendy Michealson, 25, possibly a full-time prostitute. Estimated to have been killed between Friday 12th April and Sunday 14th, discovered on 17th April. Dumped in field, badly beaten, throat cut, number five.
- Claire Atkins, 16, student, Saturday 8th June, Kings Park, throat cut, number four.
- Nikki Woods, 17, student, Saturday 8th June, Kings Park, throat cut, number six.

It stinks, it all stinks. To have so many young girls killed in what should have been safe places. It stinks to have the public giving THEM the stink eye. It stinks because someone, probably Boltz, isn't wearing enough deodorant, making the already airless room intolerable. Grimm is waiting for someone else, someone with a more 'delicate feminine nose' to suggest opening a window. Beads of sweat drip down his neck, sliding underneath his un-ironed shirt. He is going to need a spatula to scrape his clothes off tonight.

They are speculating now on why they think that the assailant may have sped up and it's quickly turning into an argument about whether or not it is The Numbers Killer again, whether there is more than one of them and how many there could be. Yet again, no one is backing down or even listening to each other. They just don't have anything solid or useful. Grimm doesn't join in the arguments, he is tired of sitting in this stuffy room wasting more and more precious time, he has places to be, children to hug close. No one is saying anything useful or new, they are growing paranoid over the possibility of a whole cult of killers, discussing "Special Measures" that have never worked before and won't work now. Grimm knows better than to point that out. Usually Colvin would be the irritating voice of reason, pointing out the obvious, but she is still subdue, merely staring into space, or perhaps she has finally realised the pointlessness of speaking against the crowd?

A whole cult of serial killers? Some people watch too much television. Grimm mentally tuts at them and their stupid theories. It is clearly one person, a male, growing in confidence and discovering new ways to be a complete bastard. He is experimenting, killing when the opportunity was easy and stalking when his prey was hiding. He is hindered only by a work schedule and Grimm thinks they should be looking for someone who works shifts. Not that that really narrows things down but it is a more realistic start than what some of the others are suggesting.

They should be focusing on Mary Angus, he eventually suggests when the others finally quieten down, trying to change the subject to something more useful. Eyes roll, there are pointed looks and mutters. She is the one most violently attacked, is his reasoning, the one who had her car stolen, the one most likely to be known personally to the killer. There has to be a connection between them. She must have mentioned something to someone about being followed or about upsetting someone, there has to be something. He is quickly talked over, the conversation changes before he has even finished thinking and then they have the audacity to wonder why he rarely contributes to these meetings. Well he is going to take a closer look at Mary Angus. He bets somewhere, on the long list of people she had audited, there will be something useful. The lucky break they have all been waiting for.

Colvin is numb. She is aware of the discussions going on around her but all she can hear is the accusing voice, "We are dying out here and you don't even care." Such an overdramatic cliché yes, but it worked. What was it that upset her the most about that comment? In the line of duty she has been screamed at, sworn at, been sick on, bled on, spat on, and squeezed inappropriately. But nothing has ever affected her like this, never felt so hurt or betrayed by those people. The people she is sworn to protect. Is it because the voice was right? She doesn't care if that particular voice is killed, well not after how she swore and cursed her in front of everyone until Colvin was on the verge of arresting her. That voice could go to hell for all she cared, a forbidden voice whispers. Colvin straightens up quickly, worrying that somehow someone heard what she was thinking or guessed what she had been thinking from her facial expressions. No, they are too busy discussing stupid 'solutions.' A quick glance around the room and she can tell no one has been paying any attention to her.

"You don't even care." Maybe it was the insinuation that she didn't care for the two young girls, or any of the women murdered so far. The accusation that she didn't feel anything, because she did, and she is finding it harder every day not to let any of those feelings show. It is too unprofessional. She works so hard to take killers off the street, sacrificing any possible hopes of a love life, or even a friendship outside of work, not to mention any hopes of a reconciliation with what was left of her own family. She just works and works and works and what happens? She gets a pat on the head and quickly dismissed if she does well, scorn if she doesn't and no matter what, eventually another innocent gets murdered, another assailant avoids justice and she gets accused of not caring, of not working hard enough! Her! Out of all of the officers on the scene today why did that horrible woman have to accuse her? That horrible vile woman, standing there with her horrible growling Chihuahua, both giving the indication that they will bite at any given opportunity. That mangy horrible woman who has now taken up permanent residence in Colvin's mind.

"You don't even care." She only has to close her eyes and she is back in the sweltering sun, standing in the park, the smell of death wafting in the air. Never again would she even be able to have a picnic or a quick lunch in that park without remembering. Even if she moved out of the city, to a quiet little village in the middle of nowhere, no matter where she goes, a sunny day and some green grass will forever be linked with accusing voices and two girls lying side by side in pools of their own blood. "You don't even care." And she doesn't.

CHAPTER NINE

There is an old saying, "Why hunt for a lion when you can kill a lamb?" but there is no challenge to killing a lamb, is there? I mean it's still fun but if you want a kill you can be proud of, you take down a lion.

They also say, we humans are pursuit predators, that through endurance, we can outpace most creatures just by speed walking. The little creatures run and run and run, overtiring themselves, overextending themselves, not looking where they are going. They pause, thinking that they are safe, that they have lost you, pause to catch their breath and by that point you have caught up and you are ready for more.

They also say that we are not human. I am happy for them to believe that.

It has been nearly two months and they still have so little. They have spent weeks going through CCTV footage, combing through, looking for any signs of Mary Angus's distinctive car. Not that the public appreciates just how hard it is even to find those blurry images, they seemed to think that an alert goes off automatically whenever a crime is taking place, capturing the right images at the right angle, at the right time and is then emailed across to the right person. They seemed to think that everything is available instantly and requires no work to find it.

Take for example, the petrol idea. The assailant had been driving Angus's car presumably for several days, the assailant also used petrol as an accelerant when setting alight to her car. It is likely that at some point they refuelled the tank, especially as Mary Angus's bank statements showed that she had last refilled it three weeks prior. So the idea was to comb all available CCTV footage of petrol stations in the hopes of finding a clear image of the assailant and, if they were really lucky, they would get the credit card details of the assailant as well.

In the city there are over a hundred and fifty petrol stations. Seventy of which operated on a 24 hour basis, the rest were open an average of 12 hours a day. It is a horrifying maths problem; how many hours of footage did they have to look through given they are looking at a possible span of seven days?

70 x 24 = 1680 x 7 = 11760

80 x 12 = 960 x 7 = 6720

11760 + 6720 = an approximate 18480 hours of footage

Then add in warrants to access the footage, actually getting the footage from over 150 different sites, the long talks with managers etc. etc. It would have been worth it if they had found something. But they didn't.

Then there was the interviewing, each interview took between 30 minutes to an hour and they needed to interview an average of sixty people per victim; roughly ten family members, fifteen friends, twenty work colleagues and around fifteen neighbours plus possible eye witnesses etc. In Wendy Michealson's case, so many hours were spent just trying to find people who would admit to knowing her. All her known associates, the ones still alive, said that they hadn't seen her in months, she was turning over a new leaf, they were turning over a new leaf, she had been trying some new kind of scam but they didn't know what. She is the one they have the least information about. They weren't even sure where she lived.

There have been eight known victims so far. Thirty-to sixty minutes multiplied by sixty people is somewhere between 1,800 minutes to 3,600 minutes of interviewing per victim, multiplied by eight means between 14,400 to 28,800 precious minutes just interviewing people or, to put it another way, a solid forty days of twelve hours shifts if one person was doing all the interviewing. Then they had to follow up all their suggested leads, check out alibis, try to comprehend the vast mountains of crime scene photos, DNA evidence and follow any leads that the forensics team suggest and so forth and still have time for paperwork, emails, meetings and coffee. Maybe Grimm should be working instead of doing the maths but he is on a roll here. Maybe he should show his calculations to Morkam, who can show them to the press and public, something to ease up the constant criticisms, the unhelpful leads, the time wasters. No, he cautions himself sternly, don't stick your neck out like that, remember what happened to Vogel.

Maybe he will take his calculations home to show his wife, proof of how hard he is working, something to combat against her suspicious glares and careful sniffing. Something to show his children as an apology for a lot of things or maybe he could just throw away these calculations and get back to work. That could be the best thing to do.

He rubs his eyes again trying to comprehend the list in front of him. Nikki Woods had been a bit of a heartbreaker and her friends had "helpfully" provided a long list of thirteen boys and nine girls who might have held a grudge against her for various reasons. All needed finding and interviewing. He scans the names again; Billy Tepper, Mohammed Setti, John Woo, Tom Parry, Caleb Bulrush, Micheal Wilkes, Andrew Yeomans, Janet Goldman, Kate Thomson and Lauren Smith to name a few. None were really the right age to be considered a possible suspect but they couldn't just be dismissed either, you never know what connections they might have. Grimm has seen before what some teenagers are really capable of and he still shudders at the memory.

"Be careful out there."
"I'll be fine, I have nothing worth stealing."
"That's what my neighbours' friend used to say. It's a shame how

they found her, minus her kidneys."

"Please call me when you get home."
"And you call me when you get home."
"I'll call you if you call me."

"Text me when you get home."
"Sure."
"Not when you are on the bus, when you are actually home."
"Sure."
"Don't you dare go near that park."
"Sure."

"Please don't go, it's not safe out there."
"You know, sooner or later, you are going to have to leave the house."
"Please, we can order pizza."
"Come on, you can't stay inside for the rest of your life."
"It's not safe."
"If anyone comes near me, I'll kick them in the balls and run away."

"Cathy, please don't go."
"I'll be fine."
"Please."
"Look, you can't go through life holding back, not wanting to get hurt. This could be a big break for me. I am not giving up on my dreams now, I've worked too hard for this."
"But Cathy"

His brother is not home yet. Adrian has no idea where he is or why he is daring to go into his brother's room but he just can't resist it. Maybe he is looking for a trace of evidence that his old brother still exists, maybe he is looking for something that will make his brother go away for a long time, to prison, or to a secure ward or even just to Grandma's house. Something, he wants to find something.

He slowly creaks open the door, carefully listening for the accusing shout. All he can smell is sweat and unwashed hair. If his mother saw the room like this his brother would be in so much trouble. She would make him pick up those torn posters and pictures and repair those punch marks that border the walls, those midnight thuds finally explained. Adrian wants to go further in but can't. His nerves are screaming at him to get out now, that it's not safe. The room and his brother are unwelcoming and dangerous, they should not be risked alone. He backs out quickly, closing the door behind him, still feeling like he is being watched. He turns around to see nothing, looks around, no one is home but still... he retreats to his own room as quickly as he can, ashamed of his own fear and cowardice.

"How did it go with the interview? With Andrew Yeomans?" Colvin asks cautiously.

"Great, learnt nothing, got no new leads and Andrew is one of those boys-" Grimm pauses, looking around to make sure no one is in earshot, "who walks around like this." He scrunches up into a hump figure, grabbing his crotch with an exaggerated movement. "You know the type Sam, their balls are so small they have to walk around holding them just so they don't lose them." Colvin smiles weakly, she doesn't want to encourage this behaviour but, at the same time, it has been a long day and Grimm knows how badly she needs to smile. The worry deepens though, no wonder Grimm is getting nowhere if he is acting like this in his interviews. No, she tries to inwardly argue, he is a professional, he knows what he is doing.

But does he though? You have to admit... a long resonating burp cuts through her inner debate, ending all argument and she laughs as Grimm pats his stomach with a satisfied look.

"That's disgusting! What did you eat??"

"Disappointment" Grimm answers, adding in another burp "Deep-fried!" There is a pause then the thoughtful "And what did you have for lunch Sam?"

"Salad" Colvin turns her face away as she speaks. They both know she is lying. It is not like she is doing it on purpose. She packed a salad yesterday then forgot to eat it and intended to eat it today after her interview with Donald "Lovie, call me Don" Johnson. Mr Johnson had been suggested to them as a person of interest. Colvin could tell why after just a few moments with him. He was an absolute creep, harmless but still. The sort of creep that leeches and leers at young female customer service assistants in a shop, "Hello there girlies", and then complains when he gets a frosty service. The type that thought Nikki Wood was a fine girl, just a shame about her terrible attitude. If they got a search warrant for his home computer, Colvin bets it would be filled with pornographic images of fine girls who were only just legal. But they *would* be legal. He was not that sort of creep.

Grimm is now lecturing her about the importance of having three good meals a day, a lecture she has heard many times before. He continues, undeterred by her eye-rolls and the fact she is blatantly not listening. A man who eats deep fried junk for his lunch has no right to lecture her anyway. Where was she? Donald Johnson- a creep. Harmless but of no future interest to the police. She pauses to remind herself not to be fooled by anyone who looks harmless. Anne-Marie Mill's murderer looked harmless, was as normal as normal could be.

"You know what you need Sam?" Grimm interrupts her thoughts. She needs many things right now; a decent night's sleep is top-of the list. She is certain that she is not going to need anything that Grimm is going to suggest but she is listening for once. She becomes slowly aware that some of her fellow officers are also listening, nudging each other and snickering. Grimm notices them at the same time, stopping abruptly mid-suggestion. He stiffly turns and walks off. Colvin did intend to follow him but is distracted by her phone ringing.

It's several hours before she sees Grimm again, head down, mouth moving as he reads an email. Maybe she has been avoiding returning to her desk, maybe she had other non-desk related things to do. He stands up before she sits down and is gone before she thinks to say goodnight. She doesn't know what is going on and she doesn't care. She has paperwork to do, lots and lots of paperwork.

Nothing is said the next morning. There is a feeling that Grimm wants to say something but only clears his throat and then clears his desk instead.

"Want to sit in a few interviews with me?" He finally asks in a tone that Colvin is not familiar with. She follows him without speaking to the interview room. There is a surly greasy youth in there, waiting for them, dominating the room with the scent of cheap body spray and hair gel. Grimm introduces them both quickly, pauses to fake a smile and assure the youth that "This won't take long."

Inwardly, Colvin begins to fume, this won't take long??? The only way that Grimm could have phrased that even worse would be to just openly ask "You didn't see nothing did you? No? Next!" She finds herself wondering again how many other interviews Grimm has conducted like this, how many hours have been wasted because the interviewees felt that they couldn't confide in this police officer, how many more hours they will have to waste, re-conducting those interviews? Grimm never should have been allowed to do this on his own.

The youth in turn gives another half shrug. Colvin tries to calm herself down, maybe it is just this one? She would probably be getting the same results, the same open hostility but maybe she should have a private word with Morkam? Maybe she should step in now, try and salvage the interview by taking over? Sometimes it would be a lot easier if she just did all of the investigating by herself, it would be a lot slower but she would be in control of everything and she wouldn't be wasting time with rookie errors. So engrossed in her thoughts, Colvin misses Grimm's next question but the teen smiles, sits back, unfolding his arms. "I dunno, man, I dunno." He says with a laugh. "But I can tell you…"

One greasy youth is swapped for another angry greasy youth. This one is one of the many boys who tried to ask Claire Atkins out but was shot down with laughter. Colvin recognises him but can't remember why. Hostility radiates from his body but Colvin does not feel the slightest bit intimidated or threatened. He is an angry little boy, trying to convince everyone he is not scared by behaving like a jerk. He won't stop staring at her but won't answer any of her questions either.

Colvin feels that if she asks the wrong question he might try something stupid like throwing a chair. A boy brimming with rage but still just a small boy. He will be trouble when he grows out of this awkward stage. She wouldn't want to meet him alone in a dark place, especially given the fact that his most angry stare has been reserved for her alone. Colvin tries to remember if they have met before but most of her older memories have been locked away by too many nights of broken sleep and the lock is weighed down by all the tiny little details of this current case.

He won't tell them anything. All he needs to say is where he was on Saturday 8th June and he won't. Colvin already knows from talking with his father that he was still in bed at the time of the murders and didn't leave the house once that weekend. This interview is just meant to be a formality. But by not saying anything he looks like he is hiding something. Perhaps his father is lying, perhaps his father is also involved? Neither are quite a person of interest just yet but something is definitely going on here.

They finally end the interview and Colvin and Grimm both lead the boy out to where his father is waiting. To Colvin's surprise his father is talking with Morkam in hushed tones and there is a tense feeling in the air. She is aware that some of the other officers are murmuring and "subtly" pointing at them. The father tries to smile, he goes to gently touch his son reassuringly on the shoulder, tries to say something, but his son only angrily shrugs his hand away and stalks off towards the exit. His father gives them an embarrassed look as if to say "Teenagers! What can you do?" then follows his son.

"Where are you?"

"Please call me back, I'm worried."

"I am sorry, I am running late, are you still at A-Maze? I will be about ten more minutes."

"Please Cathy, answer the phone."

"I am at A-Maze but I can't see you, are you in one of the booths?"

"Where are you????"

All the voices, all those pleading, whining, happy, angry, drunk voices. You just press a button and they all start to play. They rarely get to hear the victim's real voices but they drown in the voices of their loved ones. Colvin thinks darkly as she listens to the voicemails on Cathy Clark's phone. Cathy has been missing for three days now and so far they have only found her phone and house keys in the lost property box at a local pub called A-Maze.

Cathy's bank has confirmed that there have been no activities on her account in those last three days, suspicious or otherwise. Her last purchase was a drink and a side order of chips at A-Maze at 7.15pm on Friday 9th August. Hopes of finding her alive are slowly dimming down into hopes of just finding her. She could be another Number victim, she could be a victim of someone else, she could just be hiding, as one member of the public has cruelly suggested, because some people will do anything for attention.

Cathy had gone out to meet local director Maxwell Penfold, "for advice." He was supposed to meet her at seven but ran late. By the time he called around eight she was no longer answering.

A-Maze had a frustrating lack of useful CCTV cameras

with the majority of them pointed at the dancefloor or the bar. Cathy, according to eye-witnesses, had been approached when she was sitting down, eating her chips. One of the eye-witnesses was positive about this because he had just been about to approach her himself when the other guy stepped up. He kept watching because he didn't reckon too much on this wimpy guys chances and had been astonished when he saw them leaving together. He didn't think she was that kind of girl. He waited for a good twenty minutes for her to come back before moving on to another girl. He kept an eye on her chair, half watching her coat and phone vibrating on the table, her half eaten chips going cold, thinking she would be back any minute given she had left those things behind.

She must have thought she would be coming back.

He didn't get a good look at the other guy, not a memorable look. Nerdish is how he described his competition, skinny, he didn't really look past his thick framed glasses, he was more interested in Cathy not the nerd.

Maxwell Penfold, the director and actor, could be described as a skinny guy with a nerdish air. He has performed very well in his interviews, Colvin could almost convince herself that he cried real tears. She would be investigating him more closely if he didn't have such solid alibis. Over twenty people and a security camera saw him leaving the theatre at 8.15pm, getting into a taxi and arriving from said taxi in full view of one of A-Maze's security cameras. He can be seen on the same camera, leaving alone twenty-ish minutes later and reappearing at the theatre because he apparently forgot his keys.

He said that he was just meeting Cathy as a friend to give her some pointers for her next audition. Colvin very much doubts that it was as innocent as that, but still, Maxwell Penfold did not kidnap Cathy, well not personally. If he was involved then a friend must have done the actual kidnapping for him, he just lured. Nothing in his phone records suggest this and he has no known connections to the other victims, unless they were also aspiring actresses. No, Colvin knows that she is only clutching at straws here. Maxwell Penfold may not have been genuinely concerned about Cathy but that did not make him a twisted depraved serial killer.

They have other leads to follow; Cathy worked two jobs, had a very large circle of family, friends, ex-boyfriends and ex-girlfriends so there is still a chance they might find a lead there.

"You know this could all just be a hoax?" Grimm quietly says, interrupting her thoughts. "A way of catching the public's eye, a way of gaining fame." She wouldn't be the first.

"Have you seen this?" Colvin retorts, pulling out a few pieces of paper with a flourish. "This is her last bank statement." Grimm scans it quickly then returns it with a "So?" shrug. "I don't think the girl who spent her last twenty quid on a flower delivery for a sick friend, would put her same friends through this kind of hell just for an extremely small chance of an acting contract, do you?"

"People are lying cheating shits Sam! You know that, I know that, anyone who plays a few rounds at a pub quiz knows that!"

Colvin turns away angrily. It's true, some people are lying shits but she doesn't want Grimm to be right that Cathy Clark is alive and well, that it is just a publicity stunt. But then she would like Grimm to be right because she wants Cathy Clark to be alive and well somewhere. She wants Cathy to have a happy ending. Maybe she is linked to the Numbers killings, maybe she is not. Maybe they will still find Cathy Clark alive and well, maybe this has all been a hoax, maybe she will always be a little lost voice, calling "pick me" to the retreating back, the dismissed failure who never stopped dreaming.

Two weeks away with her two best friends and Jenna should be having the time of her life but they are all driving each other insane. They need some time apart but, at the same time, no one wants to be alone. Jenna keeps trying to remind herself that she is not in the city anymore, that it is safe here but she can't stop that little voice in the back of her mind from screaming that she is not safe, nowhere is safe and evidently the others feel the same. Her normally quite flirty friend is actively avoiding men and her other normally friendly and outgoing friend keeps nervously asking if they can just chill out in their room. Jenna would normally insist on at least three cultural activities that involve an art gallery or a museum but she feels uneasy every time she thinks about leaving the hotel. At this rate they will be going home just as frazzled as when they left. They probably won't even be talking to each other at that point.

Home. Despite everything, she doesn't want to go home and, every day, the knot in her stomach twists tighter as their departure date steps that little bit closer. They scan their local news headlines every day, checking for updates. Have they caught the guy yet? Have they? Have they found any new victims? Have they found Cathy Clark yet? They have all become addicted to a local website called ItCouldHaveBeenMe.co.uk. It's all they can talk about in the evening, the latest theories and rumours that have been posted on the chat boards. Jenna is a firm believer in the theory that it is a police officer, who else would be able to remain undetected for so long, especially with all the scientific advances they have made with DNA etc.? Who else would be able to strike in broad daylight without anyone else noticing? Didn't one of them make the papers last year for inappropriate relations with another serial killer? Everything just stinks of a cover up. Her friends disagree, they think it is a husband and wife team, which does make some sense but Jenna just can't picture a woman doing such brutal things as plucking out the eyes of her victims. "Well, look at Rosemary West for example," was her friend's snappish retort in a tone that Jenna didn't like. She didn't want to look at Rosemary West either, didn't want to listen anymore, just wanted to change the subject. They would have started an argument there and then if it wasn't time for Happy Hour.

Later, with three strong cocktails inside her, Jenna looks

across the crowded bar, throat tightening, tears threatening, not wanting to be here, not wanting to go home, wondering if she will ever be able to enjoy anything again, wondering if she will ever feel safe again. She tries to stand up but her legs won't stop shaking and everything feels so cold. The last thing she feels ~~is~~ are large hands clasping her from behind and seeing her two friend's scared faces in front of her. "No, not me, please don't hurt me", are the last things she thinks before collapsing in a dead faint.

"Have you interviewed Barry Jones yet?" One of Cathy's many exs.

"Yes" Grimm isn't even trying to be helpful anymore.

"Why is Seasons saying that you won't help tail Craig Barrie?" Another ex, one with a police history.

"It's a waste of time Sam, the guy's not worth it."

"He could lead us to Cathy."

"Only place he is going to lead us is to the pub and back."

"I can't believe you are disobeying orders."

"And I can't believe that you're acting as stupid as they are. I want to catch this killer just as much as anyone else but we're not going to catch him if we are wasting time and resources on nobodies!"

Colvin wants to say more, she wants to start with pointing out the stupidity of disobeying orders, especially when you are still on probation for the last stupid thing that you did. That just because you decide that someone isn't a killer doesn't mean that they aren't. She is close to pointing out that if it was up to Grimm then Anne-Marie Mills's killer would still be at large. She wants to say all this but she is aware that a. the look in Grimm's eye is dangerous and b. they now have an audience. She turns to see Morkam standing there, his face impassive, his voice not betraying anything. "My office now" he says calmly to Grimm.

Grimm is in a foul mood when he comes out. He was in there for a long time Colvin notes, both speaking in voices too soft for the onlookers to overhear. But that look on his face as he walked out, Colvin knows not to approach him. Not that she wants to. Right now Colvin is getting sick of having to tip-toe around him, of having to do most of the work, of having to share an office space with him, of having to share air with him. He is just determined to drag himself down and out and he is not going to take her with him. He is not going to distract her from what is important either, finding Cathy Clark alive and finding the assailant.

They are blaming him for their own idiocy. Grimm is well aware that he is the new Vogel, the new scapegoat and will be until he retires. He doesn't really care, this is nothing compared to his wife's antics.

They need a punching bag. They are getting nowhere and need someone to take their frustrations out on. They haven't gotten anywhere even remotely close to finding even a decent suspect, so someone must be missing something obvious and it must be the killer kisser, the murderers mate, Nicolas Grimm. Never mind how hard he worked all these years, all those cases he successfully closed, no matter who he was, this is who he really is. They will never forget that.

And it was only one fucking kiss, that's the worst part. He didn't initiate it, didn't expect it. What was he supposed to have done? Arrested her for sexual harassment? Grimm swallows his anger back down. He knows where this kind of emotion can lead, has seen too many victims of it. He needs to do something to get rid of it without hurting anyone else. Until then he just needs to grin and bear it even though his balls are in the vice and they are twisting too hard, just grin and bear it Grimm, just grin and...

CHAPTER TEN

You know what people never look that closely at? Suitcases. Suitcases big enough to fit a person into (with some bending or chopping required). And suitcases can be moved quickly without anyone batting an eyelid, some people will even help you with the hoisting. It is not as fun as playing the "my girlfriend is really drunk and I am just taking her home" game but people are less likely to remember your face.

See I just can't stop thinking of ways to improve the experience, keep smoothing out all those potential problems. How to get the maximum enjoyment out of everything. I can't stop thinking about it, about them, about how to do better next time. There is so much more we could be doing, so much more.

Still, learn by doing.

It is peaceful here. It is calm here. It is safe here. It is the perfect spot for a photo shoot Jillian thinks to herself. No, not the sordid kind, she knows what some people think. Her subject is the most perfect of all goddesses: Mother Nature. Stripping herself bare in true autumnal fashion. Jillian's hands shake in excitement. She wants to capture it all; the soft shivering waves of warm orange, the golden leaves falling from the skies like raindrops, contrasting against the impossible blue skies. She wants to start by doing everything: taking photos, writing poetry, sitting back and watching the slow elegant dance of leaves. It's unnervingly quiet here, apart from the wind howling, almost as if the whole forest is waiting for her, watching her. She giggles softly to herself, ashamed of her ridiculousness and takes a comforting sip of her green tea. Then moves, camera in hand to capture the descent of a lone, falling leaf.

Another strong gust hits with a sharp cry, rippling and rattling the ground leaves, shaking through the dry branches of trees. She sets up the slow motion capture on her camera ready for the next hit. Perfect, perfect, she is really happy with how these pictures are turning out. Hold it! What is that red? Too cheap a red to be a leaf. It must be someone's abandoned toy. How dare they! People need to stop discarding their litter with reckless abandon. It's disgusting, that's what it is, absolutely disgusting.

She stomps over to those little pieces of tarnished red, buried beneath the leaves, winking up at her. Her warm hand moving down to sharply yank away this sordid rubbish. It takes a moment for her brain to process just how heavy this cheap toy is, she didn't expect this level of resistance. She pulls harder, still not registering that the red enamel is someone's painted fingernails and those fingernails are still attached to their owner's cold fingers.

She has such pretty red nails, perfectly polished with the colour of confidence. Not a single scratch on them. Another indicator that she didn't even have a chance to fight back. Colvin stares at the nails, the hand with an unmistakable 7 cut deep. Its owner still mostly buried in the leaf debris. Such pretty nails.

The forensic team are working hard to slowly remove the leaves, not wanting to lose any possible evidence still trapped underneath. The wind keeps blowing, hurtling their equipment and more sodding leaves everywhere. Colvin and Grimm both have strict instructions to stand there and hold equipment but at least they are helping. Well Colvin is helping, she is not sure how helpful Grimm's mutterings and jokes are. "We're gonna need a bigger rake", was not his best effort.

Colvin is mostly ignoring him, spending her time wondering about the girl with the confident nails. Trying not to watch as she is slowly unearthed but not able to turn away. How did she end up here? How long has she been out here? What is her name? Who is missing her? Could this be Cathy? After nearly two months of endless searching have they finally found her? If not, is Cathy out here too? Who else could be out here? They will need to conduct a full search of the woods, search deep underneath the leaves. For evidence, for more victims, search deep to find out what else is buried under a fuck ton of leaves. Fucking leaves. The assailant must be laughing his head off knowing the man power and hours it will take to go through this wood. Everything must be one big fucking joke to him. She just wants to swipe the smile off his face and bury it deep underneath these leaves. Hell, she wants to bury his whole face, not just his smile.

There has been another one. After all these months of anxious waiting. They haven't released a name or a photograph yet but they all know she has a number. Anxiety shakes through Jenna's body making her feel sick and faint at the same time. She would be useless against an attacker she thinks to herself, her only defence would be to throw up and then faint. She can feel her skin goose pimpling in fear. She hates all of this, the anxiety, the sickness, the shakes. Ever since she came back from holiday she has been living on a steady diet of poor nerves, yoghurt and vodka. People were noticing. They won't stop giving her soft 'you will be ok' hugs and shoulder pats. They are not helping. Nothing is helping. Anxiety has dug too deep inside of her and is now bursting out through every skin seam.

She feels like she can do nothing but wait for updates on the current victim and the previous victims. Wait to see who will be the next victim, powerless to do anything except wait. Why haven't they released any more information? Why haven't they arrested anyone yet? Why haven't they done anything yet? What is it going take for the police to start taking this seriously?

"Shall we make like a tree and leaf?" Grimm asks Colvin out of earshot of the others. It wasn't funny the first time, four hours ago and it's really not funny now. They are losing light and it is nearly time for them to leave, for the next team to take over. It's been four hours and they still know practically nothing.

Red Nail Girl has nearly been completely unearthed now, but not yet taken away. They have more bits to slowly remove and bag. They have checked her pockets and found nothing, no purse nearby, no keys, no phone, not even a tissue. No means of identification. They might be able to reconstruct some of her facial features, see what she used to look like before the bruising and the swelling, underneath the blood and the dirt. Identifying her is going to be extremely hard, the assailant has found another way to slow them down or so he thinks. Sometimes when people go to unusual lengths to hide a body, to hide an identity, they expose themselves in the uniqueness. There is still hope.

Grimm is glad to be relieved, he doesn't think he can cope with the smell of blood for much longer. He is beyond cold now, the relentless wind has caused many body retractions and various clenchings. He has a bad headache and a pain in his lower back that just won't go away no matter what position he shifts into. He would give away his entire pension for a paracetamol and a hot coffee (god knows they are worth similar amounts anyway.) He would give away everything, everything that ever meant anything to him; his wedding ring, his collection of ties, his "World's Best Dad" cup, everything for ten anonymous minutes alone with the assailant, no witnesses or paperwork.

Colvin and Grimm are back for a second day of standing out in the cold, the starting members of the relay team, ready to run if something useful should be found. Colvin is pleased to note that Grimm is quieter today. Hopefully he has now exhausted his supply of dad jokes. She is also pleased that Red Nail Girl has been taken away. Colvin didn't think she could spend another day looking at her crushed face.

Now it's eyes down, looking at all the little leftover details. They think she was either killed out here or brought-here

89

whilst dying. It is what the forensic taphonomy is indicating; the greasy black stains underneath her body, those discolourings of death. The leaf pile was too large to be caused by the wind alone indicating that she was brought out here with little or no resistance, killed, then "buried" at least a week ago, probably longer.

Small scuff marks on the back of her shoe and legs indicate that she was dragged. The unbroken nails and lack of defence wounds suggest that she was unconscious. One of her shoes had fallen off when they lifted her out, it's still here waiting to be bagged. Her other shoe is missing. Colvin stares at it. It was a sexy shoe with very high heels. The kind of shoe that made you feel a certain power wearing them, the kind that were always met with appreciating or wistful looks, the kind you would wear to an expensive club not the kind you would wear if you knew you were going to take a walk in the forest. Or any sort of walk for that matter.

Expensive dress, expensive shoes, expensive nails. All ruined by mud, blood and wriggling grubs. Expensive blood splattered jewellery; the deceased had money but not enough for her disappearance to have made the papers. That's really all they knew right now. Too much money to be Cathy Clark. Maybe by the time they leave here today someone would have found a name for Red Nail Girl.

Cathy Clark, she could be out here too. There could be so many more out here. A shiver runs down Colvin's spine. She knows where they are now. Two of The Numbers Killer's victims died in this vicinity. One was a special constable, a cop just like her, someone who thought they were safe, surrounded by work colleagues and friends. Colvin's eyes meet Grimm's dark glare and she shivers again. They will be talking, back at the station and no doubt across the city, talking again about Walker, his innocence, of the similarities between the kills. There will be many more arguments, a demand for all the old suspects to be interviewed yet again. Then the complaints will restart as the men who had their lives ruined with a single accusation are put through hell again. Some old "suspects" who weren't really suspects but had been swabbed anyway just because they were suspected of being involved with a different crime. There are many men now with deep grudges against the police because of those swabs. Men who had lost families and friends because of those accusations, innocent men who now have nothing to lose. Maybe if she was one of those men, Colvin thinks, maybe she would want revenge, perhaps by showing up those accusers, perhaps by performing a copycat kill...

And now here is Colvin, caught up in the middle of it all, nowhere to turn, all eyes on her, watching her, laughing at her, waiting for the perfect moment...

Adrian has always hated dinner time. Even before. He hates the food, it is always a bland burnt offering from someone too out of it to cook properly. Even just the smell of dinner cooking is enough to unleash a thousand memories of sullen dinners. He hates chips, he hates broccoli, he hates anything that even looks like it might have moved once. Most of all he hates sitting down to dinner with his family. There, he has said it. Dinner time does not bring the family together. It just tears them even further apart. Here at the dinner table he doesn't feel wanted or loved, he just feels like a superfluous referee in a championship shrugging match.

"Guys, I promise I won't get angry about this, I just want to talk." His father may just want to talk but Adrian does not want to listen any more, doesn't want to know what this is about. His brother is already warming up his shoulders ready for a sharp dismissive shrug. "There was a full bottle of vodka in the cupboard and now it's nearly empty. I just want to know who took it." Shrug goes his brother's shoulders as he continues to stare down, neatly shredding his food. Their father sighs heavily but Adrian doesn't say anything, he only half heartily shrugs when he thinks his father is looking at him. He knows who took it, they all know who took it, just like they all know that their father will do nothing and it will never be mentioned again. There is a long silence, the only sound coming from cutlery hitting plates. Adrian hates that sound too.

"Well... er... how was school today boys?" Shrug, shrug. Adrian can tell by his father's tone that he is desperate to have a normal conversation or even just a conversation. But he also knows that the question was never directed at him and he is not required to speak. Adrian stays quiet, forcing himself to try and swallow the tasteless food.

"Did you even go to school today?" Shrug, grunt, shrug.

"I had a phone call from your teacher earlier, care to explain?" Shrug, shrug. Adrian is fairly certain he is not the one who is being asked but shrugs all the same. The food is sticking in his throat, lodging itself tightly. Adrian can barely breathe. If he does choke he knows his brother's only response would be a shrug.

"Goddamn it! What's it going to take to get an answer out of you?"

The sound of a chair being thrown back startles Adrian. He doesn't dare look up though. Another chair is thrown back and there's an agonising twenty-three seconds of silence before a slam announces that his brother has left the room. His father looks to him for guidance or maybe even an explanation. All Adrian can do though is shrug.

Third day out here in the forest, now trying to track the drag marks, the ones buried beneath the leaves whilst the wind continues to wail the lamentations of long dead girls. Perhaps Colvin is beginning to lose her mind but never once in these three days has the feeling left her, the feeling that they are not alone in the forest, the feeling of being closely watched. Despite her constant perimeter checks, her careful prods, she can't find anyone else.

When this is over she is going to take a long holiday, as long as she possibly can. Somewhere warm and safe. That is, of course, if there is anything left of her when this is over.

"She had a number seven cut", Colvin overhears. She turns, horrified to see Juda speaking to someone on the phone, not noticing she was in the room. He pauses, listening to the receiver. "No, not identified yet, I will let you know when they do."

"What the hell do you think you are doing???" Colvin screams, letting out the three days of pent up rage. Here she is, working her butt off for days in a cold windy forest, working hard to preserve and protect every piece of evidence they can find and here this asshole is, telling extremely sensitive information to fuck knows who. Not another officer, she knows they all know, someone who shouldn't know. If this sort of information is being leaked out to the press... Juda is staring at her in shock, quickly hanging up the phone. Her scream has attracted many curious bystanders who are all muttering. Juda and Colvin stare at each other and Colvin is aware that whatever is said now is going to have serious consequences. If she is right then Juda is a traitor to the investigation, to the butchered girls, to all of them. If she is wrong, and he was actually talking to someone who had a right to know, then she has shown a room full of officers that she is going to overreact to any dubious situation with the slightest bit of provocation, a trait that every officer hates.

"Who were you talking to?" She asks sternly, trying to keep her voice under control. Juda's look of guilt is noticed by every watching eye, closely followed by a look of hatred. He notices Morkam standing calmly in the corner and meets his stern gaze instead.

"Robert Leona has a right to know that his wife's killer is back." Juda says defiantly, setting off another chorus of mutterings and nods of support.

"My office. Now."

The others drift away, still gossiping as Juda calmly follows Morkam out of the room with one single backwards look at Colvin. She stalks out, head down, not wanting anyone else to ask any questions and not quite understanding what the hell is going on. She knows who Robert Leona is and he is not someone who has the right to know anything, not after what he did.

"I don't blame them for trying to find a girl who might still be alive," a deep breath, a grieving pause, "but I can't forgive them for forgetting about my girl either." Barry Williams, father of that poor Ruby Williams explains on the screen, pausing to dab at his eyes. Jenna watches at home, her heart going out to the poor man and the other desolate parents nodding in agreement. Then those sad faces are replaced by a commercial for indigestion and the moment is gone. But all those families, the public, Jenna herself are all momentarily united by a sense of shared grief and a common agenda; that they have been forgotten about, that the police are not doing enough to protect them. Jenna takes a long gulp of wine, trying to hold back the tears.

"If you were in the area, please contact us on..." Another appeal, all Jenna hears and sees are police appeals for information and especially for any dash cam or mobile phone footage, the same appeal with the area and dates changing. The same newspaper reports over and over but the victims photos keep changing. There wasn't even a photo for the last one, just a terse report. Jenna guesses that is how you know it's a really bad one. Everyone is speculating now on how bad it is, how many were found this time, why the police won't tell them anything. "Protecting their own" is becoming a popular theory. "They protect their own and we will protect our own" is a repeated message now on ItCouldHaveBeenMe.co.uk. Jenna has seen many cash rewards being offered on that same website for any copies of dash cam footage, just send them a copy before you hand it over to the police, nothing illegal about that, just helping out a desperate parent who lost a daughter, nothing more. Some taxi drivers are making a killing right now.

Jenna's electricity company is also making a killing right now. She is constantly moving around the house checking everything is locked, turning lights on and off to make it look like someone else also lives there, setting up timers. She can't even turn the lights off to sleep now, not that she can sleep. Every time she closes her eyes the panic sets in, jerking her back awake. She wants to go out, wants to enjoy life again but is always so afraid. Everyone is a possible enemy right now and she hates it. And she keeps doing stupid things because she is too tired to think about what she is doing, like drinking a whole bottle of wine by herself at four o clock in the afternoon or like yesterday; when she finally met someone, after months of trying, someone smart and funny who seemed to really like her and, for a few beautiful minutes, they could have kissed and had a Happy Ever After but then all she could think about was how he could be the one, the murderer and she panicked and burst out crying before running away. She has probably scared him away and has no idea how to even find him again to apologise. She can never go back to that bookshop again either.

"I would like to remind everyone of the importance of protecting the public and not assisting in the spread of misinformation and causing unnecessary panic." Morkam says woodenly, feeling the splinters stabbing in his throat as he stands alone against the accusatory stares and insubordinate mutterings, trying to keep his own voice and face neutral. He knows that all some officers are hearing is "Blah, blah, I am a stupid figure head and I should have retired by now, blah blah. I can't control my own staff, blah blah blah."

"If I hear of anyone releasing confidential information about these killings to any members of the public that person will be immediately suspended without pay whilst a full investigation is conducted." He tries not to look directly at Juda when he says this but he can see heads turning in his direction, more pointed stares. Juda has worked with him for over ten years now, he should have known better, should have been more discreet. Morkam isn't an idiot; he knows that all his officers talk, eventually everyone talks, these things can't stay locked inside forever but the public paranoia is growing at an alarming rate and there will be consequences.

Every time Morkam speaks Colvin can feel the resentment towards her grow, "If I hear of anyone…" With that one sentence she is back to being the outsider, not part of the true team. "She wasn't here before, she is not to be trusted" the stares say, "and don't think we have forgotten your partner, the Killer Kisser either. Neither of you are welcome here, this is our shit show not yours". How quickly they forget where paranoia and panic leads. What happened before, last time, when the wrong information was released to the public, how the fear grew, leading to the downfalls and deaths of several innocent members of the public. One poor woman is still in prison for manslaughter having attacked what she thought was an intruder entering her house, not realising in time that the intruder was just her drunk husband returning home. His blood is not just on her hands.

Colvin is aware that some of the other officers are calling her "Mini-Bullface" or "Ms. Bull" after her predecessor. Some of the "wittier" officers are calling her Cuntface or Camelface depending on their comfortability with the C-word. There will be hell to pay when one of them dares say it within her hearing. She is not going to stand for any more workplace bullying. They say she won't admit when she is wrong, but she is NOT wrong. They say she is losing, that she is out of fresh ideas, but she is going to prove them wrong.

She doesn't care what they are calling Grimm, it is his fault and he can deal with it like a big boy.

There are always good times and bad times. Even if you are not an officer of the law. All you can do is fight tooth and nail to persuade the good times to outshine the bad ones and even that will only get you so far. Right now, no matter what she does, she is stuck in a very bad time, an endless loop in which, every time she thinks they are getting somewhere, they are back to square one again.

On future reflection, she doesn't feel like she is as close

to the rest of the team as she used to be, that maybe her partner doesn't have her back like he used too. Maybe when she has caught this killer she should look into transferring again, if they don't promote her. Somewhere new, a city with less ragged scars.

A hundred and twenty officers plus a hundred very carefully vetted volunteers have stalked the streets, wandered the woods, knocked on thousands of doors and searched over nine hundred houses, sheds, gardens and, not forgetting of course, refuse sites. Over sixty people so far have responded to their appeals for dash cam recordings, each yielding between one and three hours of footage to go through.

All it had resulted in so far was a few blurry images, nothing distinctive or substantial and a couple of false leads.

There is a small hope that someone is holding back crucial evidence, either for the money or the opportunity to get the bastard before the police manage to. There is an even smaller hope that they might come to their senses and hand it over.

Some people are high risk victims; those out on the street, the gang members, the drug dealers, the prostitutes, the good boys and girls who fell in with the wrong crowd or didn't have any other option like Carly Ellis or Wendy Michealson. Some people are low risk victims; people who do everything 'right' in the eyes of the judgmental but still, through no fault of their own, end up dying prematurely like Priya Smythe or Mary Angus. A very rare few are no-risk victims, the untouchable, those with very powerful friends, families, lovers and supporters. Natalie Ivanovich was, in Grimm's opinion, one of those people. Ex-wife to a very prominent politician, a member of high class society and suspected of being the supplier of very expensive drugs. Grimm is supposed to be helping search her mansion right now but, by the looks of things, a whole legion of people have been there before them. Grimm is darkly wondering who might have tipped them off. In the time it took to retrieve Natalie Ivanovich's broken body from the leaves, reconstruct her face and finally make a formal identification, someone who was supposed to be working with them, had recognised her, told her friends and left them still struggling to figure out who she was. This shit is starting to get really tiresome now. In the unlikely case that they find anything of interest in this mansion, Grimm is going to ensure it is well documented with multiple backups because no doubt it will somehow miraculously disappear between its retrieval and the police station. Not that anything will really be worth taking as evidence, too much interference, too much cross contamination.

Here is what they do know; Natalie Ivanovich was taken from here at some point and, judging by what she was wearing and the substances found in her blood stream, Grimm guesses that she had been returning home from somewhere seductive, most likely the kind of club that no one will admit going to or seeing her there. Judging by the small amount of blood splatter by the entrance and the fallen shoe (the one they have spent many long hours in the forest searching for) Grimm thinks she had come in, taken off one shoe and had probably just unsteadily bent down to unstrap the other when she was caught by surprise. Unless that's just what someone else wants them to think? But it still raises the question how did she get taken to the forest? What have they missed? Why wasn't she missed? Why had no one reported her missing?

CHAPTER ELEVEN

"Hi there, a good evening to you. I'm sorry to disturb you on this lovely evening but do you have a few minutes to spare? We are looking for donations..." My voice sounds too sweet, too fake and she doesn't fall for it, just shuts the door with a poor apology. I don't really care, she was too old for my tastes anyway. I just move on. Maybe I will come back here one day and teach her some manners, so many people need to be taught some manners these days.

"Hi there!" A curious old lady peeks out at the next house but she doesn't even let me finish, she just quickly mumbles excuses and gently closes the door. The fear in her eyes was quite beautiful though, you should have seen it. Everyone is scared of that knock on the door, the ring of the doorbell in the dark hours. The hunting hours.

A lovely young lady answers the last door, dressed as one does when they are alone and not expecting company. She gives me an embarrassed look, wondering to herself why she even answered the door in the first place. I know by the look in her eyes that she is alone, her eyes betray the fear that she feels. Perfect. It's just so perfect. She tries to close the door on me! Another one who needs teaching a lesson or three. Lucky for her I am a patient teacher and I have plenty of time.

She doesn't even have time to think about screaming. I close the door and press down, not even giving her a chance put up a fight. She just closes her eyes and prays it will be over soon, the little broken deer caught in headlights, tears falling fast down her face.

"Please. Leave me alone. I won't tell anyone." She tries to

plea. Don't worry little girl, I am a good teacher and it's time to start your first lesson. Together we will see this through until the bitter end.

They got practically nothing from Natalie Ivanovich's mansion. Nothing but polite "I don't know" from interviewing her nearest and dearest. That and hard stares with tones of voice and body stances that clearly said, "We will handle this, you piss off and write a speeding ticket or something." So many politely but firmly closed doors. There are already rumours that those nearest and dearest have hired their own private investigator. Probably someone who will sit on their arse all day then try to take credit for all *their* hard work. Grimm wouldn't mind becoming a private detective. He has always fancied himself to be a lone wolf.

The only thing they did get was an 'encouragement' to work harder and faster because a. someone else might beat them to it and b. there was suddenly a big pressure increase from certain politicians and press. Better results are being demanded now and Colvin absolutely detests it, detests the implication that they weren't working hard enough before, detests the implication that Natalie Ivanovich's death will make a dramatic difference to their investigation. And so they get 'encouragement' and more conspiracy theories since Natalie was last seen on the 19th October and, if she died on the same day, then she died on the same day as Ruby Williams. More pressure is being put on them as it has been a year since Ruby Williams died and now more voices are demanding to know why it has taken so long and they are still no closer to catching this guy.

They got nothing from Natalie Ivanovich's death except more CCTV footage to watch, to add to the mountain of unwatched CCTV footage they already had. All officers are required to work overtime to try and help get on top of the endless digital mountain.

"I have never worked this much overtime in my life", Grimm grumbles, settling into his chair and taking a long gulp of coffee, wishing for something stronger. Colvin doesn't lift her eyes from her own screen. She barely acknowledges he has spoken.

"My wife is starting to suspect something." There is something in Grimm's voice that makes Colvin pay attention, something cold. Colvin tries not to care, she doesn't fully trust Grimm, no matter how many months it has been. He brought this on himself she reminds herself, not daring to say it out loud. She knows sometimes people make mistakes but still. She doesn't really know what to say in return anyway, it's not up to her to fix things.

"Doesn't she know that there is a serial killer on the loose?" Colvin finally replies, her voice trembling unconsciously on the word serial.

"Yes and she doesn't like it", an angry pause, "There are a lot of things my wife doesn't like right now." *Including you*, his tone implies.

Adrian is sat on the worn sofa pretending to watch the news. His father is sat opposite, pretending to be more interested in today's crossword puzzle. The top story tonight is about the latest victim found with multiple stab wounds. His father gives an audible gasp at the word "stab" and tries to cover it by asking, "Do you think your brother has been acting strangely recently?" while not taking his eyes off his newspaper. He is trying to be nonchalant but Adrian can hear the apprehension in his voice. Adrian is not given a chance to answer as an angry growl startles both of them, closely followed by the sound of feet stomping on stairs and a loud door slam. His brother evidently heard the question too and didn't like the implication. Adrian doesn't dare answer, not only because his brother might still be listening but because it was a stupid question. It is obvious that his brother was acting more than strange, feral would be one word for it. Everyone knows this, everyone who lives on their street, everyone who goes to their school, everyone knows and everyone else talks about it. But Adrian doesn't want to even think about it, doesn't want to encourage any other questions.

"I just don't know how to reach him any more. I don't know what to do." His father's voice is sad, wistful. He said the same thing once about their mother, in the same tone. Adrian didn't know then what to say and he doesn't know now.

"Usually in frenzied attacks, we find the assailant's blood on the victim or in the house, as they cut themselves accidentally during the attack. Are you certain at Mary Angus's house that you didn't see any drops of blood? Any smears on the doors that hadn't been tagged by the forensic team?"

Colvin pauses, trying to remember. So much has happened since then. Her voice is hesitant when she answers but both she and Grimm state that every single one of the blood marks were documented and photographed and that samples taken by the Forensic team. No they are sure they checked the whole house. But how can anyone be a hundred percent sure of anything? Especially when their fellow officers are listening in, nudging each other and smirking. Miss Perfect must have missed something, haha. Their interrogator turns to them next and asks "Can you say the same about Priya Smythe's investigation?"

They immediately stop smiling.

Colvin wonders if the same could be said for any of the early victims? How carefully did they go over those scenes? How do you find a drop of an assailant's blood in an ocean of victim's blood? How meticulously did they go over the victims clothing? Skin? Homes? What have they missed so far? Maybe something hasn't been missed, just delayed as they are still waiting on some forensic reports. All of the cases have now been given top priority but there are just so many samples to go through. Mary Angus's home alone had yielded over fifty samples, each one requiring time and money to go through. During the first killing

102

spree of The Numbers Killer the forensic team had been given thousands of samples and they had taken over two years to process through the more promising of specimens. Now they were having to go back to those old samples and look again, further slowing down the lab. Processing can only go so fast, despite the desperation. They are improving though, things that used to take over two years are now only taking six hundred days, give or take a few weeks.

Dismissed with one final warning to be ultra-vigilant at the crime scenes, a comment which annoys every officer standing, Colvin and Grimm get ready to head back out to the forest, to join the hunt for the missing suitcase and other evidence.

The missing suitcase is another, new, headache. It might have been taken by the assailant or it might have been taken by one of Natalie's "friends." If they hadn't had gone through her house so thoroughly the police might have realised it was missing sooner. They had been puzzled before by the rummaged through mess of clothes, toiletries and sun creams all dumped in a heap close to the front door. Then came the news that she wasn't originally reported missing because she was thought to be on holiday. Somewhere hot, somewhere where she could restock and order more supplies. A hush hush holiday that only a few people were allowed to know about. They now suspect that she packed then went out leaving her suitcase by the front door, ready for her flight the next day. The assailant, before or after knocking her unconscious, emptied the contents of the suitcase into that messy pile and then stuffed her into it, using it to transport her unnoticed to the forest. At some point she was taken out (possibly, Colvin thinks, because she regained conscious and began screaming) and then dragged to the dumpsite.

There are holes in this theory however. Colvin knows, if the assailant was in Natalie's mansion waiting for her to come home, having already emptied the suitcase, surely Natalie, even under her alcohol and drug influences, would have noticed something was wrong and panicked instead of starting to take her shoes off? If the assailant followed Natalie unnoticed into her home wouldn't he have made better preparations for moving her, rather than relying on a chance suitcase? But then this assailant seems to get lucky where ever he goes and he'd already relied on chance when targeting Lucy Swann, Priya Smythe and Mary Angus. No wonder he is a cocky son of a bitch. Everything works out so nicely for him.

If he abandoned the suitcase it must still be somewhere within dragging distance of the dumpsite. It's hard to believe that they missed it before. Despite all the leaves, one of them would surely have said "Hey, what's this suitcase doing here, I better check it out." They are not that stupid but their orders are to go back and search again. It doesn't matter that they still have many more bins to go through, more camera footage to watch, more people to interview. They have to go back out and search again because, obviously, they were too stupid to see the woods for the trees. They don't even know what the suitcase looks like. Colvin imagines it to be large, expensive but non-descript, something that matches Natalie's image but didn't draw the attention of the airport staff. Colvin suspects it had been taken by one of Natalie's friends, for its valuable "linings."

The drive down to the forest is awkward. Grimm hasn't spoken much since yesterday's overtime outburst. He is just sitting quietly, arms tightly folded, eyes shut. At first Colvin had been expecting the usual jokes about her driving, even had a retort ready, but nothing was said. Complete silence except for the steady reports coming from the police radio. On arriving he slams out the car the second she puts on the handbrake. He starts walking out towards their designated search site without even checking that she is following, barely making an effort to search as he goes. Colvin struggles to catch up, just keeps following the sound of breaking twigs as they go deeper and deeper into the forest. She stops as a muffled shout breaks ahead of her, holding her breath, waiting for another sound.

Does she call out and give away her position? Her hand reaches for her radio. Maybe it is nothing, maybe he tripped? It would serve him right for storming off ahead. Maybe someone else is out here… Does she call for back up? Or does she keep going? Her mind urges her to take precautions, to slow down, maybe start breathing again, but her body is already charging ahead. She can see Grimm now, pinned to the ground by two men, all of them struggling with each other angrily.

"You don't have to say anything…" She freezes, confused. They don't notice her, they are too busy trying to get a firm hold of Grimm. "…but anything you do say…"

"Stop!" she yells, trying to sound authoritative having found her voice again. There is no reaction from the men, but a third man is suddenly by her side reaching out for her.

"Please come with me Miss."

"No, wait, you have got this all wrong." They are too busy 'rescuing' her to listen. She doesn't know what to do or say next. Her mind is still trying simply to process it all. Are these men fellow officers? Maybe they're a gang of assailants pretending to be officers? Does she try to call for back-up or does she aim one careful groin level, self defence kick? She pulls back a foot, trying to ready herself to take on all three men when fucking Juda appears, talking into his radio excitedly. He pauses in shock when he sees Colvin's face, then takes a closer look at the man struggling in the mud. For a brief moment Colvin thought he was going to walk away but then he laughs and manages an authoritative "Let him go Collins."

"But sir-"

"Let him go." Sullenly the handcuffs are removed. Grimm stays down, trying to catch his breath.

"False alarm, stand down." He reports into his radio to the visual disappointment of the other men. "Collins, Peters, this is DCI Colvin and Grimm."

Realisation finally dawns on her "protectors" faces, then another darker look of hatred as they recognise names. Colvin is not sure whose reputation caused those dark looks. If these men are friends of Juda's then it is probably hers. All the relief of seeing Juda is quickly draining away. She was probably safer before they knew who she was.

"What the hell is going on?" Grimm finally manages to catch his breath long enough to demand answers.

"We got a call that a suspicious looking male was out here alone with a-" Juda stops to wink at Colvin, trailing off at her angry expression. Grimm manages to pull himself to his feet, shaking off mud and anger. Silently he stalks off back in the direction of the car park. Colvin can't believe he has left her here alone with these men.

"Collins, Peters, Jones, please check the area for anyone else who matches the description we were given." Juda mutters. Disappointed the other officers retreat and Juda waits for them to be out of earshot before he continues, "Sorry Sam, the guy on the phone sounded convinced that he had seen the killer out here with a new victim and you know this is one of his favourite spots." More alarm bells suddenly start ringing in Colvin's head. They haven't been here long enough for someone to have noticed them.

"When did the call come in? Did they get the callers details?" Juda gawps at her, not quite understanding.

"I'm sure it was just a mistake Sam." He pauses, instantly dismissing it from his mind as an honest mistake, lots of paranoid people out there. He takes a slow breath, distracting Colvin with his next statement. "Coincidentally there is someone here who wants to talk to you though."

"Who?" Those alarm bells are getting a full work out today.

"You need to understand, he is not a bad guy. He just needs to talk to you."

Juda, in his male innocence, doesn't know how threatening that sounds to Colvin. She wishes Grimm would come back and she thinks about pressing her panic button or about making a poor excuse and leaving. She is still shaking from Grimm's near arrest. Here, alone in the woods (except for Juda, who she is sure doesn't like her) to meet a random male, who just wants to talk to her about something? No thank you.

"You're not scared are you Sam?" He asks in a tone suggesting she was a five year old, refusing to go near the tiger exhibit at the zoo.

Jenna moves faster than she ever thought possible, her muscles throbbing and trembling with the exertion. Her chest burning from the pressure as she tries to hold on, tries to keep going as her breath comes in short gasps and sweat pours down her forehead. A yell from behind her forces her to push even harder, to keep going, to keep pushing. She is almost there and she has to make it. She *has* to. She is pushing with everything she has now, almost there, got to make it.

"Ten more seconds," the voice yells "nine, eight..." Jenna makes it to four seconds before she gives in, collapsing down hard onto the mat, reaching desperately for her water. She both hates and loves these exercise classes.

Sometimes, when she is running on the spot, she thinks about being chased in an attempt to force herself to go faster and faster. When she is kickboxing she thinks about kicking her attacker as hard as she can, trying to build up her muscle memory and automatic reactions as she raises and kicks and kicks again.

It's helping and, at the same time, it's not helping. It is helping because it is a distraction, a way of finally being able to focus her mind onto one thing and just punch everything else out. She is sleeping a little better now. Partly because of the classes, partly because of the exhaustion. It is not helping because she still feels so weak, so afraid. She might be able to run fast for thirty seconds but so what? The killer can probably run faster for longer *and* punch harder. She is not safe yet, she still has a long way to go.

"You're not scared are you Sam?" Juda smiles in what he thinks is a reassuring manner but it has a nasty predatory gleam to it. He sees the look in her eyes and tries harder. "Please? Just talk to him for a few minutes?" A few minutes? That's all it takes to kill someone! Colvin hates Juda so badly right now even for just considering putting her in this position. She is not really listening as Juda pleads. "... Once was a great officer..."

Then she becomes aware of someone else staring at her with hostile eyes. Juda is murmuring an introduction then the fucking bastard just leaves her there. Alone.

"Hello Sam." Even his voice is cold and condemning. It is hard to imagine that this person was once the best practical joker on the force, the friendliest policeman you might ever meet. But that was a long time ago and life has hardened his face, creasing what once were smile lines into a permanent frown. Colvin dislikes him already from his reputation alone, just wants to kick him in the balls and run. Then Robert Leona opens his mouth to speak and all that comes out is a half choked sob.

Colvin doesn't want to drop her defences but it is hard to see a grown man who is sobbing uncontrollably as a threat. She wishes again that Grimm hadn't abandoned her, Grimm has always been the better one at comforting people. Robert Leona, when crying, is just a faded man, in faded clothes with nothing left but fading memories.

"I am sorry." He finally manages, wiping his face with his sleeve. Colvin doesn't try to offer reassurances or even a tissue. He shouldn't have come out here. Shouldn't be here standing close to the spot where his wife spent her last hours. She was one of the searchers who came out here that day to look for some of The Numbers Killer's other victims, unaware that she herself was being watched, marked out and a few hours away from a similar fate. They say that there are still many bodies out here in the woods still waiting. They also say that there are other things still waiting in the woods, waiting for the easy prey.

Grimm pokes around the fallen leaves. The problem with any crime that happens in an outdoor area like this one is that you are never quite sure what is rubbish and what is a clue. He is still angry and possibly also lost though he would be the last one to admit it. He just wants to punch some stupid people who deserve it! There shouldn't be anything wrong with that but he is already on thin ice and this would be the last straw.

It would be worth it though! It would feel so satisfying, something that would keep him warm on those dark lonely nights. Every day he finds himself thinking of all the things he could do instead of being a police officer. He could spend more time with his children for starters; weekends and alternative holidays maybe depending on what the judge agrees to? It's not that his wife is only married to him for the uniform but one more stupid thing like getting fired for assault would mean that his bags would be packed and waiting for him by the front door before the twat even hit the ground. Mrs Grimm would know before Morkam had even finished his "I am disappointed" lecture.

He supposes he should find Colvin again, they were out here for a reason after all and he doesn't want to give her another reason to complain. She has probably stopped laughing at him by now, her and those other fuckers. He really hopes that they trip over a stick or something. Juda deserves to know what dog shit tastes like.

"Do you know what I regret the most? Not taking part in the search that day. I thought she would be safe. That everyone would look out for her." He trails off angrily, staring at Colvin's feet. Colvin knows better than to tell him that, in her experience, no one in this work-force looks out for you.

"I was just so tired, I should have just… She always had so much energy, she never stopped. She told me that she would be home at four and I waited for her. I ~~and~~ waited and waited. We were supposed to go out for dinner together and I kept waiting and waiting… and none of those fuckers…" He balls up his fists in frustration, looking angrily in the direction Juda left. "I am sorry. You start therapy and someone starts you talking and suddenly it is very hard to stop. No one can shut you up, even when you are saying stuff no one wants to hear." Colvin is the same with sympathies, you can't let yourself feel sympathies for one person because then suddenly there is no holding back.

"This is no way to live" He tries to catch her eye, tries to smile through the pain. "Suddenly nothing matters and you become dangerously reckless." Colvin's heart stops and she wonders g where he is going with this. "You spend every penny you have because tomorrow doesn't matter anymore. You start sticking your hand straight into boiling water just to see if the pasta is done because pain doesn't matter. It's no way to live." He repeats, not pausing for condolences, not that Colvin would offer any. "At first all I wanted was her wedding ring back, that's all that mattered. It was all I could think about." He pauses, trying to reconnect his thoughts. He knows he is not reaching her and he just wants to shake her. Why can't she see what a wonderful woman his wife was? How much she meant to him?

It's not that Colvin is completely un-detached or 'un-human'. It's just that she also knows about what happened to the Krill. Poor unfortunate Krill who was attacked by the same … vigilantes (for want of a better word) group that Robert Leona was-a part of. Colvin knows that Robert Leona chose not to re-join the force after his wife died but if he had chosen to come back he would have been fired for what he did. These victims are the only ones that Colvin really has any sympathies for and she owes it to them not to compromise the investigation.

They still talk in hushed whispers about what Krill went through, still use the situation as a prime example of why public paranoia should never go unchecked. Still use it as an example of the failure of police protection.

They all have something in common Colvin thinks; The Krill, Robert Leona, even Nicholas Grimm. They are all stuck in the same place, unable to go back and change anything, unable to move forward or even change the subject. Just stuck in the same loop, tormenting themselves with the same thing, over and over and over. Maybe everyone in this city is still caught up in that same hellish loop, including her?

It is the radio call that brings Grimm and Colvin back together, the suitcase, Juda and everything else forgotten by the emergency. They sit in silence on that short drive, listening to rapid firing orders, knowing that this is going to be a bad one.

They can't park close to Victoria Road. A dozen police cars have all arrived at similar times and none of them can siren through the thick crowds. On foot they group together and force themselves through to join their fellow anxious officers. Empty and not quiet empty drink are being thrown indiscriminately, more calls for further assistance are being shouted, no one wants to resort to force but it is fast becoming the only remaining option.

Colvin is still reeling from the noise; the sirens blaring, the high pitched screams, the shouting. That one woman screaming over and over as she is held back from her daughter by two struggling officers. She is not capable of words any more, just one long animal scream drawn out with desperation, anguish and anger. Colvin sees another old woman, half collapsed on the ground and being knocked over and over again by a crowd impatient to see a body. Colvin has no way of reaching the woman, she can't even reach down for her camera. She is trapped tight in a moving wall of sweaty bodies and hot hysteria. There are too many people pushing and pulling, too many shouting faces demanding the impossible from them. No one is willing to back down despite the shouted orders, the threats of arrest and the arrival of even more officers. It is only when the cuffs are pulled out and certain expressive individuals are lead away that they manage to regain some control over the scene.

Someone must have helped the old woman up and led her away for a nice hot cup of tea. The screaming woman has also been led away (probably for something stronger than a cup of tea). It took a while for Colvin to realise she could no longer hear the screaming and that it was now only echoing in her head.

They are all still shaky but trying not to show it. They know they are still being watched. Some of the watchers are trying to be subtle by peeking out from behind their curtains while others stand, defiant, in front of their windows with camera in hand. Not that they can see much past the police cordons and screens. They see enough though.

Colvin is starting to get a sense of what happened. Someone, for some reason, knocked on the door of number ten. The door wasn't locked and they unknowingly knocked the door slowly open, revealing the victim waiting inside. Their shouts and screams brought forward more people, more and more as everyone wanted a look and to take a photograph. Eventually someone called the police, who then called more police as the crowds grew beyond control.

In one bold move the assailant had ensured that everyone knew what number he had carved into the victims right hand (6) consolidating together everyone's fears into a mass panic and nearly causing a riot. In doing so the assailant also ensured that the crime scene was completely contaminated as so many people trampled into the house, tried to untie the victim, tried to perform CPR and searched the house Then, having destroyed or contaminated any potential evidence, the public stood back and criticised them for not having caught this guy yet, for fuck sake!

Now they are trying to organise themselves; organising who should search the house, who is to guard the crime scene and who is to interview any potential remaining eye witnesses. Grimm and Colvin are supposed to start interviewing immediately.

Interviews? How are they meant to interview the same people they were threatening to arrest less than an hour ago? The same people who were, in turn, wanting to drag them away and do serious damage to their skulls for not catching this guy already? For putting their families and friends at risk? How cooperative do you think those people are going to be in an interview?

Interview? How can they interview when Colvin is on the edge of a nervous breakdown and Grimm is on the edge of an aggressive breakdown? Both are burning out with the overload. Colvin would sooner go back to the forest and to its hidden dead then spend more time with the living. She is not even fully sure she knows what is going on here. The only thing that she knows for certain is that the victim's name is Sarah Grieg, she was twenty-three and she died sometime within the last 12 hours from exsanguination.

Six houses, that's all they have to do. Divide and conquer with the other officers, 'While you all are here and the memories are still fresh, you might as well' orders. The resigned orders.

It is a slight relief that no one answers at Number 4. Colvin and Grimm wait patiently, pushing the doorbell a few more times then knocking just in case the doorbell didn't work, using these few precious moments to breathe, recompose. Grimm's hands are still shaking and he really wants to talk about what the fuck just happened but knows he has to save it all for the drive back to the station where things can be said off the record. Slowly, reluctantly they give up on Number 4 and traipse towards the next house, Number 6.

It is the first time that Colvin has ever seen a well-polished, gleaming door knocker before. Grimm obliviously raps it, leaving behind a small trace of mud and sweat. The door opens quickly as if its occupant had been waiting for them. Prim is how Colvin would describe the woman, prim and proper with not one hair out of place. Someone who presumably still starches. Colvin holds out her identification badge in defence against Ms Prim's disapproving stare. She can almost see her internally debating whether should she let them in. Her eyes slide to the small splotches of mud on both of their shoes, a small degree of panic registers as she takes in the sight, inwardly debating with herself. "No don't let them in…but they are the police…but mud… but police.." Her eyes widen in dismay as she sees the mud stains on Grimm's knees and Colvin is thankful that he left his very muddy jacket in the car, otherwise is there every chance they would have been introduced to a bucket of soapy water.

"Come in" is finally said, whilst her mind thinks of all the cleaning it is going to take to remove their presence at the end. Bad things are not allowed in this house. Colvin stops Grimm from going much further than the welcome mat, allowing just enough space for them to softly close the door behind them. She takes in the clean white hallway, the spotless white floor and tries not to move.

"This won't take long, we just have a few questions."

They talk softly, awkwardly still standing on aching feet. Ms Prim doesn't really know Sarah Grieg at Number 10, could only just recognise her as a neighbour with a vague smile. She hadn't really spoken to her in weeks. No, she didn't hear anything unusual last night nor has she noticed anyone strange in the area. Colvin finds this quite interesting as she suspects that Ms Prim is the type of person who would notice someone acting suspiciously, perhaps even record their comings and goings in a neatly written ledger. They are about to wrap up the interview when Ms Prim casually mentions that a charity collector did come to the door last night. She only looks embarrassed when they ask which charity. She had not let the young man get that far in his explanation. No, sorry she couldn't describe him as she didn't really look at his face. They were around here all the time and she didn't feel like she had anything left to give. She awkwardly wishes them good luck with their investigation as she ushers them out the door leaving Colvin and Grimm alone to exchange a series of glances.

The elderly couple at Number 8 already know about their poor neighbour. Such a shame, such a nice girl although bit quiet. A sensible girl with such a nice boyfriend, bit loud at times, a bit shouty, but young love you know? They last saw her yesterday as she always put their bins out for them, it's hard for Roger to move them when they are full, he just had surgery on his knee. No, nothing seemed out the ordinary, she didn't seem upset or unhappy. Maybe a little scared but they all were, such a dreadful time, you know how it is at the moment dear.

Colvin does know "how it is" at the moment, she sees the "how it is" up front and still bleeding. But that is what makes it so strange that in these times of hyper vigilantism no one in this neighbourhood noticed a persistent stranger or anything else out of the ordinary. Colvin takes a deep breath and tries to ask nonchalantly if they saw the charity collector last night?

Oh yes dear, we get them a lot. What was that dear? Sorry

I don't know which charity, maybe around half seven-ish? What did they look like? There is a long pause, memories are not what they used to be, people aren't who they used to be. Eye witnesses tend to remember certain details in accordance to their own experience and expertise. For example, a fashion designer may notice the clothes more than the face, Ms Prim only really noticed that the man was clean and considerate enough to wear plastic gloves. The elderly couple at Number 8 only really remember the glasses and the predatory smile.

The lady at Number 12 will never truly realise how close she was to becoming a victim last night. She is the trusting type, the type who will invite someone in for a cup of tea before looking at their ID badge. Grimm eagerly accepted her offer of a drink since she insisted that it was not too much trouble. They make small talk as they take reassuring sips of the best tea Grimm has tasted in a long time. Colvin is less relaxed having realised now, on their third interview, the smell of stale beer and flat coke isn't coming from the houses. It is coming from them, a lingering result of being pelted with drink cans. She longs to go home and shower, rinse away the smell of distrust and disappointment. What must these people think of them? Do they still trust them? Do they still believe in them? She has wanted to ask each interviewee, each passer-by, how are you feeling right now? Perhaps she has a hidden sadistic streak or perhaps she wants reassurance that people still do believe in her or perhaps she just finally wants it to be said to her face- how truly afraid people are and how little they trust the police. Or perhaps she just wants to see how well these people can lie. After all any one of these people could be hiding something.

Morale wise, Number 12 provides a much needed booster. Answers wise, they got nothing. She was out last night so didn't hear or notice anything was wrong until she saw the crowds gathering. She didn't really know Sarah Grieg, she only started renting this place two months ago and is out a lot. She was sorry she couldn't be of more help.

Colvin recognises the man at Number 14 as someone who

was throwing cans with poor accuracy. He notices her disappointed gaze and looks down in shame. So that's the type of man he is thinks Colvin, aggressive on the streets but a mouse in his house. She makes a point of taking his name and writing down all his details slowly. Not that she suspects that someone whose house stinks of bacon and body spray is really going to turn out to be a serial killer. She just wants to see that worried look appear in his eyes.

He is polite as he tells them that no, he doesn't really know Sarah Grieg, not that well anyway. He knows her by sight, she was really sweet, always gave him a cheery wave but nothing more. No he hadn't really noticed anyone on the streets, he is a recent divorcee himself and he can tell you from his recent pub jaunts that no one is really out much on the streets around here (except for when you are trying to cause a riot, Colvin whispers to herself, not wanting to start something but still needing to say something.) No, he didn't see anyone from a charity last night, no one came to the door, he is positive of that.

They were slowly walking back to their car, giving small goodbye nods to the other officers when Colvin just happened to look up quickly, into a bedroom window opposite, catching the wild stare from its occupant. He is staring straight at her, eyes glinting with anger, fists curled. Colvin recognises him immediately as the Angry Youth. That rejected boy, rejected by Claire Atkins all those months ago. Colvin doesn't think it is a co-incidence that he lives here. She returns his stare with her own best intimidating look.

"It just feels like the police have forgotten us." Grimm turns off his car radio with a sharp jab, spending the last twenty minutes of his commute home in damning silence. If someone cared enough about him to ask how he is feeling right now his answer would be a tired smile and a thumbs up. But if he was going to give them an honest answer then it would be that he doesn't even know how to begin describing how he feels right now. He is not angry, just disappointed. No, he is angry, he is just one move away from erupting as fiercely and as deadly as a volcano. He is tired. He was tired three weeks ago and now he is teetering in unknown territory far beyond exhaustion. Most of all, he is defeated and feeling all the shame, humiliation, hatred that comes with defeat.

When he arrives home he goes straight into the shower, turning the water up to high temperatures in an attempt to desperately burn away the feelings, the sweat, the mud, the lingering smell of blood. Rinse, lather, scrub, repeat and then repeat again. Those feelings, those smells can't come in to the house. Finally he towels off, easing himself into his comfy daddy clothes, taking his work clothes straight to the washing machine for similar treatment.

"Daddy! Daddy" comes the joyful cry from behind him, startling him with its happiness. Grimm gently lowers his aching body down to hug his little daughter. This is what makes coming home worthwhile he thinks, wrapping his arms in tight, then freezing as he inhales the unmistakably smell of vapour rub. He wants to cry, wants to push away that disgusting smell and its reminding flashes of Mary Angus's house. The world that he tries to protect his daughter from is here, smeared across her skin and he has to just grin and bear it. She can never know.

Colvin goes home to nothing. No one awaits her at the door. She has a hot shower then she eats dinner alone, reheating a two day old take away that she eats without really tasting or thinking about. What to do now? Listen to the news? Non-stop audio criticism of their actions or lack of actions. She could call friends and go out for a drink if any of them still dare to venture outside. But if they do meet up, there will be only one thing they will want to talk about. At times like these, Colvin isn't so much a friend as a potential source of information and she has to be very careful about what she says.

Colvin walks past the stack of boxes, into the study come

junk room. She promises herself once again that she will unpack those boxes soon, when she is definitely sure that she is staying in the city (it has only been a few years since she moved here). She flops down onto her desk chair having decided she will research useful things tonight and use her time wisely to research previous serial killers. Maybe she will find some kind of introspective that might be useful for breaking open the investigation? Almost immediately though she is drawn into typing the latest victims' names into the search engine and seeing what comes up. There are no shortage in the stay-at-home sleuths, hundreds of hits pop up with each name. *"Don't do it, don't look"*, she tries to urge herself, *"don't click, there is nothing on these pages that can help you"*.

Click.

C-A-T-H-Y C-L-A-R-K

Click, click.

She is immediately drawn to the message board on a site called ItCouldHaveBeenMe.co.uk. It is a website set up shortly after Walker died as far as Colvin can tell. It was originally to discuss the The Numbers Killer cases and how close certain commentators came to being a victim (hence the domain name) but now the website has expanded and expanded into articles and discussions about all serial killers, past and present. On it, amongst many other interesting articles and chat boards, is a long continuous thread on Cathy Clark. Someone with too much time on their hands has taken the time to Photoshop every possible 'disguise' Cathy Clark could be using. Colvin finds herself studying each image carefully, trying desperately to recall if she has seen anyone who looks like those images. One image could pass as a distant cousin to that nice girl they spoke to today at Number 12 or maybe she is simply imagining things?

She is not the only one who is imagining things.

The person who posted those Photoshop disguises has also asked another person, StarShiner3000 who has identified themselves as Cathy's flat mate, for images of the clothes in Cathy's wardrobe so they could further expand their theories on what Cathy might have changed her look to. Colvin really hopes that StarShiner3000 does not comply. That is if StarShiner3000 is who they say they are.

Colvin tries to think about that flat mate. Was she really the type to call herself StarShiner? Colvin remembers a very worried girl, endlessly nasally repeating the phrases "She shouldn't have" and "I shouldn't have". Constantly blaming herself for Cathy's disappearance. Colvin remembers her calling two days ago tearfully asking for updates, for more information. Oh and here is her latest message on the chat board a complaint about how the police won't tell her anything. "This is why we don't tell you anything." Colvin says out loud to an empty room with a derisive snort.

According to the website Cathy has been spotted in over thirty different locations, some thousands of miles away from each other. She has cut her hair, dyed it purple and then she has gotten hair extensions. Or she has a really good supply of wigs. Colvin is filled with a quiet desperation that someone out there is actually taking this website and these amateur 'detectives' seriously.

She is considering finding some of these people and having a really stern talk with them. They are crossing that fine line between investigating and stalking. Take this one person, DWThides, who has posted a month long commentary on Maxwell Penfold, his whereabouts at all times, his possible 'alias,' his next possible victims, a very embellished link between him and Natalie Ivanovich and then finally, a long list of possible places he might have dumped Cathy's body. Places like King's Park, near or in the pond, the field close to where Wendy Michealson was dumped, the abandoned farm close to the forest. Though she really doesn't believe that Maxwell Penfold has anything to do with Cathy's disappearance she makes a careful note of those places. Most are already under constant police and public surveillance but still...

The main commenters on the site are already going into overdrive attempting to analyse the details surrounding Sarah

Grieg's death. Colvin wishes that they had been able to seize every single mobile phone and camera from that mob because now there were over twenty different published images of Sarah tied to her chair, most of them were thankfully quite blurry but still, Colvin rubs her face in disgust. Who thinks it is a good idea to take a picture of a dead girl and then upload that picture on a website that can be seen by anyone with an internet connection? Who? And what was wrong with them? And what is wrong with the people who are taking great delight in analysing every little part of those photos? Why are they asking questions like 'How is Sarah held to the chair, can anyone tell? Is it rope? Cable ties???" "I think it might be her dressing gown?" "What exactly is she wearing?" "What do you think the six means??" (She still saves each picture as Sarah had been moved before they got there and they had nothing to show what her original position had been as so much evidence had been lost by people interfering) Colvin also makes a note to see if legally, they can order that these pictures are taken down.

"I am familiar with the street that Sarah Grieg was murdered on. You may all remember my theories about that crazy cop bitch and this adds to my theory in so many ways. You may recall that I think that bitch killed J. Walker to protect her own husband Barry. Barry lives on this street! Who's the paranoid now?" Aanderson101 posted ten minutes ago. Colvin thinks she has a good idea on who Aanderson101 is referring to. No wonder people didn't trust the police when there's people like this trying to convince them that the police are all out to get them.

Colvin clicks on another link trying to find Aanderson101's original theories, then another, then another. Then she sees herself. Video footage from that day in the park five months ago, standing guard as they try to process the last of the remains of Claire Atkins and Nikki Woods. That horrible woman, the one she is constantly trying to drive from her mind, yelling at her all over again. She still remembers it all, can still feel that prickly heat, the swarming sensation of the flies crawling on her skin, that self hate and humiliation as that woman yells. "Well, do something. We are dying out here and YOU DON'T EVEN CARE!"

It plays over and over on a loop. Angrily Colvin mutes it, focusing instead on reading down into the comments, noting how many commenters were personally attacking her and her 'ineptitude.' There is something soul destroying about spending your entire life working so hard to protect people, sacrificing everything you have, pushing yourself harder and harder to protect people and in the end, all they do is turn around and criticise you and the size of your nose. Well fuck them. Colvin goes back to the top of the page intent on closing it and maybe even writing a letter of resignation. She pauses, looking back on that video again. The camera operative had taken that moment to scan the crowd and it was all paused on one now familiar face. She hadn't noticed him there that day, wouldn't have even known who he was. Robert Leona in yet another place he had no reason to be.

She had almost forgotten about him, this morning seems another world away now. She needs to talk with Juda, find out why Robert Leona was even out in the woods today. The area was supposed to be off limits to civilians. She also wants to know who called the police on Grimm? Or was the whole thing just a prank? Maybe it was orchestrated by Juda as punishment for getting him into trouble with Morkam? That was a large possibility. The sort of thing Juda would do.

Maybe Leona was also on this site? Maybe he was Aanderson101? Leona is still utterly convinced that his wife's killer is still alive and that Walker was completely innocent. She had asked him before outright if he had any physical evidence to exonerate Walker? And his answer was just a defeated "I don't have access to the case files." And that was FOR A GOOD REASON Leona, you don't have access because you got so caught up in paranoia that you helped attack an innocent person. Colvin pauses in her memories, the irony is not lost on her. Look how close she had been just now, how caught up she was getting in paranoid theories, risking and compromising her own cases. She shuts down with an angry click.

CHAPTER TWELVE

Dear Detective Dipshits,

I do hope this letter finds you well and not too stressed from having to do some work for a change?

Do you know, the funny thing about the world is that it's very, very large and very hard to find things? It's hard to find people too, if you don't know where to start looking. They can be anywhere, under any rock or hard place. It's hard to find them when they keep moving around but sometimes it's even harder to find someone when they are not moving at all. You only seem to find the easy ones don't you? It must be so hard to be this stupid that I almost feel sorry for you. So I am sending you a small hint. A little reward from me to you, for working so hard and yet failing so miserably.

Can you guess what I am planning to do tonight? I am going to have so much fun doing it too, knowing that you are too stupid to stop me.

Hugs and kisses
BTY

The sender had thoughtfully included a map, marked with a big X and marked with what looked to be dried blood. Frantic efforts are already being made to analyse the "blood" and check the paper for fingerprints. Judging by the frantic calls coming through, this letter had not just been sent to them.

The X on the map is too big and smeared to show exactly where it is pinpointing but it is somewhere around Ware's Old Farm, about twenty miles away from the station and right on the outskirts of the city. Grimm drives out as part of a long police convoy with Colvin sitting in the front seat, half dozing and two other stony faced officers sitting silently in the back

This has to be a hoax, Grimm thinks knowing that they are all going to look like stupid idiots for responding. But if they don't look... They have to look in every cranny, dirt mound and puddle, knowing they are not going to find anything. It is just a hoax after all. He would be willing to bet serious money on that. A stupid hoax thought out by someone with little imagination like an ex-colleague or an ex-suspect perhaps? Someone who wants to get petty revenge in a petty way.

Fat spots of rain hit the windows and howls of wind shake the car. Grimm turns the heat up trying to make the most of these last warm minutes. He has not felt properly warm for weeks, not since they found Natalie Ivanovich back in mid-October. Day by day everything seems to get that little bit colder and meaner. It's Thursday 21st November and they should be thinking ahead to Christmas, protesting that those Christmas songs are being played too early but still singing along. He should be mocking those who are already buying mince pies but still eating them anyway. But he isn't because no one is sharing or even smiling and they are far, far away from preparing to welcome jolly St Nick into their homes. Not even that well known old man is going to be allowed through those barred, bolted and double locked doors this year.

Halloween, his second favourite holiday, was a quiet and private affair this year since Sarah Grieg was killed some dark moment between the 29th and 30th of October. It was normally a busy night for them, Halloween, and it was still fairly busy, just not in the way they expected. No one went trick or treating and their main calls were polite requests to remove strangers/friends of friends from Halloween parties. No one even wore a mask this year. Grimm had been looking forward to taking his kids out trick or treating but had to be content with watching a few age appropriate 'scary' movies while sneaking bites of buttery popcorn under his wife's disapproving watchful eye which wasn't quiet as fun.

He is familiar with Ware's Old Farm or Old Ware's Farm as it was known by some depending on how local you were and which legends you had heard. It is a place to go if you wanted to catch teenagers smoking weed. Only the braver, older teenagers though as the younger ones were scared to go too close, having grown up hearing all about the legends of Old Ware and his special pickling jars and Widow Ware's "special" stew. Both Wares were long gone now. Grimm doesn't know who technically owns the farm now or if anyone would ever consider it worth buying, given how often it floods. Not even property developers want anything to do with this place.

Grimm pulls into the property with an audible curse. Over twenty cars have beaten them here, their cameras poised and carefully pointed. Orders are now being barked through their radios and all Grimm can think is who are these people and why don't they have anything better to do?

It takes nearly an hour of precious daylight to shoo those people away. Those who insist that they know their rights are still waiting past the police screens and wardens, pointing their cameras at anything that moves, still poking around in the mud despite the rain. Some others have decided to go home now the police have FINALLY decided to do their jobs. Two or three are just quietly sitting in their cars, waiting for who knows what. Grimm, with a polite nod recognises them as the private investigators hired by Natalie Ivanovich's friends and he hopes to hell that they haven't already found some vital evidence and hidden it away. For that matter he also hopes the same can be said for the other idiots who had been in the area. They have already destroyed any chance the forensic team had of getting decent tyre track markings out of the mud, once again contaminating a potential crime scene. When will they bloody learn? Grimm angrily mutters to himself. All these crime documentaries and they are still absolute idiots! He is really going to be annoyed if this turns out not to be a hoax. Not as annoyed as he will be if it is a hoax, which it is. All these police officers are badly needed elsewhere right now, they shouldn't be poking around amidst all the mud, broken bottles, used condoms and cigarette butts. They shouldn't be collecting any of these "samples" of teenage wasteland and overloading the Forensics team. They shouldn't be wasting their precious time over a prank whilst the cold trail of evidence around Sarah Grieg's death begins to freeze. It's just another distraction! A hoax! A bloody stupid... OH FUCK!

Grimm slides forward on the mud, catching himself before he plummets face first. If he fell here the photos will haunt him for the rest of his career. He has already noted how many people were specifically watching him before. More onlookers are turning up now, late for the party, looking as if they might cause a riot. They will have to call more police officers out here soon, more officers here means even less officers in the city and no one wants that either. Except for maybe one person.

Rain penetrates through Grimm's thick coat, trickling down his neck. He wishes for a hot coffee, all these people and not a single entrepreneur selling hot food and drinks! What is the world coming too? This would be so much easier if it was summer. If it was then all they would have to do is follow the flies. At least it is not as bad as Autumn and the Forest and having to sieve for evidence through all those fucking leaves. Winter does have some advantages though; everything is bare but covered in mud and it would have been so much easier to see the little disturbances if it hadn't of been for those pesky curious onlookers trampling the scene.

What was worse? Coming out here and checking everything carefully, only to find out that it was just a hoax? Or missing something small and receiving another gloating letter? Perhaps a letter with even more obvious directions, truly showing everyone how incompetent they are? Grimm grits his teeth, he doesn't think that they are doing this right. Everyone is everywhere when they should be griding off areas and working more carefully. No one wants to be seen as idle in front of their critical audience (not that their audience can see much past the screens). No one wants to slow down and think.

Colvin spotted Robert Leona lurking in the background when they first pulled in but then, thankfully, later saw that he'd retreated to his car. Less thankfully, he went to his car with one of the private investigators. No doubt to trade information. He looks like he is willing to wait all day just to talk to someone, hopefully not her. No, she hasn't had chance to review the information against Walker yet. No she doesn't have any updates (not that she would tell him if she did, she is a professional after all.) She has been a bit busy trying to investigate the last hours of Sarah Grieg's life.

Sarah Grieg; what an interesting puzzle and, by interesting, they mean a complicated, mystifying nightmare. Only three people reported seeing a charity collector in the area that night. None of those people could give a description of the person or name the charity. They have contacted over two hundred charities to date, none of which will admit to having staff or volunteers in the area that day or even that week. If it was the assailant posing as a charity collector then that just raises more questions. Did he really get 'lucky' after just three houses? Or did he know the street that Sarah Grieg lived on but not her house? Or was he targeting someone else but chose her instead? Compare and contrast this to the attacks on Priya Smythe and Mary Angus where the assailant seemed to know exactly where they lived and when they would be home alone.

Judging by the evidence, Sarah was attacked and killed in her front room. They can't tell for sure but nothing suggested that the assailant went into any other room in the house. He brought his own knife this time, borrowing only Sarah's chair and dressing gown belt. That was one thing; Sarah had been wearing her dressing gown and pyjamas. She probably hadn't been expecting anyone. Colvin won't even answer the door if she is wearing her pyjamas, she couldn't see Sarah inviting a stranger in but no one heard any indication that the assailant forced entry. There was no evidence of a disturbance as far as they can tell but, the trouble is, they are relying on what they can see in the blurry website photos where the focus is more on Sarah. Their own photos are fairly useless given how badly Sarah's would be rescuers damaged the crime scene.

Not that that is an acceptable reason for them to have gotten nothing and nowhere, especially according to Sarah's father who just can't understand their lack of progress and is appearing on chat shows everywhere, to say so. He is especially angry at their inability to censor those pictures, which are also appearing everywhere.

They have been searching for nearly an hour and the mutters that this is just a hoax are getting louder as fingers grow numb. Colvin doesn't think that this is a hoax. She knows something is out here, maybe it was left by the person who sent that letter, maybe it wasn't. But something is waiting here.

She pauses, trying to think of everything they know about the assailant. She thinks he would have left something in an obvious place but somewhere that is easy to miss. She thinks about underneath the long lines of parked cars; the assailant would love that, so close and yet so stupid. But then that would mean the assailant arrived here first to play at parking attendant, carefully manoeuvring the vehicles. No it is too farfetched but, maybe, one of them has accidentally parked over something vital. Maybe she will check carefully before she leaves... but then she can't dig up an entire field by herself... and she is tired and cold... and last thing she wants is for Grimm to drive off without her, promising to come back for her, leaving her alone to dig her own grave... no! She can't think like that.

She moves back into the barn. Someone has already searched in here but a second look wouldn't hurt and she needs just a few minutes in the dry to compose herself and shake off those unwanted thoughts. She takes a few more steps inside. She was wrong about it being dry in here, half the roof is leaking, the other half is missing. Ugh, why can't she catch a break for just a few moments?

In answer to that question the barn door slams shuts, sealing her alone inside. She takes a deep breath and tries not to scream. Maybe the wind blew it shut? Maybe some other officer shut the door on purpose, wanting to knock the teacher's pet down a few embarrassing pegs? They are probably waiting for her to scream, waiting by the other side of the door snickering to each other as one of them holds the door shut. As scared as she is, she won't give them that satisfaction. She braces herself, expecting a jump scare; someone hitting the walls, or scratching at the windows or someone to come creeping behind her, their knife sharp and ready. She turns around shining her torch in all directions over and over until she is really sure that she is alone in here, wishing that her heart would stop beating so hard. She keeps still, listening for that tell-tale creak. Nothing except that distant mutter of those other officers worlds away and the howls of the wind. *"Don't scream. Don't Scream!"* She tells herself firmly. *"All you have to do is walk over to that door and open it. You can do that. Just lift one foot slowly and then lift the other. Something you have done over a billion times before. There is nothing here, nothing to be afraid of! Now move!"*

"Fine, don't move. You are here to search the barn so search it! Shine the torch round and round again and again! Can you see any disturbances in the dust? Any mud tracks not caused by you? No? The only disturbances are by the door and the odd areas where the roof has caved in. Then what does that tell you? The other officers didn't search in here very well, they stopped by the door, no one but you has come this far. The others must have just shined a light around, saw nothing was out of place and moved on, you know, the sensible option?" One that didn't put them at risk of falling through a rotting floorboard. It is not like her to take such a stupid risk, what was wrong with her? What was she thinking? *"Maybe Sam"*, she tells herself strongly, *"you should get out of here before the rest of the roof caves in? Come on, move it! Before they all go home without you. Come on, move!"*

She moves her torch in one last full circle around the barn, stepping forward as she catches sight of something dark behind the door. What is that? She creeps forward slowly, finally regaining use of her wobbly legs, forgetting the danger. *"Don't!"* her mind warns, *"don't look, don't, just get out of here. No, you are an Officer of the Law, you can't be scared of just a... what is that? A large battered suitcase! You can't be afraid of a suitcase!"* She moves closer, ready to take one last final look before she leaves the barn, when the thought strikes her- what is a suitcase doing here?

Well, thinking sensibly about it, a suitcase could be here for a number of perfectly good reasons. The Wares could have left it behind for instance although this one doesn't look that old. It is battered and muddy but not old. It could have been brought and abandoned here by an entrepreneur of the opiate kind. Yes, it was probably just used as an easy way to bring beer out here or something vaguely illegal but not illegal enough to be worth bothering with. Probably nothing to do with why they were out here today. But, she thinks, as her heart begins to race again and her breath comes in and out in raggedy hisses, she should probably check. Her fingers tremble as she reaches out to touch it. *"Please be nothing"* she begs, noticing an address tag on it and shivering as she reads the words.

N. Ivanovich.

Oh fuck.

Does she open it? She pauses for a moment. The correct thing to do would be to tell someone it is here and get the forensic team in, but then she will never know.... but she could destroy some potential evidence... but then this could be nothing. This could be a bygone relic from some ancient farm visit. Could be nothing and it's just a co-incidence that they are searching for a suitcase belonging to someone with the same unusual surname.

In less than a month Jenna has gone from feeling really positive about her exercise classes to feeling even worse and even more vulnerable than before. Now the killer is watching from behind every corner, waiting for her to let her guard down, watching everything she does with a mocking grin. Jenna has come so close to snapping, to screaming at random strangers on the street to just do it and get it over with! She has spent too many nights clutching her kitchen knife, twitching and reacting to every single sound.

And she was doing so well before! What happened to trigger such a relapse? Well, it might have something to do with the fact that Sarah Grieg was her fitness instructor. With her death suddenly everything felt hopeless again, what was the point in the work outs? They didn't help Sarah, not one bit. Everyone knows exactly what happened to her; the pictures are everywhere she looks. Grieg is still hot news on itcouldhavebeenme.co.uk, continuously reminding her how easily it could have been her. That she could be next...

"We can't just sit around, waiting to be picked off, we have to do something."

"We need to let the police handle this."

"They can't protect us."

"Everyone please settle down."

Jenna originally didn't think that it was a good idea to join a gang. Well, it wasn't really a gang and she didn't so much join, she was dragged there by her concerned friends. This is a different kind of class they said, focusing more on how to fight back. The poster said it was a meeting group for women who wanted to be taught how to defend themselves and was funded by the Fran Lizzie Taylor memorial foundation. She mostly enjoys the group meetings; they begin with yoga and positive chanting, then they progress to shadow boxing and self-defence. Those parts are fun and it's mostly an exercise class with defensive purposes which is really helping to relieve her anxieties. But only when the class is in session.

"Tonight we should go out there together."

"And get ourselves killed? No way."

"No, listen."

But then, afterwards, before they carpool home they talk, a group therapy session without a therapist. Jenna keeps telling herself not to listen but somehow always manages to get caught up in the conversation. She doesn't mind socialising, it's just they can only talk about one thing. And tonight they have all seen the letter. They all know another body has been found. The letter was posted on itcouldhavebeenme.co.uk and Jenna has read every line over and over again, trembling with every word. *"I know this is hard to read"*, the moderator said, *"but I think you have a right to know what kind of person is hunting us, that we cant rely on police protection"*. Everyone here tonight has read that letter. They are all talking about patrols, about getting him before he got you. Jenna doesn't want to join in but she doesn't want to go home to an empty house either.

"One of us could lure him, then the others could trap him."

"That's a shit idea, you're going to get yourself killed."

"Now ladies, there is no call for that kind of language."

"Fuck you."

They could never co-ordinate a plan to catch the guy Jenna thinks, they can't even get along for ten minutes.

When it truly comes down to it, Colvin will always choose the sensible option. She radios in and says she has found something, her hands still itching to undo the zip and take one little peek, just to assure herself that it is nothing. The others arrive quickly, thankfully not asking why she is searching the barn alone with the door shut.

The forensic team are called in, painstakingly finding nothing on the suitcase itself. Then they slowly begin to unzip the case as the other officers jostle for a better view. Everyone seems to be holding their breath, ready to laugh at nothing…

There is a sad collective sigh at the sight of the beautifully plaited dark hair.

More people are called in while others are ushered out. They make a pronouncement of death and take more photographs. Two sombre strong officers carefully lift the suitcase, its occupant still inside. They take her away to the awaiting morgue van, leaving with most of the forensic team. Despite playing the star role in finding the said suitcase, Colvin is relegated back onto guard duty with Grimm. Their role now is to make sure that those curious bystanders stay curious.

Colvin is quietly furious about the whole thing; that once again she is in the freezing cold, guarding nothing, while more incompetent and less experienced officers are doing more exciting things. She knows why, even after a year, a certain officer is still not to be trusted with anything too important, not when other officers are available. She patrols the area on a fast brisk circuit, trying to stay warm, trying to find something else that will break this case wide open, ensuring that no higher-ups forget her name.

She barely speaks to Grimm when they finally get to leave hours later, replaced by those truly unlucky ones who will stand guard all night. There are no updates when they get back to the station. They haven't identified suitcase girl yet and all they can say is that it is likely she died between two and three days ago. Their more pressing concern right now is that second part of the letter, *"Can you guess what I am planning to do tonight? I am going to have so much fun doing it too, knowing that you are too stupid to stop me."* Whilst that could mean anything really, most have taken it to mean that he will kill again. Tonight. As such they are focusing all their efforts on how to stop him.

Adrian's brother has a new bad habit. Knife flicking. The sound of it is most disconcerting, as it's meant to be. Click, the blade is out, ready for that moment. Click and, with a flick of the wrist, it's gone again. Click, flick, click, flick, in, out, in, out, click. Adrian knows his brother is sitting alone in the dark. Click. Flick. Who knows what is going through his mind or what he is planning to do? Click. Flick. He is unreachable, unavoidable. Adrian tries to shut him out, tries to ignore the distraction but the clicks seem to be getting louder, closer every time.

His father is no help. Every time he confiscates a knife his brother just seems to grow another one. What did their mother used to call them? Cain and Abel and everyone knows what Cain did to Abel. Click, flick, CLICK.

Colvin is not invited to join any of the teams who are patrolling King's Park tonight or any of the street teams for that matter. She is not sent back to the Forest or even back to Old Ware's Farm. Whilst Grimm is asked to stay on a little while longer, she is merely sent home with a 'well done for finding the suitcase' pat on the back. It is about four hours after her shift was supposed to have ended but still, despite her offers, despite them deciding to implement her Stop and Search idea, it was still go home Sam, we have got this.

She thinks about patrolling on her own tonight anyway. She'll show them who's tired, who needs to rest up as tomorrow is going to be a very busy day, no matter what happens tonight. She'll show them all! She thinks about it for a few more minutes. She thinks about smiling triumphantly, her handcuffs securely wrapped around the assailant's wrists, those jealous yet bitterly admiring looks on her colleagues faces. Then she thinks about what happened to the last woman who went up alone against the assailant and decides to head home.

She eats without really tasting her food. The feeling of cold despair still clings to her and she is too cold to move and too awake to sleep. Only one thing she can turn to now; she has managed to keep away these last few weeks, she was doing so well, but she will only look for a few minutes whilst she winds down and warms up. Have a little chuckle at the latest paranoid theories, pan through the bullshit for some interesting nuggets of information. Time for a little itcouldhavebeenme.co.uk.

You can almost hear the audible snap as she takes in the latest hottest thread. The snap of her body jerking to full attention; tiredness, coldness and aching muscles all forgotten as she sees a copy of that letter posted for the whole world to see. How the hell did they get a copy of it?? And what possessed them to post it??? What is wrong with these people???? They just make her want to scream. She rereads the letter again. Yes it's exactly the same as what they were sent, word by irritating smug word. The moderator posted it along with some comments about how the local newsgroups refused to publish it but they think the public has the right to know, comments that make her blood boil. She just wants to find this moderator and slap some sense, some accountability into them. Have they no idea why the newsgroups 'refused' to publish it? Have they no idea what they have done? Yes they have added a perfunctory paragraph about staying safe, about not putting yourself in danger and letting the police do their work but, judging by the comments below, no one had read that bit. Those comments have formed into a full raging debate covering all areas from a long long debate on whether it was a genuine letter or just bullshit, to speculation on what the police found at Old Wares Farm (must have been something important as some of them are still there, someone reported less than ten minutes ago). Other comments are from people suggesting the arranging of 'hunting' groups! Colvin looks at her watch. It's nearly midnight so too late to warn any of her colleagues that they might have company tonight. With a sigh she reads on, reads all the criticisms and dismissals of the "Stop and Search" policy in place tonight, the discussion and updates about where the police are patrolling and the places that they think the assailant will strike. (Obviously not the same places, as according to these people, the police don't know their arse from their elbow.) She has a strong sense that the wrong people are going to be arrested tonight which will a) piss off the police, b) piss off the public even more, possibly inducing another near riot and c) waste everybody's time which is exactly what the assailant wants to happen and is why he posted those letters in the first place. He did everything he could to make sure that as many people as possible saw it.

She wonders how and when the moderator of this website received a copy? Who else it has been sent to? She knows it was sent to a large number of television studios, radio stations and newspaper offices and there are always leaks but was it sent to the website directly? If the letter was posted, how did the killer know the websites owner home address? If emailed there might be a digital trail for them to follow and she makes a barely legible note to find out in the morning. Judging by the time stamps on the comments it looks like the letter was posted on here around midday, just in time for the lunch-hour rush.

Safety in numbers. That was the theory; always making sure that the weakest had the most protection. So many husbands, fathers, boyfriends and some very tough girlfriends are talking about going out together to hunt for this guy, to teach him a very important lesson- one that will leave him permanently taught. There was just one small drawback to this plan, it meant going out and leaving someone important home alone. Easy pickings.

Some decided not to go out, that they would have a normal evening then go to bed after carefully locking every door, window and barricading the bedroom door. Others still went out, leaving a loved one home alone, sobbing in the dark. Some didn't even think about what they were doing until it was too late to turn back. Jenna's 'gang' had a different solution. Safety in numbers. All those who had to stay behind or lived alone, they are going to have a little sleep-over in the most secure house, providing communications support to the stronger troops going out. Once the pizza has been collected the doors are going to be locked, bolted and alarms will be set. Unless an alarm is raised no one is going to return to that house tonight. The 'troops' are going to stay out the entire night, using a different house as headquarters.

Ava has spent the last four hours wishing constantly that she had called in sick today. Not that it is much different to her usual work day but, today, she really means it. It is not helping that one of her other bar staff members, Louise, keeps muttering "We shouldn't be here" over and over, whilst keeping her eyes firmly fixed to the television. The other team member Georgia is just texting someone constantly. Normal behaviour for her but, today, she is being a lot less discrete about it almost as if she was daring them to send her home early. If only Ava knew five hours ago what she knows now. If only she visited the same websites as Louise or had friends like Georgie's who just know everything, she would have kept the place shut tonight consequences be damned!

"They don't care about us, we shouldn't be here, no one else is here." It was a good point when Louise said it the first time but now she is on her eighth repeat and Ava's temper is really beginning to fray. Three hours left to go. Business is slow tonight, not just at the bar but Ava's other business as well. The people out on the street are moving with purpose, only in packs. Sure some groups of men have come in for "pick me ups" and are still huddling in corners, sipping their beers and talking in quiet voices. These groups aren't really the type Ava sees as potential heroes. There have been more serious, slightly dangerous looking men coming in for coffees and whiskey chasers before leaving quickly and quietly. Ava just thinks they are pretending to be tough. She hates them all. If they weren't out here tonight trying to be something they are clearly not she could have gone home early. If they were her usual crowd she would be too busy to be worried, but no, these people are just sitting, sipping, making their drinks last and wasting time. She is going to lose it if they start ordering tap water or stay long after last call. Not tonight boys, not tonight.

"Just three hours left", she tries to tell herself, *"it will be alright, just three hours left to go and everything will be alright"*.

One particular commentator has really irked Colvin. Appropriately named PunkMaster7000 their comment reads: "It has been a year now and we have gotten nowhere. Why don't the police just give this guy the keys to the fricking city and be done with it!" First of all, Colvin thinks, they haven't gotten "nowhere", they just haven't gotten a name or a strong suspect. They have other things though and it is only a matter of time. Second, no one has a master key to an entire city, that's just a crazy myth. Thirdly, you try catching him if you think it's that easy. Finally, fuck you! Colvin doesn't normally swear at members of the public, even when no one else can hear her, but sometimes these things just need to be said.

It still annoys her that they didn't realise that Natalie Ivanovich most likely died on the anniversary of Ruby William's death. They didn't realise until that embarrassing moment when a reporter pointed it out at a press conference. Not one of their finest moments really. She still wonders if the assailant purposely chose to kill on Saturday 19th October because it was the anniversary or merely because there was an easy picking that night? Did he try to kill again on the anniversary of Carly Ellis's death but couldn't find a suitable target? Or did he kill someone but they just haven't found the body yet? And today is not an anniversary, well it's eleven months since Lucy Swann was murdered, but that's not quite the same. Colvin would like to convince herself that it must have been a co-incidence before but she gets the feeling that this killer doesn't go in for co-incidences.

Grimm is wishing he had worn thermal underwear today. It is hard to look serious, commanding and authoritative when you can feel your balls retracting. He is fairly sure that his fellow officers are feeling the same way but that still doesn't mean he's going to share this information out loud.

Their orders are to look for anyone who might be carrying a weapon or anyone who looks out of place, which is pretty much everyone. They have imposed a Section 60 tonight giving them the power to stop anyone within a few certain areas and search for weapons. So far they have stopped around twenty men and confiscated everything from baseball bats to makeshift knuckle dusters. It seems that they are not the only ones hunting today. Grimm is wondering if they do this every night or if someone has tipped them off. What do they know that he doesn't? He just wants to leave them to it and go home. If they want to be this bloody stupid then let them. He has been partnered with Seasions tonight. Seasions has already spent most of his career looking the other way so he-won't get any complaints if he calls it a night.

Stake-outs were a lot easier when he was a younger man but then that is another thing he is not going to admit. He is lucky in the respect that he is one of the visible officers, one of the ones walking around in uniform, laughing at the "under-cover" officers who, despite their best efforts, are sticking out like sore thumbs. They are too well-groomed, too much shine on their shoes, too cop like and don't not even mention the ones who are giving themselves away with their walkie-talkies.

Grimm thinks that it is all a waste of time anyway. Either that bastard sent the letter having already killed someone- (the letter said "tonight", but that could mean last night or even the night before, who knows when he actually wrote it? Who knows how long it had sat in their mail room, despite what they say?) or he sent the letter already having a target marked out, in a private home somewhere. He wouldn't have sent the letter and then left it to fate and chance to provide him with a victim, he wouldn't be that bloody cocky would he?

Or even, thinking about, if you had sent a letter hinting that you might kill someone, you know that the police will have to react, that there will be extra police out on the street tonight, so who do you target? Their wives who are left home alone.

Well if that's the case... Eh fuck her!

One hour to go until closing and the drinking crowd has gotten a lot meaner. Ava has seen a lot of odd glances, menacing flexes and curt nods. She has seen the nervous glances between Louise and Georgia increasing. They too are more alert, holding their breath as they wait, whispering more urgently whenever they pass each other. There is a feeling in the air, quietly suffocating them all. Ava has never felt this unsafe before, never saw the need for a security guard or a silent alarm but tonight... Ava is now mostly worried that some of these men are just wait-ing around, waiting for them to close. Her team are just sitting ducks. She needs to get her team out quickly and home safely.

Colvin finishes reading a very compelling 'Top Ten Reasons Why Walker is Innocent' section and rubs her eyes, her mind wide awake and buzzing with conspiracy theories, that little reading has left her wondering if she does truly trust Juda, Seasions, Leona or even Morkam, they all have unexplained question marks against their names. So does another one of the lead investigators on The Numbers Killer case, not the one who went crazy, the other one, Fletcher. Not many officers will even mention Fletcher these days and there must be a reason for that. Fletcher certainly left the police force in a hurry, has a few strong reasons to hate women, specially the one he was married to, but then always that one question remains, if this truly is The Numbers Killer back again, why come back now? She tries to think of reasons while she reaches for her very cold coffee, why start again now? It is now nearly 1 a.m, her back is beginning to hurt, her eyes burning from the monitors glare, just one more section, she tells herself, then she will go to bed.

She clicks another link. This one brings up a photograph, little blurry and out of focus, but the subject is unmistakable, it is the Angry Youth. Why is there a picture of him on here? Even digitally, he seems to glow with anger as he scowls unknowingly into the distance.

She reads on, he lives close to where Sarah Grieg died, he has been seen on numerous times storming around King's Park. The person who posted the photograph also has it on good authority that he was rejected by Claire Atkins and he didn't take that very well, told her she would be sorry. Another person has added that his name is Caleb, he has been suspended twice for bringing knives to school.

Knives! That was it, she has seen him before! Around two years ago, she had busted him in front of his whole school in an assembly, embarrassing him in front of all those hungry eyes, all those jeering and laughing teenagers. What did she think of him before? A boy brimming with rage, but still just a small boy.

Well maybe she was wrong, maybe he is a precocious boy. She reads on, learning all about how his mother went crazy, killing herself and an innocent man. His father should have been arrested for assault but was saved by his friendships with a number of high ranking police officers. (Probably Juda again, Colvin guesses) There was no hope for Caleb with parents like these. Apparently there is an older brother too, another misguided soul. People worth investigating, or at least having a private chat with. Colvin breathes in deeply, trying to soothe her paranoid mind. They need something more substantial than a few paranoid theories from people who can't even spell the word suspect. Besides Caleb is too young... unless he was really working with his father, like a few other people have suggested, learning the family business. Colvin remembers the father too, a tired looking man, prematurely aged, probably by the stress of raising a teenager. Not someone she would think of being capable to lure and murder eleven women. But then that was probably the last thing his victims thought.

Adrian and his neighbourhood have been listening to his father and brother arguing for the last hour. Adrian sits alone in the dark, drinking his stolen vodka, wincing with every loud bang. You would think it would be a relief to finally hear the front door slam, but really it only makes it worse. Now he is left wondering who has left the house? Has he been left alone with his brother? What is his brother going to do next? Who is his brother going to hurt next?

Colvin didn't realise how many friends and families of the victims were on this site, providing confidential information, defending themselves from accusations, plainly losing their minds and still being dragged to pieces, disgusted she reads on.

Sarah Grieg's on and off again boyfriend has been on here, giving long passionate pleas about how those pictures are hurting her friends and family and to please take them down, this is not how they wanted Sarah to be remembered, she was a much loved friend, fitness instructor and member of the community, she didn't deserve to be exposed like this. In response to this plea, some commentators are asking him questions like:

"Do you have an alibi for that night she died?"

"Is it true you two had a massive fight before she died?"

"Care to explain why you were arrested last year?"

"What kind of car do you drive?" (Colvin does know the answer to this one, and no, he doesn't drive the white van that you are looking for. A white van had been noticed in the neighbourhoods where Priya Smythe and Mary Angus died, but do you know where else white vans were? Everywhere! There are two on her road right now!)

Some commentators are really making a big deal out of the fact that he hasn't answered those questions. There is a reason why he doesn't want to reveal his whereabouts, Colvin knows why and these people really don't need to know. She really can't believe the audacity of some of these commentators, some of them are even privately contacting some "suspects" and then publicly posting any responses they get, analysing every word of those responses, pointing out any "mistakes," making a huge fuss if someone doesn't immediately reply or tells them to go away, treating those responses as signs of guilt. Colvin likes the one lone commentator J-Girl-Down, who posted "OMG these people are grieving, leave them alone." and dislikes the shout down that they got in reply. All with a common theme of "THERE is A MURDERER OUT THERE, excuse me for doing everything I can to catch them, NOT LIKE SOME people!!"

Nikki Woods's mother started posting nearly two months ago about what a sweet girl her daughter was, desperately appealing for any eye-witnesses to come forth, if they haven't already. She is now defending herself against people who are calling her rude and unhelpful, demanding to know why she is "protecting" Mr Woods. Colvin found her last message heartbreaking to read:

"Rude? I lost my fucking daughter, you have no idea how much that still hurts. I don't even have the words to begin describing how bad everything hurts inside. Of always having that insufferable never-ending well of sorrow digging deeper and deeper into your stomach. It's screaming "Leave me alone" when you want a hug. "It's get the hell away from me" when you can't stand to be alone. Every word you want to scream, clogging in your throat, muting you, choking you yet needing so badly to talk. I just want one more hug with my daughter, one more minute together and that minute never to end

I used to spend every single day with my daughter, and now suddenly she is just gone, I spend every moment of my day waiting for her to reappear, for this nightmare to be over. For her and Claire to come home. I cant stop asking where are they? Why aren't they here? Why did they leave me? Where did they go? And I don't understand why you keep harassing me, I have told you everything I know!!"

It was clear that Nikki's mother needed to step away from the chat-boards, she needs help coming to terms with her grief, yet Colvin knows she won't step away, just in case she misses something important, but she really does need people to stop harassing her, she needs a good night sleep. She needs her daughter's killer caught, Colvin thinks, her chest tightening with shame.

There was one man who caught Ava's eye tonight, partly because he is the only man in here on his own, pretending to be a lone wolf, carefully positioned in the corner, watching everything, partly because of that but mostly because he gives Ava the creeps. Ava learnt a long time ago to always go with her first instincts on these matters. It's not that he has done anything wrong or unusual, there is no reason for the alarm bells he sends ringing in Ava's stomach, but still. Ava wishes that he would do something wrong, something to warrant her kicking him out the bar. If only some of her regulars were here tonight, someone like Toothy Tommy or One Finger Bill or even Clive, someone capable of 'discouraging' him from ordering another drink and 'encourage' him to go find another bar, without saying a word out loud. She wonders why they are not here tonight, on the one night she wants them to be, they practically live here, why have they abandoned her tonight?

It was a great relief when 'Creepy Lone Wolf' finally drained the last of his stirred-not-shaken martini and left. Ava waited a good five seconds before nonchalantly walking over and locking the door. Georgie was given very strict instructions to man the door, not to let anyone else in, no matter how desperate they were. The stragglers must have seen something in the look in her eye, or by the tone of her voice, because at that point they all decided to call it a night and leave. Then it was just a case of a quick clean up, dishwasher load before she carefully released Louise and Georgie to their waiting rides home. Neither of them asked her how she was getting home and she didn't tell them her plans. Instead she waved goodbye, locked the door, then wrapped her smiley face scarf tighter around her neck and began to walk.

Jenna's gang did so well at first, they did a few calming yoga poses before breaking out the Chardonnay, eaten pizza and then talked about signing up for the next marathon. Then one of the "ground" units had suggested going to a local pub and conducting some surveillance there, leading to a brief but furious argument between him and his wife. Now she was sat, talking furiously and privately with a few close friends, while the rest of them stood around awkwardly.

There is a weird feeling in the air, these were once women who proudly walked in "Take Back the Night" campaigns, swearing that they would no longer be afraid. They took self-defence classes, supported each other, did everything right and by the books, so why were they now hiding away in here?

Jenna, the most recent newcomer and still an outsider, finds herself repeatedly missing her "old" gang, those friends who always seemed to be busy these days. She wishes again that she could just go back in time, warn Sarah not to answer her door that night, tell those girls to stay away from Kings Park, then she wishes she could jump forward in time, to a point where this is all over and stops hurting. Just get to a point where she can finally exhale and relax again, she wishes for something, anything just to end this nightmare, please get her out of this endless miserable loop of life, get her away from these people.

Jenna is desperate to go outside, to just be alone for a few precious seconds. It's all she can think about since they locked the door, the more she thinks about it, the more she wants it. Maybe it is time to do something drastic.

Colvin has finished reading the complaints about Mary Angus's brother, who apparently sent some commenters on a wild goose chase, and she is still wondering who they spoke to, as Mary Angus didn't have a brother. She has read the speculations and body language "translations" about Sarah Grieg's father and how he acts when giving interviews. "He seems uncomfortable" "He seems to pause for long periods of time" "I think there is something he is not telling us!" Half of them are clearly not experts on the matter. She is now reading a thread started by Priya Smythe's brother, which started innocently enough, thanking people for their support and answering a few innocent questions but then it quickly devolved into a fight, as he insisted that his sister did not know the killer and did not invite any strange men into the house, EVER! Colvin is noticing a pattern on here, noticing that when some of these commentators believe so strongly in their theories, nothing you can say or do will convince them otherwise, to them it's just more evidence of why they are right. They are attacking him now, asking him questions like

"Why did the police keep you overnight for questioning?"

"Is it not true that your fiancée left you because of your anger issues?"

"Why were there 8 missed calls on her phone when you said she was out of your life?"   She wonders how did these

144

commentators find out some of this information, how the hell do they know this? Colvin suspects that there must be another leak in the force or something similar.

"People keep asking me How R U? You want the fucking truth? I feel like it's my fault that she didn't come home and my arms ache, just wanting one last soothing hug. I miss my baby gurl!"

Barry Williams posted that last week and has only attracted comments from well-wishers. Colvin finds this slightly strange given the amount of scrutiny that the others were under, but then maybe it's because Barry Williams is the only one who looks like he is ready to break off the limbs of anyone! anyone! who dares to ask him questions about his daughter's "business" and then beat them to death with their own limbs. Maybe thats the secret to getting sympathy on the internet.

You just know when someone is talking about you, when they keep looking over, to make sure that you can't hear them, smiling those tight smiles. Patel and Bolz have been discussing him for at least ten minutes now and Grimm is just longing to go over there and put them to a degree of unease. Instead he just decides to show them that he knows, with a smile and a cheery wave.

One day, when the cameras are no longer pointing at him all the bloody time, when people like that twat Robert Leona, who isn't hiding quite as well as he thinks, when those people have stopped stalking him, he will get his own back, teach them a little lesson about respecting your superior officers, but right now all he can do is smile and keep walking.

He thinks they have stopped around fifty idiots now, it is hard to tell, they all blur into the same idiot after a while. He is sick of their poor excuses, their miserable outright lies and their flaming cheekiness. He looks around again at his fellow officers, Seasions, Dalbiac, Patel, Anderson, Bolz and wondering how the hell Juda got out this particular duty, unless he is around the corner, planning another ambush and arrest. Grimm's raging monologue is interrupted by the sound of running feet, a lone girl gasps into view, visibly distressed, attracting the attention of every single male within a two mile radius.

"Are you ok?" He calls, using his gentle dad voice, she starts to move closer, close enough for Grimm to see the little smiley faces on her scarf, then her face flushes with recognition, and just as quickly she turns and runs in another direction, still running as if her life depends on it.

"Go make sure she is ok." Grimm commands to their fastest runners, Patel and Bolz, who thankfully do so without argument, while he waits with the others, waiting to see if her chaser is foolish enough to run this way.

Its now two a.m. Colvin has spent over three hours on this website, only taking brief breaks to refresh the local news websites, just in case there has been an update. She keeps telling herself not to be sucked into these paranoid theories, that there are reasonable explanations for most of these "accusations" but she is not seeing them because these are just one-sided arguments with no hard evidence to back them up, She knows she is in danger of becoming like those she has scorned previously for fixating on the wrong suspects.

Colvin blames English Literature, not the books themselves, just the school classes. She thinks that people are being taught to look too closely at the smallest details and then to present persuasively worded arguments about those tiny details, using frail evidence without analysing it carefully first, without looking at the bigger picture. She blames the media for teaching people to over-sensualise anything that might be remotely interesting just to get attention. She also blames English teachers for not teaching some people on here how to punctuate. She knows that strictly speaking it is not their fault, not even slightly their fault but she is tired, angry and hurt, her head is throbbing and it just feels good to shift the blame onto someone else for a change.

She knows she should have gone to bed hours ago, she knows that she never should have even looked at this site, that one wrong comment could compromise their investigation, but she just can't stop looking. Someone with the username G0liath, has updated the "Possible Suspects" thread whilst she was looking at the other threads, and she feels that it is within her best interest to at least look at it. She clicks and stops abruptly, staring at a photo of Nicolas Grimm, clearly taken recently at Old Ware's farm, posted with a very long list of possible reasons why it could be him. She can feel the familiar beat of panic drumming through her, the burning bile rising in her throat. She can't even bring herself to read the reasons, she just shuts down in a panic, not wanting to believe what she has just seen.

She went too far, there is no way she can sleep now, all she can do is lie awake, alone in the darkness, all those thoughts colliding in her head. Her mind trying to rationalise why it couldn't possibly be Grimm, not after everything, but every reason she can think of, has a tiny little 'but he does' 'but he has' tacked on the end of it. Then she drifts into the realms of fury, who do those commentators think they are? They have no right to post these things, she should track down every single one of them and arrest them! Charge them with attempting to pervert the course of Justice! Ha yes! That would teach them! She tries to distract herself with images of arresting all those righteous little pricks, whilst trying to drown out that voice, the one that has been praying constantly all night and is now getting louder with worry. "Please don't let there be another one. Not tonight. Please don't let there be another one."

CHAPTER THIRTEEN

When everything gets too much and you are constantly asking your-self "where can I go?" and "what should I do next?" just take a deep breath and tell yourself "one body at a time". Give that body all the attention it deserves but don't take too long because there are still so many more precious little lambs in need of a lesson and it's not polite to keep them waiting.

Our game is not just to overwhelm the police but to humiliate them. To destroy them completely, hit them with body after body until they are crushed into misery. I want them to know how easy they made it last night, how they sent that bad little girl straight into my arms. I want them to suffer sleepless nights, to spend every mo-ment in fear. I want to be on their mind wherever they go, to consume their every moment whilst showing the world what utter idiots they are.

It hurts so much. She is trying to hang on but everything hurts. She can see headlights lighting up in the distance, speeding to-wards her at thirty miles per hour then zooming past, not stop-ping, not even braking slightly. Why can't anyone see her? She tries to move but the rope is too tight, tries to scream but chokes. Oh god it hurts so much. Another row of lights appear; an illu-minated moving sign. A bus! Please someone, please let this be your stop, please get off the bus and help me. Please someone see me! She hears the roar as the bus passes by, tears streaming down her face. Everything feels darker, colder. She just wants it to stop hurting and for someone to stop and see her. Please? Please?! She thought she would be safe. She was so close to home. She never should have trusted... she had been so careful. That guy... he hurt so much... why? Why her? Please, someone help. Please!

Colvin knows that she looks like crap this morning. There is nothing she can do to disguise it; she just keeps sipping her coffee and hopes that it will take effect soon. She hopes she still looks vaguely professional but is pleased that she is not the only one who looks exhausted although the others probably didn't waste their evening reading absolute nonsense on the internet, they probably did useful things like formulate action plans or even spend time with their families. *"Stupid, stupid Sam"* she silently berates herself, still cursing her past self for not going to bed earlier.

There is some good news. No one died last night. The extra police presence on the streets must have worked. Her colleagues have finally done something right! Go team! Colvin is trying desperately to believe that no one died, really trying. She knows it is possible but... Maybe she will believe it in a few days' time? Maybe her tiredness is making her paranoid? Besides, someone must have died last night. Someone, somewhere in the world, probably more than one person for that matter. But they didn't die of unnatural causes, here in her city, at the hands of a serial killer. How nice it would be if she actually believed that?

This mornings' briefing is not really making any sense but, from what she can comprehend, they have at least identified 'her' suitcase victim as twenty-one years old Kate Drake; an investigative journalist still working the 'for exposure' assignments. Colvin wonders if Kate Drake was also a follower on the ItCouldHaveBeenMe website. If she saw the speculations about Old Wares Farm and decided to poke around thinking that she might get her lucky break? Her 'one hell of a story', not knowing that she was about to become one hell of a story herself? Maybe she arranged to meet someone out there for a private tour?

Maybe someone followed her out there? Either way it means that now there are more leads to follow, more sodding interviews and CCTV to trail through. Someone needs to find Kate's mobile, laptop, i-whatever, notepad and pen, whatever she might have used for her reporting. Someone needs to talk to her family and friends, talk to the person who reported her missing two days ago and apologise for not talking to them sooner (Colvin really really hopes someone else is given that job). Someone needs to look for her car and someone else needs to closely examine all those photos of those crowds yesterday, log and follow up all their number plates. They all have a lot of work to do but here they sit, all trying desperately not to make eye contact with Morkam, praying to themselves that they aren't given the shit jobs.

"Juda and Colvin" What the flipping fuck? Did she hear that right? She barely listens to their assignment to return to Old Wares Farm and search for Kate Drake's car. Juda? She has to pair up with Juda???

Grimm got home at some time around 3am this morning. It was nearing 4am by the time he got the feeling back in his toes. He tried to be quiet when he came in but, judging by how loud his wife slammed the breakfast items around this morning, he wasn't quite as quiet as he had hoped. Either that or she just didn't care. He listened, eyes still firmly sealed shut, as his children squabbled noisily over something trivial, continuing as they were loudly urged out of the door which was then slammed shut just to make sure that he was definitely awake. Thank you dear. Where were they off too? School? Nursery? Swimming Classes? What day is it today? Has he forgotten yet another important celebration or is she angry about something else? Grimm isn't even sure what the date is, everything has just stretched into one endless void of death, disappointment and denial. He is only certain of one thing right now and that is, no matter what happens, no matter who he meets, what he does, he is never ever going to get married again. EVER! Women are just not worth it. He tries to go back to sleep but can't. Stomach rumbling, he tries to get up but his body refuses to move, he can feel so many protests of pain bubbling from his back, knees, feet, shoulders and even his fingers all warning him of the dire agony that will erupt if he dares to move. It's best to just lie here a little longer. He wonders idly what Colvin might be doing right now, tries not to think what his wife might be doing and he is definitely avoiding thinking about that girl with the smiley face scarf. If she was still alive... Damn it, don't think about her. Don't think about that look in her eyes, or about what she was doing out that late at night. Alone. He hopes she got home safe. Patel came back after about twenty minutes saying that he had lost her, not looking like he had even tried looking for her. Bolz took thirty minutes and had been equally useless.

There is an awkward silence as they drive down. Colvin had wanted to take separate vehicles but felt too tired to drive or argue. She just hopped in the passenger seat, put on her best 'I-am-not-in-the-mood-for-your-bullshit' face and pulled out her phone.

It's a well-known trick that, the easiest way to get someone's attention, to get them to start talking, is just to simply ignore them. Some people will crack once they feel the spotlight fading, maybe it is because they think they have got away with something and can't resist a final comment or maybe they think they are being played? It doesn't work for everyone but then, nothing does though, does it? Colvin is determined not to let it work on her. If Juda is not going to say anything then neither will she.

Juda, the rapidly greying ladies' man, still thinks himself to be a bit of a fox, even when he is only two years away from retirement. He has less of the 'world-has-just-bitch-slapped-me' look that Grimm has. Juda, the man who thinks he can charm his way into anyone's good books. Juda, the officer who is hiding the most. At least according to what she read last night. Should she ask him about it? *"Ha, don't be a fool Sam"*, she inwardly chides, *"never ask difficult questions in isolated areas with no back-up, that's the fastest way of getting yourself added to the Have You Seen Me? Missing files"*. Not everything she read last night could possibly be true anyway. Juda wouldn't still be working here if it was, no one is that forgiving, not even Morkam.

They are getting close to the farm now. Does she break the silence to talk strategy? They are essentially just performing guard duty, a double check for that a fifteen-year old rust bucket of a car and a half-hearted last sweep just to make sure that nothing else has been missed. Colvin would feel slighted by this normally but today she really doesn't care. She just wants the day to be over, to go home and go to bed.

It takes a few moments for Colvin to realise that the car has stopped. She turns to see Juda staring at her intently, a hint of malice in his eyes.

They stand close by. They talk, they yawn and they distract themselves. They have all noticed her but they are pretend they haven't. No one wants to be the one to wake her up. That hunched up, pathetic looking sleeper leaning against the bus shelter frame. She might be crazy, she might be aggressive or she might start screaming so best just to leave her to sleep. All they do is silently pity her, it was a cold night last night and not a good night to be sleeping rough. Then they think of other things instead, whilst they wait for their bus. When it arrives they leave without her and forget all about her, knowing she won't be there when they return.

A police officer tries to move her on, tries to shake her awake. It takes a few moments before they realise that no amount of shaking will ever wake her up.

Grimm should have had today off. A recovery day from working so hard last night because, if they had done their job correctly in the first place, there would be no need for them to come in today. The other officers can continue the investigation of Suitcase Girl whilst he, Seasions, Dalbiac, Patel, Anderson and Bolz could rest easily, knowing that they saved a life last night. It would have been a more successful evening if they had actually caught the scum, but still. They are heroes now, brave officers who put their own life at risk to protect the innocent (and the stupid.) That was the theory any way. Grimm doesn't dare turn on the radio or the television in fear of finding out the reality. He keeps checking his phone, not because he's expecting a summons from work or anything but on the off-chance his wife sends him an apology. She doesn't. He showers and dresses quickly, not lingering too long or relaxing. He is eating a hearty brunch when the phone finally rings. That desperate 'Can you please' call from a number he has begun to fear. "Of course," he says, not ready physically or mentally. "I'll be right there," he promises, leaving his dirty plate in the sink while pouring the last of the coffee down his throat. *"Please not that girl"*, he thinks, a fear gripping him from the belly up, *"not that girl. Not her"*.

Juda is not a man who is used to being told no. When he gives an order he expects it to be done without question and he really can't believe that Colvin still hasn't done anything to help Leona. What excuse could she possibly have? All they are asking is that she takes another look at the original Numbers Killer cases. Just what is she playing about at? Has she even looked at the files yet?

Colvin, for her part, just can't understand why, out of everyone on the force, Juda is so insistent that she should be the one who helps. Out of all the old officers who have familiarity with the old case and its suspects. Out of all the new officers, some of whom had already made a point out of studying those cases closely, why her? And, after what she read online last night, she is more convinced that this could be some kind of trap.

But, right now, they have a job to do and, thankfully, it doesn't require them to be on speaking terms. With the onlookers from yesterday long gone it was very easy to spot Kate

Drake's car. Colvin is now working closely with some of the Forensic team to process it whilst Juda and some other officers are performing yet another sweep of the area. The problem is blood, or rather, the lack of blood. The post mortem revealed the true extent of Drake's injuries as well as the numbers engraved into her hands. All those wounds would have caused a lot of blood but there was little in the suitcase and no splashes in the barn. It's clear she wasn't killed in the barn, so where was she killed? Well that's Juda's job to find out, just like it is someone else's job to figure out what that deep number 8 in Drake's left hand and that equally painful number 7 in her right hand means. More numbers for Micheals, an officer who is dedicated to trying to crack The Number Killer and the "BTY" killer's codes. Her desk is covered in calculations, theories and formulas as she works on this twisted math's puzzle.

Colvin doesn't have the easiest job to do. To put it delicately Drake's car is absolutely filled with crap and, when Colvin first peeked inside, she was convinced that the assailant purposely filled it with junk just to slow them down or to put them off completely. Now they are starting to go through it, it is fairly obvious that most of this stuff *does* belong to Drake after all. With all this stuff filling the car there is no way she drove someone else here with her. There just wasn't enough room. Not unless they (or she) was strapped to the roof. Colvin looks at the thick coat of dust coating the car's roof. No she came here alone. This whole area is flat apart from the barn and dilapidated house with nowhere to hide a car (except in a large fleet of other cars, like yesterday) and Drake would have seen and heard another car approaching so why didn't she raise an alarm? Unless the assailant caught her by surprise? But, if he did that, then that would mean he was waiting in the house or barn the entire time with the suitcase ready and waiting for someone else to come out here. But she wasn't killed in the house and she didn't try to fight back.

She must have planned to meet someone here, but she wasn't killed out here. But she drove her own car... it doesn't make sense! What are they missing? What don't they know? *"And don't say a lot!"* she thinks to herself whilst still noting and photographing the contents. So far they have found about two weeks worth of fast food wrappers and associated debris (which explains the smell), scattered CDs and numerous empty cases and four spare changes of clothes; one set so Drake could dress up and look respectable and the other set so she could look a lot less respectable. Colvin wonders where she ~~has~~ had been going to need such costume changes? Then there was the reporter or wannabe robber tools of the trade; bolt cutters, screw drivers, sharp knife on the driver's side (*"why didn't you take this with you?"*, Colvin thinks). There is camera equipment hidden under a blanket, tissues, steering lock... it strikes Colvin that Kate had plenty of makeshift weapons in her car so she must have felt safe here to leave them behind. Also puzzling was that Drake left her torches in the car, indicating she was here during daylight hours so even harder to catch her off guard. Then there were phone charging leads but no phone and no phone had been found on her or in the suitcase.

What interests Colvin the most, what she is taking the time to photograph individually, is the copious amount of hand-written notes. Probably not going to be as helpful as Drake's phone or computer, but still. Colvin has already seen several names repeated in the writing, Bulrush, Fletcher, Juda, Walker, Leona along with some names Colvin doesn't recognise. She is thinking about how much she is looking forward to reading through Drake's research later on when her phone starts to ring.

Please not that girl, the one with the smiley face scarf. Not here, not today. You know they are just going to blame him. Please not her, please. Oh.

You would think that Grimm would be pleased that his prayers were answered and that the girl at the bus stop was not the same girl. Instead Grimm only feels disgust, disgust with himself for feeling relief at the sight of a dead girl. Disgust at the hordes of onlookers who keep trying to inch forward, thinking that the police are too stupid to see what they are doing. Disgust at the cameras, disgust at the gawping. Gather around people, Officer Grimm has plenty of disgust for you all!

Grimm arrived at the scene about two hours after the body had been found. Credit was due to the first officer who found her, they didn't scream or bring attention to themselves in any way, they just calmly requested assistance asap. They kept everything calm until the assistance arrived and they quickly got the scene taped off, the screens up and strategically placed the police vans which arrived. No members of the public got to see anything substantial but, sadly, neither could they be convinced that nothing was happening. They waited around, watching. Then they started talking, tweeting etc. bringing more bloody people to the scene. If only the police had some form of camouflage, an invisible cloaking device, a mind control device, something to keep all those cameras away and all those mouths shut. Don't even get Grimm started on what he would like to use for crowd control.

It would have been nice to be the hero, just for a little while longer.

Juda, in Colvin's mind, is driving too slowly. In reality he is breaking the speed limit but, to Colvin, he should be going faster!

Not that going faster will change anything. The information they have been given is that the girl has been dead for hours. Any trail has probably already gone cold and, knowing this assailant, it has already been contaminated by onlookers. But still, Juda should be going faster.

"So what do we know?" She even hates the way he asks that. There is no "we" Juda. Not anymore. There are only I's here. No teams.

"Female found dead on Park Road. Forensics are at the scene..." Another officer begins warbling and Colvin closes her eyes. It feels like the same scene is repeating over and over again just with different victims. The victim is probably displayed openly for all the public to come and prod and stare and trample over her crime scene. She hopes that today no one will throw drink cans at her, she hopes that Grimm will be at the scene just so she can ditch Juda and she hopes that no one will yell at her. She hopes that she can finally catch a break today. She hopes that at some point soon, she can get a pint of coffee.

Jenna didn't think she would survive the night. Everything just became so tense and at any moment she thought someone would snap. She is never doing something like that again she promises herself on the quiet ride home. Next time she is just going to tough it out on her own. She promises herself she will be stronger next time, over and over, right up until she puts her keys down in her empty house. It is too quiet in here, she needs to check every room, clutching her kitchen knife tightly while making sure everything is where she left it. Then she checks yet again that the door and windows are all still locked. She is supposed to be working from home today and she will, once she has checked all the news websites for updates and of course itcould-havebeenme.co.uk. On the official sources the only news so far is that a man was assaulted on Church Street last night. *"Serves him right for being out"*, Jenna thinks whilst casting her eyes over the article, reading the lines: "Chief Constable Morkam would like to remind concerned residents that a special task force of over 80 officers has been set up and not to approach anyone behaving suspiciously. Please leave it for trained professionals to handle. Please trust the police to do their job." Jenna rolls her eyes, like anyone would trust the police now? Half of them are idiots and the other half are morons. They couldn't even stop a man from getting beaten up last night, what use are they?

> *"Enough of this, time to work!"* Jenna thinks, absent-mindedly pressing the refresh button for the fifteenth time. This time a new headline appears.

> "Police and forensic officers in Station Street as part of 'ongoing investigation'"

She knew it!

The article is brief but it's enough. Jenna ignores the line that reads "We are asking people not to speculate online about the nature of the investigation" and goes over to ItCouldHave-BeenMe.co.uk to join the other hundred or so commentators in an animated frenzy of speculation.

CPR was not attempted on Bus Stop Girl, she had been dead far too long. The officer who found her concentrated all their efforts into preserving the scene. Even now they are taking the uttermost care in preserving every little detail including keeping the knot of the scarf which held her to her seat on the off chance that a piece of the killer's skin might be trapped inside. The result of taking so much care however is that they are working very, very slowly to the consternation of their audience. Their audience who couldn't see anything but are still dramatically speculating, complaining loudly and demanding to know what they are messing about at? Grimm, despite everything, feels hopeful. The killer had obviously expected a large number of people to destroy the crime scene, to cause anger and chaos like he had at the other locations. Maybe, just maybe because he was expecting that, he wasn't as careful as he should have been.

Bus Stop Girl's name is Rachel Kelly, they have found her Student ID tucked inside her pocket. Just that, no mobile, no purse, keys, backpack, shopping bag or anything to indicate why she was out here alone or how long she might have been here. Nothing to indicate why she had been left, tied to a seat with a number eight cut into her right hand. Don't get Grimm wrong, he is happy to have a name and a dedicated team at the station working to find her family and an address, he would be even happier if the police manage to reach her family long before the gossipy panic does. He would be even happier if she was still alive, but it is puzzling. This killer has a habit of taking stuff usually any means of identification etc, anything to slow them down, so why leave her ID card? Did he not realise it was there?

Did he just take her bag but not bother searching her pockets?

Grimm looks up and down Station Road again, why was she out here? Most of the student accommodation was on the other side of the city, closer to the University. They are still a ten minute walk away from the train station, was she going somewhere? Coming home? Was she meeting someone? Someone who hasn't reported her missing? Why was the killer out here last night? Why this area? Yes there was less chance of getting caught here, admittedly they had concentrated their stop and search efforts more in the city centre, but there was also a lot less chance of finding prey here. Maybe he was just waiting to see who was in that last train home crowd before moving on to a different spot. Maybe he was in that crowd, volunteering chivalrously to escort the vulnerable to the bus stop? Maybe he was waiting for her specifically? Let's see now; they are going to have to do a bin seize, everything within about a thirty minute walking distance, also seize the CCTV footage from the nearby train station and any buses that might have passed this way last night.

The angry murmur of work is a welcome change in atmosphere from the accusing silence of Old Wares Farm. Everywhere Colvin looks someone is doing something; some officers had formed barricades completely closing off the street despite being greatly outnumbered. The protective screens are up and the Forensic teams are performing their dance. Almost makes Colvin wonder why they were needed here. She looks around but can't see Grimm anywhere. Her jaws tightens as she realises where she is. Parks Road, just a five minute walk away from Kings Park, his old hunting ground. An area where they had large numbers of officers patrolling last night. Who was out here? Why didn't they see anything? Why didn't they hear anything? Why didn't they bloody do anything?

The only thing Colvin can't see is a body. They have been led to a row of houses with high brick walls. She can hear some of the Forensic team working, even thinks she recognises a voice or two but, until one of them stands up, does she realise where the body is. Discarded and out of sight behind the walls, *"this isn't right"*, Colvin thinks. Where is the big 'Fuck You' display? Where is the show of arrogance and contempt for the whole world to see? Is this even the same assailant?

"Found about an hour ago by the home owner." It annoys Colvin that the officer is speaking to Juda and not her and that they are waiting for orders from him not her. Juda dutifully sends off officers to conduct door to door interviews, adds others to the crowd control, someone else to get him a coffee, someone to find so and so. Then he turns to Colvin with a challenging stare, gesturing towards where the body was now being loaded. The Forensics team are trying to be discreet, trying to avoid drawing any more attention but they are as subtle as someone trying to open a bag of sweets in a crowded theatre.

"Go with them, see if you can get an ID." Colvin's stomach twists painfully, a betraying look of fear shimmers across her face but "Fine" is all she says.

Adrian is trying to power-stance, trying to look calm and in control, trying to look like a man. Like a hero, like someone not related to his brother. He is doing this in response to two people; that guy who has nonchalantly walked past the house at least six times now, taking an intense stare each time he passes and that woman in the blue car who is pretending to be lost, peeking down at a map every time she notices him looking and aiming her camera when she thinks he is not. Adrian doesn't know what is going on but he is trying his best not to be intimidated. His best however is not nearly good enough.

His brother might know what's going on if Adrian could dare to ask him. He locked himself into the bathroom nearly forty minutes ago. Adrian can hear the tap going, mutterings of curses and a constant scrubbing noise. Adrian is almost certain that his brother didn't come home last night. He expected another argument about it or, at least, for his father to order him

out the bathroom but his father seems to be ignoring everything.

Finally his brother slams the door back, clutching his
shirt in his hands and defecting all possible questions with an
angry "What the fuck do you want? Get out of my fucking way"
before storming off downstairs with angry loud stomps. Not
caring that Adrian saw the bloodstains. Downstairs the volume
on the television is purposely turned up, the news team abruptly
announcing that another two women have been found dead
today, as if his father was accusing his brother without daring to
say the words.

Despite Grimm's politest requests, his award winning smile and
his old but still great jokes, despite his best interviewing efforts,
he has been met with nothing but curt dismissals and open hostility, not even one offer of a cup of tea! It would be enough to
make a lesser man question why he had just spent the whole
night outside in the freezing cold, guarding the streets when he
could have been at home with his equally cold wife. It would
make a lesser man more inclined next time just to bugger off
to the pub when called upon to do his duty. Or perhaps, that
lesser officer might be inclined to start issuing petty citations at
the smallest of illegal grievances. Really, what else could he do?
He is giving his everything right now and they are just spitting
in his face, some of them quite literally. He should point out to
some people how much easier everything would be, how much
smoother last night could have gone, if people stopped trying to
take the law into their own hands!

Grimm takes a deep breath, regretting for the tenth time
answering his phone earlier. He tries to remind himself that, just
because everyone thinks you are the bad guy, that doesn't make
you the bad guy. Tries to remind himself that his children still
believe in him, that they are proud of him, that they still love
him. Even if they have forgotten what he looks like. But then the
doubt cuts in. If he is such a great guy then why did that girl run

away from him? What did she see? Why did she have to do that in front of everyone? He needs to stop thinking about her, it's not like he is ever going to see her again to ask her.

It's not that Colvin is scared, she has stood by plenty of dead bodies so she isn't about to faint or wax lyrical about cold dead staring eyes. It's just, well, she is tired, her mind is still buzzing from the contents of Kate Drake's car, all those far away glimpses of a happy life and those notes that might mean something. Someone else could have done this job- she would have been of more use if she had stayed on the Kate Drake investigation. Even though it's the same investigation. Maybe she is a little over-whelmed right now, a little more than paranoid, even a little hungry? She didn't get a chance to eat lunch and, once this van stops and they unload and stoically get to work, she won't want to eat for a long time. Also she would have liked to have stayed at the scene and had a closer look around. Something just isn't feel-ing right. It doesn't feel like the same guy. She would have like to have spoken to the homeowner, found out why it took them so long to find this victim, since Forensics are estimating that she has been dead for several hours now. She would have been more useful if she stayed on the scene, not that she isn't grateful to get away from Juda. Being sent here was his way of punishing her for not doing what he wanted her to do.

"Busy today." One of the Forensics remarks, Colvin gives a tight nod in response, not knowing what they know. "Let's see what we have here." The bag is unzipped, cause of death seems fairly simple enough, even to someone who is not med-ically trained. A deep cut, heavy across the throat, no hesitation marks, no defence wounds, no other signs of the usual assault. Maybe this is the work of a copycat, maybe it was just because of the police patrolling nearby? A deep number 9 cut into her left hand. Colvin tries to concentrate on her notes, getting ready to note personal effects, anything that might give a clue on the vic-tim's identity.

Colvin can't help sneaking glimpses at the victim whilst the others swab and poke. The victim looks to be in her late twenties. There is a certain hardness in her face, even in death. Perfectly applied dark red lipstick, a matching hair-slide holding back her short, dark hair. A tiny silver hoop in her eyebrow, the kind Colvin had when she was seventeen. Odd splashes of blood higher up on her face, suggesting that her mouth had been covered during the attack, by a hand, Colvin suspects. She would even go as far as to predict that the assailant would have made a point to go past at least one police officer without wiping off the blood, nothing too obvious, but enough, maybe even give a friendly hello to them, pretend to be coming back late from the pub, making jokes about a furious missus. A taunt he wouldn't be able to resist.

It's only when they remove the bloody rag from around the victim's neck that Colvin realises that it had once been a scarf, tucked into the victim's jacket, giving clear access to her neck. She can even see the smiley face motif on it, something that didn't quite fit the rest of the tough girl image. Someone must have given her that scarf, a Secret Santa or a birthday present perhaps? Either way it was a present from someone she cared about enough to wear it, at least for a few weeks. There was something else around her neck too, a work lanyard with a key-card attached. A work ID for an Ava James, bar employee at the Butcher's Arms. A pub familiar to most police officers. Colvin is about to leave the room, about to call someone to notify the family and begin the interviews dance when they start emptying out the inner pocket of her jacket.

CHAPTER FOURTEEN

Now you are really getting it. I am proud of the progress you are making.

It had been on the same level as a hard slap to the face. Colvin had felt the full force of it, smacking through her cheek, tearing through her body, leaving behind deep welts of despair. Despite it, she still had to smile and carry on, keep working, work even harder if such a thing was possible. Even now, a week later, she is still feeling mentally bruised and shaken. It had started when she had called base to update them with Ava James' identity. In return she had finally been informed about the second victim, Rachel Kelly, that sudden suckerpunch from someone who never physically raised a hand.

She was done, that day, right then and there, she was done and she is still fucking done! She is still going through all those crucial motions, waiting and waiting, waiting for it to be the end of the day so she can go home and cry, waiting for someone to take her aside and tell her that her efforts were appreciated but now they want someone else to take over. This would never have happened if she had been allowed to patrol that night, why couldn't anyone else just do their job properly for once? What was the point? She never should have listened when they told her to go home, never believed them when they said they had got this, never should have listened to their bleats about safety, that utter bullshit about being a potential target. She should have been out with them, protecting the people, instead of staying home, reading that paranoid waffle.

Grimm had known something was wrong the minute he walked back into the station. It was if the building itself had stopped to hold its breath, silently accusing him with the thud of the closing door. But this time it is not just him being accused; he was just the ring leader, the corrupter, the one to be fed to the drooling lions.

Imagine getting hit by a shoe and then another shoe, one that had been stood in dog shit, then another, then it's not shoes any more, it's bricks; falling one by one, leaving you intact on the outside but utterly disintegrated on the inside. Imagine being flayed into small strings of skin, then spun on a sharp spinning wheel into a fine cloth which is then used as a towel for someone's sweaty balls. Imagine all that and you are just beginning to understand how Grimm felt that day. That was over a week ago now and he is feeling worse now than he did then.

He has been questioned endlessly along with every other officer on patrol in that area that night. Over and over until he began doubting his own memories, constantly having to mentally run through the details to convince himself that he was innocent and had done nothing wrong.

Then they had come under more heavy fire for not getting a valid name and address for every single one of those thousands of faces that they had stopped that night. For letting some people anonymously go with just a warning to get home. And they were in trouble for not stopping those other trillion or so people who moved in clusters, loitering politely on the sidelines, the non-threatening people. For not stopping and getting their details. For not remembering what they all looked like. Who should he have stopped? He tries to think back, never mind the weapons they confiscated, the people they had sent home, who did they miss? Who didn't they look at more carefully?

Those women? The other police officers, those security forces, the people they thought were there to help? Who did they miss?

Why did Ava James in her smiley face scarf run away from him? Why did she seem to recognise him? They ask out loud the same questions Grimm torments himself with, the questions he has no answers too. Grimm remembers faces and he is certain he didn't know her. He'd never met her before, he was certain of that on that first round of questioning and he was still certain when they asked him for the fifth and sixth time.

He wasn't the one who followed her, he never went out of sight of the other officers. He only ordered Patel and Bolz to follow her, a move which has seriously damaged all of their careers, another move he is going to spend a lifetime paying for.

In that week they have gone through the usual steps; other officers were still hunting down CCTV footages, chasing leads and hot tips but all they have learnt so far is Kate Drake, left hand number 8, right hand number 7, told none of her colleagues, friends, followers etc. that she was going out to investigate Old Wares Farm. Efforts to investigate her call records and her emails had yielded over a thousand "useful" tips as hundreds of people had contacted Kate with their thoughts and suspicions but there were no messages that proposed a meeting or a search of the farm. She was last seen alive early morning on Tuesday 19th November buying a cup of coffee to go. That is the last time she paid for anything on her card or appeared on any CCTV footage they could find. Colvin still has the copies of Kate's notes to go through but is not optimistic about finding anything useful. She thinks that the assailant would have taken the effort to destroy the car if he thought for a moment Kate Drake had anything that would link back to him.

Analysis of the "Dear Detective Dipshits" letter had yielded very little and the analysis of the red X proved that it was dried blood, blood that had previously belonged to Cathy Clark. Some officers think it means she is still alive and working with the assailant but Colvin thinks that she is dead and the assailant is storing her blood somewhere. It worries her, usually at 3am, exactly how he is storing her blood, perhaps even her body, and why, out of all the victims so far, he chose to keep her. She also is scared by the thought that the other officers *are* correct and that Cathy Clark might *still* be alive. Alive and his prisoner.

Rachel Kelly, right hand number 8, had been coming back to the city on the last train home after spending a few days with her girlfriend. She had promised to take a taxi home from the train station. Rachel was spotted leaving the train station at 11.25pm on the CCTV footage. She'd been alone, hurrying with head low and no one noticing her or following her. That was the only footage they could find of her. Rachel's friends had insisted that she would never have talked to a stranger, that she would walk a mile in the wrong direction if she thought someone was following her, she didn't even smile in a public place in case it led to someone trying to take advantage. Her friends had lamented over and over that she would Never! Ever! Trust! A Man! and she was too afraid of giving the wrong impression after that incident years ago.

Ava James, left hand number 9, had closed The Butchers Arms at 1am. The staff had left the building around 1.20am and she had been seen running on the streets sometime between 1.30am-1.45am. Running in the direction of her home. All officers in the area swear they didn't see anyone following her or hear anything suspicious. She just appeared suddenly and disappeared just as quickly. Ava's body had been dumped one street away from her house. There had been some useful content on Ava James's phone but it was only of interest to the Narcotics officers. Her work colleagues at The Butchers Arm thought Ava was being picked up by someone and that she was going straight home. They thought she could take care of herself and so they never thought to ask how she was getting home. If they knew anything about Ava's side business they weren't telling.

The biggest puzzle was that they couldn't figure out where the victims had been attacked. The blood found on the scenes was inconsistent with the victims' injuries. They know it had taken a while for Rachel Kelly to die as she had been attacked and then tied to the bus stop on Station Street and left to bleed out. They estimated that she had died somewhere between an hour to two hours after she had been attacked. In contrast Ava had died fairly instantly. It was the same with Kate Drake; they could not find any evidence of attack or blood anywhere at the Farm. The popular theory is that the victims had been dragged into a large vehicle, killed inside it and then dumped. White vans had been noticed by eye-witnesses in both areas but they were a common sighting everywhere, no one had thought to note down their number plates. Two different residents of Park Road had remembered hearing a vehicle door slam around 2am but thought nothing of it. The other theory pointed out that assailant had enough time to walk from Station Street to Park Road but that would also mean that he walked around blood stained, carrying a weapon in a heavy patrolled area without being stopped. No one wanted to believe that theory.

"He has a strong hatred of women" No shit Sherlock! Really how much money did they waste on this consult? Grimm knew this would be a waste of time and it is. The clue was in the name, consult; a word made up of two concepts, to con and to insult. Sadly, judging by the furious scribbling of his fellow officers, Grimm is the only one who feels this way. Nearly every spare officer they have is sat in here concentrating, all three of their brain cells overfiring.

"He is likely to have been humiliated by a woman in the past, perhaps a bad divorce or an overbearing mother." Even the speaker notices that everyone's eyes are turning towards Grimm who looks down, pretending to make notes. He turns slightly to see Colvin is also staring at him, a look of horror in her eyes. *"You too?"* he wants to ask, *"after everything?"*

"This is someone who might try to insert themselves into the investigation." Colvin immediately thinks of Robert Leona.

She hasn't thought about him for a while but, if they had chosen that moment to ask the room to the name the person trying their hardest to insert themselves into the investigation, she would be waving her arm in the air like a child. Oooh Oooh! Pick me! Robert Leona! Then she might also suggest the private investigators hired by Natalie Ivanovich's friends. Those investigators didn't so much as investigate as just follow the police around everywhere. Maybe they should take a close look at their credentials?

Grimm thinks that was just another statement that means nothing given that pretty much everyone has tried to insert themselves into this investigation, including most of the general public. So far all they have really confirmed is that the police are looking for one mean motherfucker and they already knew that anyway. Money well spent. Back in his day people were only brought in if they were useful. These people are just hazarding guesses and stating the obvious.

Colvin had hoped that they would say more about geographical profiling, something that has always interested her but they barely touch on it, only saying that due to the distance in locations the suspect is likely to be using a vehicle, lives close to or exercises around Kings Park and he is likely to work unsociable hours, possibly a job that involves a lot of local travel.

"Hey Grimm, what's your relationship with your mother like?" Some cocky little just-been-promoted upstart dares to ask when they are all trailing out, the other officers trying to subtly stay in listening range whilst attempting to keep a straight face. Grimm wants to reply with a short and sweet, "Fuck you" but he knows that is exactly what they are waiting for, more evidence for termination. One of them probably even has a tape-recorder already recording, just waiting. Even now they are still trying to drive him out. Still blaming him for what happened to Ava Kelly, still questioning how he really knew Wendy Michealson.

"I have a better relationship with *your* mother." He retorts instead with a wink and a hip thrust. There, that shut the little bastard up.

There is not really time to start anything else after the consult. Grimm refills his coffee cup and heads back to his desk, hating everyone around him. He is intent on catching up on paperwork and emails. Colvin follows him quietly, slumping at her own desk with a defeated sigh. The consult didn't motivate her, didn't inspire any new plans or offer any advice to lure the assailant. Grimm thinks the most infuriating thing about it was the implication that they weren't really trying. If Grimm had a pound for every interview he had conducted, for every minute of CCTV watched, every suspect he had personally investigated then not only would he be able to retire, he would be able to buy a nice boat too.

Grimm is trying to think of something not work related to say to Sam. He knows she doesn't have a partner, no known children and asking about her parents has always been a big no-no. He tries to think if she has ever mentioned any hobbies or interests that he could weakly enquire about but nothing that he can remember. That is a big problem with her, she is too work-orientated. She needs to lighten up, like he does with his... erm … well at least he has a loving family's support... ah damn it all! Maybe he should suggest a spa day to Colvin but he is sure that would go down like a fart at a funeral. He just needs something to break the silence without bringing up the consult. The sooner that is forgotten the better. Something to make her smile or something to ensure at least five minutes of quality conversation, something they haven't had in days. He thinks again of that look of horror during the consult. He needs to start the conversation, needs to remind her that he is not a monster. He had tried to do that on Tuesday and had joined a group of sullen faced officers standing around the coffee machine, tried to break the silence by jovially asking if anyone had seen the Station Ghost, the one with a face like a scowling bull? He'd gone on to say that he'd heard some officers swearing that they'd seen her by the photocopier where she monitored its usage with a glare while others still insisted that she patrolled the corridors, listening carefully to each conversation to ensure no personal comments were being made on paid time. Some even believed that the ghost had never left the station and that she would haunt it forever, trying to help catch the serial killer that eluded her grasp.

It did not get the effect he was hoping for. Of the officers standing there none of them found it interesting or amusing. None of them even believed in ghosts and, those who knew who Bullface was, didn't appreciate being reminded of her. It had sparked off a long rant from one of the officers about the improbability of ghosts; how there was always a simple explanation for any ghost sightings and that it was just paranoia, fuelled by tiredness, hysteria and, of course, idiots. The rant ended with the officer saying he couldn't believe that some of the smartest minds in the city could be fooled so easily into believing such nonsense and, if they are fooled by such things, it was their own fault. By then it felt like they weren't just talking about ghosts anymore. It had become a personal shot about how he shouldn't have been fooled so easily by a certain woman. A reminder that they hadn't forgotten and they hadn't forgiven. At that point his phone had gone off and he was grateful for an excuse to depart from the conversation. Grimm scowls at the memory, abandons all thoughts of trying to make conversation and buries himself in his emails instead.

Colvin knows she should talk to Grimm but, frankly, what was the point? She has heard the other officers proclaiming, with a certain satisfaction, that 'It's only a matter of time before he snaps.' They even have a betting pool going, Colvin had politely declined to place a bet, suspecting they have similar bets going regarding her. The feeling that someone is going to do something stupid is in the air and she doesn't know what to do.

They had had a good conversation shortly after Ava James had been found dead. Colvin had found Grimm at his desk, head firmly buried into his arms, still questioning over and over why Ava James had run away from him. Colvin had considered telling him about itcouldhavebeenme.co.uk and the articles and theories based on him but, instead, she focused on first getting his version of events. After that she'd told Grimm that maybe Ava had run away from the sight of his uniform, rather than his face, because of the large quantity of drugs hidden in her pockets. The conversation had visibly helped and had even inspired him briefly to do some work.

Colvin no longer really suspects Grimm of any wrong doing. What she suspects is that, maybe, he was purposely planted in that area by the assailant or someone working with him? Someone who knew which way the fingers would point, a perfect distraction. She had tried to subtly question Grimm about who divided and placed the patrols but the only real important information she has discovered so far is that Juda was not on patrol that night although he had been sighted in the area. There was probably a perfectly reasonable explanation but she doesn't want to talk to him to find out.

Colvin has been thinking a lot lately, despite being done with it all. She has been thinking about Robert Leona, Juda, that Incredibly Angry Youth (she really should find out his name), Morkam, Fletcher and Walker. Fucking Walker. She has also been thinking a lot about therapy, sleeping pills and yoga. Anything that might mean she can sleep at night, although she draws the line at chamomile tea.

On one of those sleepless nights she asked herself why she was so reluctant to even consider the possibility that Walker might be innocent? Is it because of what it implied and because she didn't want it to be true? Proving him to be innocent would also mean confirming the rumour about the woman she replaced. Her predecessor would not have been the first police officer to take an innocent life nor the last but Colvin just didn't want it to be true, not about her. Maybe it's because she feels so close to cracking herself? It could just so easily happen, the wrong word said in the wrong tone of voice and who knows what it could trigger? She also didn't want to believe that her colleagues would perpetuate such a cover up (who could believe that they would be that smart or that evil?)

Maybe Walker had been another diversion tactic? But

then if Walker wasn't the original Numbers Killer and the original had now returned, why the massive time gap? Where had they been? What had they been doing? They had obviously been spiralling out of control before, how did they manage to suppress that? Go into hiding whilst framing someone else for their kills? Why have they chosen to go public now after so many years of operating secretly in the dark?

She suspects that this killer is just someone familiar with the details of the original Numbers Killer, someone just using those details to cause confusion, reignite old hurts and grievances and mislead the police. And it was working so fucking well! It was another stupid test, another opportunity to divide them and cause chaos whilst all the while laughing at their stupidity.

Colvin has also spent sleepless nights wishing that they had come up with a better name than The Numbers Killer. Normally serial killers gave themselves a nickname or, if not, the press would invent one for them and there was something wrong about that Colvin thought. They should let the police publicly name the killers. After-all, what killer would continue if they were branded "That Flowers Guy" or "The Wee Bastard"? Colvin was up for calling this one "The Guy with the Tiny Penis" or GWTP for short. Something suitably uncool and which didn't invoke fear like the "Yorkshire Ripper" or "The Boston Strangler" and so on.

Then she started thinking about the "Dear Detective Dipshits" letter. It had been signed BTY but what on earth did that stand for? It had immediately brought to her mind the BTK killer who said that BTK stood for Bind, Torture, Kill. What could BTY stand for? Bastards Torture You? Bitches Take... something beginning with Y. Colvin is sure it will eventually be explained to them in another condescending note. Perhaps it was someone's initials or another clumsy attempt to frame someone like Brian Young or Brett Yeomans?

Who is BTY? Walker's partner? An admirer? A lover? A son? And who trained them to be so good? To avoid detectives,

CCTV, the public and their ever present cameras? To lurk in the darkness, seizing women without detection? But why now? Why after so many years, why now? Colvin feels if she could find the answer to that question she could find BTY. Was he waiting for someone to come out of prison? Waiting for someone to grow up? Waiting for a target to become accessible?

One of the victims had to mean something, she had decided. They had to be missing something, those victims couldn't all be chosen randomly. Those numbers cut into their hands had to mean something, something obvious. That's what she needs to do; take another long, close look at Walker's victims and BTY's victims. Someone must have been targeted for a reason.

Now the biggest question is does she confide her theories and thoughts with Grimm? He might try to talk her out of them and call her crazy or she might be wrong to trust him and he might actually be reporting back to Morkam, Juda or someone else. He might just stand over her shoulder making unhelpful comments and dismissive sighs like he had in the consult briefing today or he might come up with a new insight that she didn't think of, see a connection she missed. Too late, it's home time and he is already out the door. Maybe she will start looking on her own tomorrow morning, see if she can find something interesting.

For now she can drive herself crazy all night, thinking of where to start. Does she start having another look at the numbers? The victims themselves? Kate Drake notes? Try her own attempt at a Geographical profile? So many factors, so many unanswered questions and she needs to think carefully about where to step.

Colvin walks into work the next morning, trying to hold her shoulders high, her head up and smile. Her fellow officers greet her, wondering if she is on drugs or just constipated. Either way they don't really care. Colvin walks briskly to her desk having already decided on an action plan, a backup plan and another

174

plan just in case. She is surprised to see Grimm is not at his desk but doesn't dwell on it. She has work to do. Starting with the numbers.

2, 22, 28, 30, 34, 36, 38, 40, 42. Those are the numbers that the original Numbers Killer used. They know one number is missing from this sequence because he was interrupted before he could brand her. There were others, unofficial victims and everyone knows that there are more Polaroids locked securely away, seen by only a small handful of officers, who even now, won't speak about them. She would need to speak with Morkam if she wants access to those.

Polaroids, the original Numbers Killer documented each one of his kills with Polaroids. He sometimes left Polaroids of previous victims with new victims, a grand 'look what I did' gesture and he took things as well, mementos, trophies, wedding rings, jewellery. BTY takes things sometimes as a way to slow down identification. Colvin wouldn't be surprised to find those things have just been discarded somewhere, dumped without any real thought. Tossed like Kate Drake's phone which had been found trodden into the mud. The only exception being Mary Angus's car which Colvin still thinks was taken just for the thrill of being able to drive such a sleek shiny sports car or perhaps something to use to lure the next victim.

These are the numbers used by BTY so far, depending how you interpret the two hand kills:

1,2,1,32,43,5,64 (or 6, 4*),5,7,6,87,98 (or 9, 8*)

or
1,2,1, 23, 34, 5, 4, 46 (or 4,6*), 5, 7, 6, 78, 89 (or 8, 9*)

*depending if you counted two kills on the same night to be a joint number or a separate number.

Neither code make sense to Colvin and she's fairly sure that neither The Numbers Killer and BTY use the same codes as The Numbers Killer only used even numbers. She needs to look at the numbers in a different way.

She starts pulling out pictures from The Number Killers file. Here is the left hand of Isabel Hilarie, the number 34 cut deep. Colvin knows from memory that mess of pink and purple felt tip on her wrist is the top of a slightly lopsided dinosaur. Hilarie had drawn beautiful images all over her body in a fit of drunken boredom before leaving the house for snacks. She had been an art student at the university and if she was still alive, she would have graduated by now. Perhaps the world would have known her name for a different art-based reason?

Madison Albrook was another student. Her right hand had been felt tipped with a number 36 and she was the only victim he didn't have time to properly brand, going for a shock kill in a busy area and not wanting to take any chances of being caught. Then there are more hands with deep, to the bone cuts that showed what he was really capable of doing when he had the time.

She puts all the hands in a line then starts pulling out the pictures of the BTY's victim's hands. She tries to focus on the numbers alone but it strikes her how different each hand was. Each had a little mark of its owners identity. Left hand number 1: Ruby Williams. Normally the first kill is worth looking the most closely at, there is a reason why they were chosen, a closeness, but this "first" kill didn't really feel like a first. Instead it seemed the work of an already practised killer honing his skills. Colvin stares hard at that number 1, partly etched into a dark bruise.

Left hand number 2: Carly Ellis. The picture is a close up shot, Colvin can clearly see the tiny rose tattoo had been cut by the number.

Right hand number 1: Lucy Swann, her gold painted nails, her gold ring still shining through that layer of dried blood. A hand that earlier had been used to greet, cradle drinks and gesture as its owner laughed, joked and traded presents. Colvin tries to compare the deep numbers on Priya Smythe's hands with The Numbers Killer' victims, but is distracted by the fact that Priya was obviously a nail biter. Had she been scared nights before the attack had occurred? Had she known that she was being watched and lay alone in the darkness, nervously chewing, waiting? The 3 on her left hand and the 2 on her right don't quite look the same as the numbers on Madison and Hilarie and Colvin couldn't tell if they were done by the same person or by someone new. But then the 4 on Mary Angus's left hand and the 3 on her right hand don't quite look like they were done by the same person who cut Priya's hands either.

Mary Angus. There has never been another attack quite as brutal as what happened to Mary Angus, the kills really vary in their brutality, the assailant seems to constantly be moving between aggressive kills and shocking kills, always experimenting. Some officers are focusing their efforts investigating Mary Angus, Priya Smythe, Natalie Ivanovich and Kate Drake's backgrounds as they are the victims that he seems to have spent the most time with. Those kills felt like they were personal attacks. Colvin is not quite so sure.

Left hand number 5, Wendy Michealson. The first of the 'look at what I can do victims', if he hadn't of set Mary's car on fire in that field, if he hadn't of purposely drawn their attention, who knows how long it would have taken to find Wendy? He could have left her there, her left hand slowly rotting away, so they would never know what number she was, just like the original Numbers Killer had done with some of his victims. But no, this killer wants them to find his work, that's what made Cathy Clark's disappearance so puzzling. Colvin only knows the basics of forensics and she idly wonders if that baby pink nail polish on Wendy's fingers would have disintegrated in time. What would have been left of her cheap jewellery if they hadn't found her?

The next set of hands are the hardest ones to look at. Claire Atkins and Nikki Woods–with matching sparkly manicures, friendship bracelets and matching cheap rings but not matching numbers. Claire's right hand cut had been a 4 while Nikki's left hand had been a 6. Memories of that summer trickle in; that heatwave where their every working moment was spent waiting for that explosion of anger from the public, waiting for the riots. After those two young girls were killed though there was nothing, the heat was turned down and the anger set to simmer. Now they are in winter and people's patience has been burnt dry, goodwill burnt into an unrecognisable crisp stain and the only thing left is bubbling hatred, ho ho ho and a Merry Christmas. Oh and of course those memories of that woman shouting that she didn't even care. That still hurt.

No hands picture for the next victim, Cathy Clark, if she was a victim that is. Colvin wonders why, out of all the victims, the assailant had hidden this one? They have exhausted all their possible leads into her background but still some officers are still insisting that this is *the* one. The victim that needs studying closely. Colvin wonders if maybe this is just another one of the assailant's traps, ensuring that they spent more time on this one and not the others? It was odd, hiding her body. The Numbers Killer purposely hid bodies, relished in the confusion and panic. BTY didn't, BTY liked to relish in the fear, liked to show off and everything, from the victims at Kings Park, the sunbathing girls, the home invasions, was a show of force, a demonstration of different skills. Some officers think BTY has more hidden victims and they want to search the forests and fields. Colvin has no doubt however that there won't be any more buried bodies with this one, no matter what the others say. If they make a show out of looking, this assailant will purposely plant something for them to 'miss.' Her explanation for Cathy Clark would be that maybe he was just proving that he can successfully bury a body, keep it hidden from them. Maybe he was saving it for another gloating letter and another twisted treasure hunt?

Which also leads to the question of what would have happened if that random photographer hadn't found the body of Natalie Ivanovich in the woods that day? The assailant had purposely left her hand peeking out of the leaves, those perfectly painted red nails on show. Was the assailant planning to send them a letter about that one? Had he been surprised that she had been found relatively quickly? Why did he kill on the anniversary of Ruby Williams' death only to go to the effort to hide the body? Surely if he was killing because it was the anniversary, he would leave the body on show? And why make Natalie so hard to identify? Was this one personal as well? Or just proof that no one was safe from him and no one could think themselves to be untouchable? Colvin had read a theory on ItCouldHave-BeenMe.co.uk that she had been picked because she had dirt on certain police officers. That a certain police officer may not have killed her but may have picked her to be the next to die. That same theory had also hinted about Colvin's own imminent demise.

To add to the already long list of questions, why did he make Sarah Grieg's death so open and prominent? Was her death another attempt not just to control the police but to provoke the public? Had he expected a bigger reaction from the display of Nikki Woods and Claire Atkins? Had he wanted to publicly remind everyone that they were not safe? Right hand number 6 for Sarah, the cut just above an old burn scar. Her family had told them that it was from a kitchen accident and that Sarah had liked to bake cakes. Colvin feels that maybe she would have been happier not knowing that.

She is only getting more questions from doing this, just a headache and heartache. It is hard looking at the reminders that all these victims were once humans. Girls who had a future ahead of them. Girls who deserved better. Speaking of girls who deserved better the next victim is Kate Drake, a number 8 on her left hand and a 7 on her right. Colvin has now read Kate's research notes which turned out to be nothing but 'hot' takes on the same old, same old, fleshed out with some 'creativity.' Kate had been trying to track down the families of the victims of the previous Number Killer. She was having trouble tracking most of them down and the ones she did find didn't want to talk to her. Colvin had listened to the brief recording Kate had made of her interview with Jennifer Taylor, the mother of Fran Lizzie Taylor. Jennifer was a known associate of Leona and part of the same vigilante group. Founder of that vigilante group even, then, later, the subdue founder of the Fran Lizzie Taylor memorial foundation. It had been a shock to hear her slurred voice on that recording, angrily asking Kate, "Do you people have any idea of the damage that you do?" Kate had been planning to use this quote as the basis of a new article.

She has the photo of Fran's hand here. Fran had been the first victim to be publicly displayed by the Numbers Killer with a very precise 22 carved into her hand. It had been carved with something sharp, possibly a scalpel, by someone not in a hurry. It didn't quite match the numbers on Madison or Hilarie and it definitely didn't match the 2s on Carly Ellis or Priya Smythe.

Kate did have some interesting research on Walker however and had been planning an article entitled "Just Your Average Joe". It was based on an interview with a sadly anonymous friend of his (Colvin would love to know who) who was still insisting that Walker was innocent and that he was not capable of such cruelty. Kate also had supporting statements from various members of Walker's family and other friends who said that the Walkers were a sweet happy couple and he would never have done anything to hurt her. There was an interview with another friend, Barry Harris, who said that he had seen Walker on the day that Stella McQam had been murdered, an hour after the time of death. Walker had been too calm and collected, he remembered, insisting that there was no way he could have just killed someone. Then, to counterbalance the article, there had been a quote from former police officer Aaron Fletcher which simply read "Walker was guilty as fuck" with no other explanation.

Most of Kate's notes looked like they had been lifted straight from ItCouldHaveBeenMe.co.uk, word for word, right down to the spelling mistakes. Unless Kate had been the one who had written them in the first place? Perhaps Colvin is being a tad cruel here but she thinks, if Kate had lived, she would have been considering a career change within a year or so moving towards something more suitable for her creative talents.

Sighing heavily, she pulls out the pictures of the last two hands. Ava James, a number 9 cut in her left hand and a reminder written on her right hand to call Barry. Rachel Kelly, right hand with a number 8 cut and a brand new engagement ring on her left. Colvin finishes placing the pictures in a row, still feeling like she is missing a photo or perhaps the bigger picture. She still has no idea what the codes could mean. She mixes the photos up, all the numbers together, then all the different ethnicities together but it still makes no sense. Clutching at straws she tries organising them by nail colour and then, finally, all the left hands together followed by all the right hands together. Stopping suddenly, she stares down. Is it really just that simple?

Some officers believe that BTY has killed more victims than they know about and that victims might still remain in the forest, park or at the farm. So many people on itcouldhavebeen-me.co.uk are theorising that he killed someone on the anniversary of Carly Ellis's death as well, they just haven't found her yet. Colvin doesn't think so. She thinks the only other victim is Cathy Clark and would even go as far to say that Cathy Clark is dead and that she has a number 5 cut in her right hand. The answers have been staring at them this entire time, another laugh against them that they couldn't see.

It explains so much too, how Natalie Ivanovich had been moved without drag marks, how Claire and Nikki had been attacked without one of them reacting and how Mary had been restrained during the weapons hunt. Two killers, one marks the left hand, 1,2,3, the other the same on the right hand. Each keeping count of their kills and when they kill together, they mark both hands.

CHAPTER FIFTEEN

Don't rush me, I don't like to be rushed. Today is a special day after all and I want to enjoy it.

I hope you appreciate how easy that one was. I keep telling you, you need to learn how to be polite and helpful, yes I know, it's beneath us, but women, they can be so cooperative when they think you are going to help them.

Jenna stops everything when she hears the thump, the one that came from somewhere upstairs, her bedroom possibly? She stays still, her heart punching a hole in her chest with rapid pounding beats, listening carefully for another tell-tale noise. It could be nothing; someone next door dropping something heavy or slamming a door a little too hard or it could be someone moving inside her house. She waits, what does she do now? Get out the house? Get a kitchen knife out the drawer? Do absolutely nothing, pretending everything is alright right up until the moment the killer's knife pricks through her skin? Does she call the police only to find out that it's nothing and forever be branded a crazy time waster? But it's today of all days, everyone knows something is going to happen today, everyone has been talking about it. She can't hear anything else but if she moves, she might miss any new sounds...maybe she will just stand, shaking in her kitchen, paralysed with indecision for the rest of her short life?

It's probably nothing she tries to reason with herself. There is nothing to be afraid of, you know all the doors are locked, as are the windows. No one should have been able to get inside the house. *"Should being the key word there"* her mind counter-argues with itself. Many things should not have happened, but they did. She reaches out a trembling hand, pulling open the utensil drawer. *"Go ahead"*, she tells herself, *"Grab the biggest knife if it makes you feel better. Take a deep breath in and out, try not to think about how blunt that knife is and how you should have sharpened it years ago. Breathe, just breathe. Everything is alright, there is no one upstairs waiting to torture you, waiting to kill you. No one waiting silently, smiling with anticipation. Everything is alright, just breathe"*. Her hand twists tight around the knife handle. *"It's probably nothing"*, she tries to smile and even tries to laugh a little at the imaginary monster. "It's going to be ok" she tries to tell herself as all the lights go out, plunging her completely into darkness, Jenna has no choice but to scream and scream and scream.

He shouldn't have driven home, he knows that, keeps repeating it to himself as he drives, extra carefully to compensate. *"Please don't let the police see me, please don't pull me over, please just let me make it home. I will never do it again, if you just let me make it home"*. He knows he should have stopped after one pint, he's not normally this stupid. *"Please just let me get home without killing anyone, without the police stopping me, please, just let me get home"*.

It is with a great sigh of relief that he sees home approaching, he just needs to successfully park this thing in the right spot, without dinging or scratching any other cars and he is home free. He can do this. He just needs to take this nice and slow, take his time, that's it, that's it. Done! Never again! He promises himself, stepping out the car with elation and immediately dropping his keys. He can't see where they landed as it's too dark, they should fix some of the lights out here, he pays so much in rent and the management just skimp on everything. He fumbles for his mobile, turning on the torch function and dropping unsteadily to his knees to look. *"Nothing, nothing, ah here they are! Right in front of these bloody fingers... oh shit!"*

It has been a good week so far, perhaps even too good? Call her jaded but Mrs Brown is always scared when a week like this happens. It usually means that something is about to go horribly, horribly wrong. Perhaps a grandchild is about to announce a divorce or a drugs charge, a neighbour might die or something will bring her whole world crashing down on her because that's what always happens to good times, they never stay good for very long.

Mrs Brown brought a lottery ticket (just in case) and waited, jumping each time the phone rang. A few more good days go by and she even wins a small amount at bingo (nothing life changing darling, just enough to buy some new curtains.) Nothing else remarkable happens however. Perhaps she is wrong this time? Perhaps the good times are finally here to stay for once in her long life? Maybe everything is going to be ok and life isn't about to take a massive shit on her happiness? She starts to smile at her sudden good fortune.

Then the phone rings again.

It's daughter number three. Not her good daughter nor her bad daughter, just her indifferent daughter. They don't talk that often due to too many unspoken resentments and years of sibling gossip and Mrs Brown wants to hang up the minute she recognises that voice, knowing that this was going to hurt. Her daughter's voice is growing in urgent hysteria as she shrieks such awful words to her mother. Mrs Brown's happiness drains out of her body leaving nothing but a cutting chill in her bones. She puts the phone down still not quite comprehending then begins to softly cry. Her next happy day is a life time away.

It is amazing how people's wants and needs change as they grow older. They go from wanting the big things like fast cars, money and diamonds to just wanting a decent plumber and not to be murdered on a Saturday night out. The City knows the drill but still ignores the rules. More "For Sale" signs pop up every day and more overseas visa applications are sent but those who aren't leaving or hiding are watching, plotting and whispering. On the night of Saturday 21st December over 5500 calls were made to the police reporting suspicious noises, prowlers, loiters, white vans. Over 5,500 calls and yet not one single person even heard Amy Brown scream.

Sunnyside Apartments on the Avenue was a popular area to live in the City, mostly because it sounded posh. Children didn't play out on the streets here but they were allowed to walk unsupervised to the local shop. People didn't know their neighbours' names but still acknowledged them with tight smiles. It didn't used to be as nice as this, three years ago the locals called it 'Suicide Apartments'. Grimm thinks that in less than two days they will give it a new nickname. He can't see the current forty or so residents wanting to continue living here or anywhere else in the city. Even though the blood has been washed away something dark still remains.

Amy Brown died here sometime between 7.30pm and 8pm on Saturday 21st December. Saturday had been Grimm's day off and he had spent the day with his wife, frantically Christmas shopping whilst his children were being spoilt rotten by their grandparents. That day, despite the stress and people repeatedly treading on his feet, had been a good day. It had earnt him a few brownie points with his missus for starters, now he is only at minus two hundred or so. She had even smiled at him! If he is lucky and she likes her Christmas present he might even get a decent conversation with her, now that is really living the dream!

But first he needs to live a little reality. It's not Christmas here, despite the decorations. It's Monday 23rd December and they have a few questions to ask.

Colvin also had Saturday 21st off. Not just 'off' but really off, off. No internet, no news, nothing but watching Christmas specials on the television while eating handfuls of popcorn and trying to feel something she lost a long time ago. Then at 4:30pm? she left the sofa to go to work having promised Grimm that she would take SaturDAY off but not SaturNIGHT. Not that it was any of his business anyway but Colvin, in a slight fit of madness, had agreed to help cover the phones overnight. That night they needed all the help they could get.

It had been a non-stop night and it had left Colvin feeling mentally, physically and emotionally drained as a convoy of calls ceaselessly hit her one right after the other. There were the usual fights, it being Christmas after all, those domestic calls and those dark calls from people who had lost all faith in Santa, Jesus and every other religion in-between.

Then there were the tipster calls, reports of white vans everywhere as those last minute special deliveries were made. Prowler calls, so many prowler calls in fact, that Colvin suspected that even the assailant was calling, just to send them in the wrong direction. The 'neighbourhood' patrols really didn't help either as large groups of men patrolled 'their' streets, often coming into contact with other large groups of irate men, all talking loudly at each other as they urged each other to move on, get the fuck out of here and don't come back.

Colvin was regretting so much, not seeing an end to those calls, hearing voices echo in her head, jumping with each shrill voice. She never should have done this, never should have volunteered. She was close to tears as THAT call came through, the one with the woman screaming continuously in the background. Colvin had rushed the closest patrol car to them along with some paramedics, the screams were unbearable to listen to. Ten minutes of those screams, trying to assure the caller that the police were coming while thinking of every possible worse scenario, only to find out that the screamer was ok. Well mostly ok, a faulty Christmas tree light had tripped some fuses plunging her into darkness and she panicked. Eventually they got through to her, got through the screams and got her to put the knife down. It had been such a relief to finally disconnect the call.

She didn't answer the Amy Brown call. Some other volunteer got that one and it changed everything in the room. The atmosphere slumped into defeat but they couldn't do anything else to help, they had to keep answering the other calls, knowing. The callers became even harder to cope with they were so irate, so drunk, so chilling, so unhappy. The only joy Colvin felt that evening was when she disconnected her last call and finally went home.

But then work followed her as it always did. She can't do anything to get her mind off that topic. Colvin can't stop thinking about her theory that there are two killers out there, working together, training each other. She is fairly certain of her theory but just doesn't know how to prove it. But, wouldn't they have found more evidence if it was true? And that 'Dear Detective Dipshits' letter, said 'I' not 'we' but then they know this assailant likes to fuck with people's minds. It just doesn't add up though. She doesn't want to talk to Morkam until she has more evidence. She knows she is not the only officer to believe that there is more than one killer but the others... their ideas are suspiciously similar to ideas that Colvin would consider to be crackpot, ideas she doesn't want to associate with. The problem wasn't evidence, they have plenty of evidence, all that circumstantial, contaminated but might still be useful evidence. They have suspects, plenty of suspects and a whole team working on those suspects as well as on surveillance, cross checking alibis and thoroughly investigating said suspects. They even had confessions, time wasting, attention seeking confessions and general just something isn't right here confessions. What they didn't have was evidence linking directly to even one suspect, let alone two. She needs something, something more than a theory.

Until she has that she has no one she can talk to. If she draws up a list of people that she trusts enough to talk to and who are willing to listen to her, without laughing at her or stealing her ideas and taking credit for them or just straight up dismissing her, she is only left with one name and even that name is written in pencil with a big question mark next to it.

It doesn't help that the more she goes online the more

it feels like something is being kept secret from her. Something which has been kept from her from the start. A secret about Morkam or Walker or Fletcher or even Leona. If only she had worked here in those days, if only she knew what really went on. Sometimes she has to remind herself that she has something that those online commentators do not have- actual facts and experience of solving real crimes.

She had to go online that Saturday night, well at that point it was early Sunday morning. All she knew was that there was another victim and where she had been found. She needed more details! By the time she went onto ItCouldHave-BeenMe.co.uk they already had a name, Amy Brown, a location (Sunnyside Apartments) and a photograph of the victim (thankfully this time it was not a photograph of her corpse) as well as several rapidly expanding theories. They did not know how she died, just that there was a lot of blood and that the man who discovered her body was telling everyone about the deep number 10 cut into her hand. They were also talking about a blood trail that led inside into the building, a trail that the police were doing nothing about!

Colvin hoped victim's family had already been notified by someone official and that they didn't look at this website. She spent the rest of the morning wondering how the hell they had gotten that information so fast. One commentator called 'El Perro' had posted a name within about ninety minutes of the victim being discovered. The photograph had followed about thirty minutes later from a different commentator, 'Punk-Master7000'. Then a few more commentators down 'G0liath' had posted that former police officer Aaron Fletcher also lived at Sunnyside Apartments, one floor away from Amy Brown. Fletcher's name appeared over and over in their "Suspects" lists. Then 'SunshineSue' chimed in saying that the Fletchers used to live near her and that they were famous on the street for their arguments. One day the wife (Catherine? Claire? Clarabell? Something beginning with C) just disappeared. Then, a few days later, Fletcher was gone too. 'SunshineSue' never saw either of them move out. 'SunshineSue' is also friendly with the new owner of that house who has told her all about the badly plastered walls, the attempts to hide fist sized dents.

Other commentators, especially 'J-Girl-Down' and 'Punk-Master7000', were already making a big deal about the date, Saturday the 21st, being the one year anniversary of Lucy Swann's death. Those commentators are trying to convince people that they know when the next death is going to be and are also blasting the police for not noticing the pattern sooner but somehow managing to omit explaining why the killer didn't strike on Carly Ellis's anniversary.

The blood trail was first mentioned in their Monday morning briefing. It had been fairly obvious in the crime scene photos. The first officers on the scene must have thought they had struck gold; a victim with a trail of footprints right next to her leading into the building. They'd followed it eagerly thinking that they finally had a lucky break, especially when it led to a door that had no known association with Amy Brown. They'd knocked firmly on the door, readying themselves for a fight with back up just down the corridor. Much to their disappointment a lady in her late forties had answered and it was clear she had no idea what was going on.

The quickly obtained CCTV footage showed Amy Brown, a divorced 29 year old florist, leaving the foyer at 7.22pm. Then it showed the other lady leaving the foyer at 8pm to have a smoke outside before re-entering at 8.12pm. They could even see her leaving that bloody footprint trail as she returned on the CCTV footage. The smoker apparently was completely unaware that she had walked right up to the victim and stood in Amy's blood for a good few minutes. She hadn't even noticed the bloody footprints on her own floor.

The CCTV footage of the carpark was completely useless due to several light failures. They could only see when a car was moving around with its headlights on, and no, the assailant hadn't made that mistake. Colvin suspects this area was targeted because the assailant knew that the lights were out. Perhaps he'd broken them himself? But still, it seems odd again. Amy Brown not only had a number 10 cut into her left hand but also, unknown to a certain website, she also had the number 9 cut into her right hand. Now, if her theory was correct, this would mean that both killers worked together on this victim. But, when they worked together they are brutal, inhumane. Personality wise Colvin thinks if there are two assailants then maybe one assailant is more aggressive than the other one? The other one is more of a showman, the condescending one. But this kill had been more restrained. Amy had been presumably grabbed, her assailant going straight for her throat before cutting the numbers in her hands. Still nasty but there was no beating, no metaphysical slap to the face and no trickery. Had the assailant(s) been disturbed? Or was her theory wrong? Had they missed something obvious? Had they missed another victim, one who was still in plain sight? What were they up to? Had they been interrupted by someone? It couldn't have been the smoker as they could have easily overpowered her. Colvin needs to interview the smoker herself and ask her carefully if she remembers anyone standing close by, perhaps brushing past her or even asking to borrow her lighter?

Had they picked this victim for a reason? Was Amy Brown someone to them? A rejection? A grudge? A witness? Work of an ex-husband or current lover seeing a cover up opportunity? Or, going back to that stupid website and those stupid theories, was it just because it was another anniversary and she just happened to be standing there?

As they walk down the corridors of Sunnyside Apartments Colvin can almost hear their every movement, their presumed thoughts being narrated by the other residents and watchers eager for something to add to the online speculations. She resists the urge to give her audience something to really talk about and keeps moving to the beat of typing fingers. No doubt later she will be able to read all about her day on itcouldhave-beenme.co.uk and how she and that notorious Grimm had been spotted inside the building heading towards the door of noted suspect Aaron Fletcher.

She could easily write her own article at this point. She would open by saying "Some say that the more confident a killer gets, the closer they get to home and we all know that this S.O.B is more than confident." Then she could add some bullshit gibberish about the contrasts of the niceness of the apartments and brutality of the crime. Maybe if she writes a couple of these articles, Colvin could quit the police force and start writing her own crime novels which would probably be a more rewarding career and, possibly, better paid. She could start by building up an online following on itcouldhavebeenme.co.uk with a few embellished articles, a publishing contract would soon follow and then fame and glory would be hers.

Grimm isn't thinking about fortune or fame as they walk, brushing pass the Christmas decorations that feel so out of place right now. He thinks that this will be yet another waste of time but what can you do? At least he wasn't stuck outside like some poor saps. From what he has heard about Aaron Fletcher, the guy is nothing but a spineless coward, another cop who couldn't hack it when things got tough. The best description Grimm has heard of Fletcher is that he is a man who is too afraid to look down, in case he saw his own cock. Grimm doesn't need to hear anything else although, from what he has also heard, being part-nered with an officer like Bullface for several years would be enough to install a deep desire to kill in any reasonable man. Per-haps they really should be talking to Bullface's husband?

When you hear so many rumours and stories about one person for so long you begin to build up a mental image of them. Colvin is expecting Aaron Fletcher to look weedy as it is his most talked about trait. Perhaps he will have an awkward haircut, a slight nasal twang in his voice? The man who answers the door is taller than what she had been expecting and has that same tired smile she sees every day in the mirror. He is also wearing *the* most ugliest Christmas jumper that Colvin has ever seen.

There is a wariness in his voice as he asks to see their identification and he takes his time to carefully study each ID badge. Whilst waiting from the doorway Colvin glances around at what she can see in the apartment. From here she can see three large overflowing bookcases and can just about make out some of the titles. Each section is neatly organised, each sub-topic grouped together. Heaven forbid that the large number of criminology books, the books on serial killers, sociopaths and criminal psychology mix with the learning to love yourself again books. They must be kept separate by the books on philosophy and science fiction. She can see only a few concessions to the approaching Christmas holidays including tinsel half heartily draped over the shelves and two Christmas cards carefully placed in the centre, one to a "A Wonderful Son at Christmas." There is an odd odour in the air of something burnt and spicy.

Fletcher finally invites them inside with a noticeable resignation, even goes as far as to offer them a drink which is politely declined. Colvin and Grimm carefully perch on the sofa whilst Fletcher retreats to the chair behind his desk. Grimm produces a notebook and starts up with the standard questions then moves on to:

"Did you know Amy Brown?"

"Not that well, I asked her out once on a dating site about a year ago, that was before I knew she lived in the same building as me." There is an embarrassed flush on Fletcher's face as if he didn't want to tell them that, didn't want to admit to knowing her at all. He knows how it sounds and what it indicates to them but he is a former police officer, he knows how deeply they will look into Amy Brown's past, her computer records. If he doesn't admit it now then it will only come back to haunt him later.

"Which website was this?" Fletcher names two, not quite remembering which one. He hasn't really been that active on them recently, too many men and too many female accounts slowly deactivating one after another.

"When was the last time you spoke to her?"

"I haven't really seen her in months." They had never really spoke face to face. There was that awkward period when she realised who he was, then he didn't see her for ages, almost as if she was avoiding him. Then there were overly cautious smiles when she did see him. Fletcher wasn't bothered by it, she was just one out of many rejections, nothing to dwell on.

"Have you noticed anyone suspicious or acting strangely?"

"No." Fletcher said almost instantly. He had never stopped watching people, could happily stand for hours by the window, watching the world go by, music playing quietly in the background. He is not an officer anymore but he still sees himself as a protector. Not enough to go hunting for the new killer but enough to keep his eyes open for anything that might aid the police in their investigation, anything that might help him redeem himself. Amy Brown's death had felt personal, a blow to his already deflated ego.

"Can you account for your whereabouts on Saturday 21st December? Between the hours of 6.30-9.30pm?"

"I left here at 5pm. I'm taking a philosophy course full time at the University and it was our Christmas social. I was with them from 6pm until 9pm then I came back here." That Christmas social was another sore point. He had been looking forward to it for weeks as he didn't get many invitations anymore. No one had asked him to leave early but even he could see how uneasy he was making some of his classmates and he had no idea why. The police were already there by the time he got back and he had been politely but quickly escorted through the cordons to his front door. He didn't ask any questions at the time, he didn't really want to know what was going on.

Grimm inwardly snorts to himself at the mere mention of Philosophy thinking that Fletcher is just another fan of Nietzsche, full of admiration for that overly banged out quote about the abyss staring back. In Grimm's opinion, if you stare too long at the abyss, it tends to get nervous and start talking about calling its lawyer.

Grimm wanted to finish the interview there, having gotten enough information to establish an alibi. Just as he had suspected this had been a waste of time. Grimm's heart sinks as he hears his partner ask "Do you mind if I ask you a few questions about Walker?"

Yes Fletcher did mind. He has spent years trying to make sense of what Walker did, trying to forget the accusing stares, the victims. His life had changed so much because of The Numbers Killer, changed him into a person he himself no longer recognised. It had made him a vegetarian for starters, he couldn't stand even a glimpse of butchered meat now. But he is still Fletcher and he still can't say no.

"Sure" he says in a mechanical tone, ready to recite those same old answers. Robert Leona, Morkam, Juda, Seasions, all those officers who worked the original The Numbers Killer case, have a haunted look permanently etched in their eyes, an 'I can't face any more of this shit' look. Colvin has started noticing that look appearing more and more in those also working the BTY case, that 'old before their time' look. When it appears everyone knows that stress leave, early retirement, alcoholism and marriage breakdowns are in their future. Fletcher didn't have that look until she mentioned Walker's name.

"What was Walker like as a friend?" That was an unexpected reminding blow. Fletcher visibly winces at the word 'friend' but then regains his composure. Suddenly Grimm thinks Colvin might be on to something interesting here. Fletcher takes a long pause trying to figure out how to phrase his answer.

"He was a great friend. He was always ready to quietly whisper in your ear that, as a friend you should know... He was a textbook sociopath, a back stabber, a shit stirrer...oh yes, he was a great friend in that way that only pure evil can be." Even Grimm is impressed by the bitterness in Fletcher's voice.

"How did you discover that Walker was The Numbers Killer?"

"... I didn't." Colvin waits, for the usual denial that Walker

194

was The Numbers Killer, despite what Fletcher had said to Kate Drake. "My partner Victoria figured it out." It takes both Grimm and Colvin a moment to remember who Victoria was. This is the first time Colvin has ever heard anyone say Bullface's real name with respect. "I wish I knew how. I came so close to catching him once and still didn't even realise. He was meant to be one of my best friends and I never suspected he was even capable of... But I do know that Victoria wouldn't have acted unless she was a hundred percent sure, that's what kind of cop she was, a great one..." The sudden trailing off of speech said everything. Victoria Bulrush *had* been a great cop. Fletcher on the other hand had merely been adequate.

"I know a lot of cops like Leona and Juda don't believe it, I don't think they want to because of what it implicates." Fletcher wasn't going to come right out and say that he didn't think Leona could cope with the fact that his best friend killed his wife and that Leona may have aided him to kill another innocent woman. If these officers have done their homework then they would know that anyway. Fletcher doesn't blame Leona, he can barely cope with the memory that he had made a serial killer his best man.

"How sure are you that it was Walker?"

"100%" Colvin really wasn't expecting that answer either. "His fingerprints matched to partials we pulled from various scenes, his DNA matches blood found on one of the victims, a strand of his hair on another victim. Hell we even matched his footprints to a certain scene. We found the knife he used, in his HANDS, with various victims' blood on it. We found burnt remains of his polaroids collection. I am a 100% sure that Walker was The Numbers Killer." Colvin isn't going to start sharing with Fletcher those theories about planted evidence, circumstantial evidence or contaminated on purpose evidence. She doesn't want him to know what they suspect. Instead she tries to continue asking questions as innocently as she can.

"And this new killer?" Fletcher finally meets Colvin's gaze.

"Copycat."

"You don't think that Walker may have had an accomplice?"

"No, I was asked this when the killings first started." Colvin immediately wants to ask who by? but refrains from doing so. "We never found any indication of a second person, if you look at the original crime scene photos, the gaps in blood spray, they only indicate one person." This sends alarm bells ringing in Colvin's head. *How* had she missed looking at that detail in this current case? "We only ever saw one person on the CCTV footage. Eyewitnesses, including myself, only ever saw one person."

Grimm, if he had been there alone, might have asked Fletcher if he thought that a washed up police officer might be responsible? One with a lot of built up anger towards women, who might eventually benefit from stepping in at the "last" moment to save a victim which would of course rebuild his shattered reputation and regain his access to easy prey in one move? Just to poke the bear a little, see what his reaction would be.

"Did you ever figure out what the numbers mean?" Colvin is also testing him here and suspects he might reply with a subtle gloat or an over-willingness to help. She feels uneasy asking him these questions but he seems oblivious.

"It's really simple once you work it out, too simple, so simple... you doubt yourself when you realise, thinking it couldn't be that easy, that you must have made some kind of mistake. Meanwhile he was laughing at us because it is so simple and yet we *couldn't* figure it out." Deep breath, all those bad memories resurfacing again in his eyes. "Once we found the burnt remains of those polaroids... it confirmed it. He only used even numbers, we should have realised sooner when we found 22 left hand, 24 right hand, 26 left. Left, right, left... never any even odd numbers. It's so simple in hindsight but we thought it must be some kind of code, something more complicate. We thought there were more victims, we just never thought... It was just something to confuse us, distract us from the bigger things. I could be wrong..." he trails off, deep in unhappy thoughts.

Colvin notes that Fletcher isn't even trying to find out any information about their current killer, doesn't ask what the new code is. He isn't trying to prove he knows more than them or distract them with more babble about Walker's innocence. He knows this is not his case anymore, his case is firmly closed. He doesn't want to talk about the eleven known victims of The Numbers Killer or the others, those unknown, still lost that those polaroids hinted of.

Colvin was about to thank Fletcher for his time when a familiar logo caught her eye on a business card, pinned to Fletcher's noticeboard and slightly hidden by coursework reminders and take away menus. She asks Fletcher about it but he is dismissive and smiles a smile that creeps Colvin out. Apparently a man wanted to interview him about Walker for a book he is writing about him. Fletcher had said no to the interview and he had meant to throw the card away. No he doesn't mind Colvin taking it. Colvin carefully puts it in her notebook knowing she will have some explaining to do with Grimm. Did Fletcher purposely leave this on show? Or is he really that oblivious? The paranoia creeps back into Colvin's mind. Maybe this was his idea of a hint, one he thought they would be too stupid to see? Perhaps even a little joke? She tries to shush those thoughts as they smile and say polite goodbyes. She knows that business card will turn out to be nothing but she has taken it now, it was too late to change her mind.

Fletcher eagerly closes the door shut behind them refusing to allow himself even the slightest bit of curiosity. He can almost see his former partner, Bullface, standing there, her permanent frown creasing deeper into her face as she studies his book titles. "Nietzsche has a lot to answer for" she would say with a disapproving sniff. He knows how much he is letting her down by not getting involved, but he just can't. He can't pretend to be something he isn't, anymore.

CHAPTER SIXTEEN

Walker was an artist and, like all artists, he was misunderstood, misinterpreted and underappreciated. He was a treasure taken from us too soon but it is a great honour to continue his work, to take his work to new heights. No one will ever forget his name... or figure out ours.

What we will do tonight, it will take time before it's truly appreciated, before they learn. We are going to teach them to respect our work. Teach them that we are not going to go away, even if they close their eyes. We are here to stay and we have so much work to do.

Sunday 19th January, how did they get into January? Colvin remembers little about Christmas or the New Year. Mostly she spent her time trailing through Amy Brown's online love life. Amy had signed up last January and, over the course of a year, had spoken to sixty-eight possible suitors, including of course, Aaron Fletcher. Amy had blocked twelve outright, rejected another fifty-two without meeting them and didn't go on a second date with the remaining four. But still, each one of those sixty-eight had to be investigated. Colvin still can't believe that there were so many and had been tempted to sign up for online dating herself once this was over. But then she started reading through the messages and pictures Amy had been sent. It is going to take a to get those images out of her mind. What made it worse was there were more as those sixty-eight were only the men who had contacted her online. More unknown males had asked Amy out at work which meant more likely suspects. Amy's work colleagues had told them about the twenty or so men and how some had been persistent repeat offenders. Her colleagues' descriptions of these men weren't much to go on, just vague descriptions like "wedding ring guy," "that dork guy with glasses," and Colvin's favourite "oh you know, *THAT* guy." It has been a very frustrating few weeks.

What was more frustrating was that, despite their repeated searches, they had not been able to find Amy's hair slide much to her mother's great distress. Apparently Amy had always worn a flower hair slide. It had lots of fake diamonds and had been made for her by her sister. Amy's mother had wanted her to be buried with it. It could be seen in Amy's hair on the CCTV footage and they had searched the car park for it but with no luck. The assailant must have stolen it but then, in Colvin's mind, that leads to more difficult questions. As far as they know the assailant had never stolen anything so personal before. When he steals, he steals identifications, phones, car keys and things to slow down their investigation. In a way the hair slide had slowed their investigation down, as they searched for that sentimental item but what was so special about Amy Brown that he felt the need to take her hair slide from her? It had no real value, only sentimental. Did it mean that Amy symbolised a personal rejection to him? If so did that mean that the other victims were in fact connected? Had they all been picked for a very specific reason? Even the ones that they thought were opportunistic kills? If so, why? What can't Colvin see? Trying to think in a different way she is also carefully watching ItCouldHaveBeen-Me.co.uk closely in case it had been taken by some other trophy hunter.

That incident changed Jenna. Even though they were nice to her about it (it was even worse than that, they were understanding with her) and used those extra special voices when talking with her which made their kindness even harder to cope with. It made Jenna so angry with herself, her anger growing with each pitying look. Never again, she has told herself, never again will she have a screaming melt down in her kitchen (or anywhere else!) just because a light has gone out. Next time she would face the dark alone. Never again does she want to feel so weak, so powerless and so helpless. Never again!

She has committed to this New Years resolution with a pure determined vengeance. She is determined to face facts. She is not safe, she will never be safe. They are never going to catch this guy. All these years television has lied to her about the power of criminal investigation. She knows now that eyewitnesses aren't reliable and, although it's not their fault, memories can be subtly modified and remoulded to suit beliefs, pre-conceptions and biases. CCTV is blurry, DNA is circumstantial. They can only be sure of one thing in this heaving mass of uncertainty and that's that the police don't have a fucking clue. No one is going to protect them but that's ok, because who needs the police anyway? Not Jenna.

She is not going to live in fear anymore, not going to allow herself to be afraid of anything, including spiders! Yes, she has said it before, but this time, this time she means it! She has returned to the gym and reunited with her gang. She is determined and can feel herself growing stronger every day. She is getting really good at shadow boxing now, can feel the power behind every punch, pure strength in every kick. She will never feel scared again she promises herself, drawing back her fist for another punch.

It's a manta now, "I am not afraid. I am not afraid anymore". She repeats it as she waits at the bus stop with the other women, chatting casually. She is fearless on the bus and, even at night, when doubt falls with the darkness, she whispers to herself over and over. She is a fighter now and she is not afraid. She feels good, even though she still has trouble closing her eyes.

Her phone bleeps, breaking through her thoughts. Another message from her gang with more photos of men to be aware of and an update about that father/son team; a pair to really watch out for and avoid at all costs. Another bleep, someone has the partial number plate of a white van and people begin to warn each other about going out tonight or organising teams to go out together. Tonight is the anniversary of that day when that cop went crazy, all those years ago. She is responsible for what is happening now. They think there will be another attack tonight. Bleep, bleep, bleep, Jenna closes her eyes, clenches her fists up tight and whispers that she is not afraid.

"Marika Martin went missing shortly after this photo was taken." All officers intently study the photo. Across the city, across the country, across the world, countless other people are doing the same. The photo's main focus is a pretty girl in her early twenties Colvin would guess. She stands out in the gloom of the photograph not just because of her bright purple hair or her bright purple lipstick smile. Standing behind her, as if he had been caught following her, was a boy. One with a scowl embedded on his face. A boy Colvin recognises as Angry Youth.

"The boy behind her is Caleb Bulrush." Most of them already knew that, they know him as the boy who was rejected by Claire Atkins. The same boy who lives close to Sarah Grieg's old home.

"A team was sent to take Caleb into protective custody earlier but he ran away. Caleb is possibly armed and considered to be at risk." A pause. "He is not considered to be a suspect in Marika's abduction but because this photo has somehow been circulated across the city already, I would like to bring him under police protection." Colvin can feel the resentment build in the room and she knows many of the officers here believe that Morkam is trying to protect Caleb for all the wrong reasons. They whisper about the boy's mother and of Morkam's relationship with her.

Their orders are simple; search for the boy and the girl, search for the girl. Marika went missing somewhere between three to four hours ago whilst surrounded by people. She went missing somewhere between a popular shopping area and King's Park. A patrol is already searching King's Park. A similar disappearance to Cathy Clark. It makes Colvin doubt her theory about there being two killers. Now she suspects there might possibly be three of them; one who likes to show off, one who just likes to kill and the one who likes to hide.

"You should avoid approaching Caleb." Grimm's stern warning punctuates through Colvin's thoughts and she looks at him confused. "I don't think he has forgotten that time you had him suspended." It all suddenly clicks. She had forgotten all about that, too wrapped up in the Anne-Marie Mills case. She knew she had recognised him! Shortly after Carly Ellis had been found they had been ordered to do a talk at a local school on knife awareness. She had busted him for knife carrying, in an assembly, in front of his entire school, without thinking. He gave himself away that day, obviously nervously, always twitching his hand towards his pocket as if looking for reassurance from the wrong thing. There was a reason for his dark looks of hatred after all.

Still, given that apparently most of the city seems to be gunning for his blood, she has a duty to at least try to help him, regardless of how he feels about her. But she thinks it would be sensible to take Grimm's advice about not approaching him alone.

The dark room lights up with blue flashes reminding Adrian of the night his mother died. A police car or an ambulance is outside the house. He wishes it was an ambulance. The driver turns the lights off quickly but the neighbours have already been alerted and are in full peeking mode. Adrian can hear his father talking downstairs saying words that Adrian never thought he would hear him say.

Then, just as quickly, they are gone and Adrian can hear the tell-tale sounds of his father's car starting up and driving away.

Adrian shivers, realising he is now alone in the house. What will he do if his brother comes home? Why didn't his father take him with him? Why didn't he even tell Adrian he was going? Adrian pushes his chest of drawers in front of his bedroom door and crawls back into bed, pulling the covers up high over his head. There, alone in the darkness, he cries a little and wishes for the thousandth time that his mother was still alive.

He hates his mother for dying. He hates his father for leaving him alone. He hates his brother for being a weird twat. Mostly though he hates himself for feeling this scared, this alone and this helpless.

He used to want to be a police officer just like his mother. He used to spend his break times in the playground protecting the weak. Until that bloody day when he was forced, by fists, to accept that he was the weak one. How did everything he ever wanted get so far out of reach? As he curls up tight wishing that everything will be over soon be over, a brick smashes through his window.

The city has made its own fighters; those who have had enough of living in fear.

One minute everything was calm, peaceful even. Colvin was out patrolling, carefully shining her torch into dark corners, alleyways, suspicious spots. Anywhere where a body, a boy or a killer might be waiting while trying to ignore how cold, tired and hungry she felt. She made the mistake of thinking about how quiet it was, not realising that it was only quiet because the city was holding its breath, building itself up for that long overdue scream.

Then someone threw a bottle, someone yelled and someone else screamed. *"He is here!"* Colvin remembers thinking, frantically looking around for someone, someone just staring at the chaos with a pleased expression on his face. All she could see however was the crowd. Descending on them, outnumbering them, consuming them... Colvin felt a hard blow to the side of her head, the shock knocking her down to her knees.

It feels like she has been frozen like this for hours. She can feel something warm slowly dripping down the side of her face and the pain in her head-exacerbated by the noise of a thousand people all screaming at once. People are falling all around her and she doesn't understand why. She thought they were all on the same side... why are they all fighting? She looks around confused, not understanding the danger she is in, still struggling to rise up off her knees. Strong arms grip her firmly, pulling her back to her feet.

"Go home lass!" A voice shouts in her ear, pushing her to move, its owner already moving on to grab at the next struggling mess of limbs. She really wants to take that advice but she can't even see a way out of the crowd. She is not sure she even remembers how to get home. She wants to do something to help, join those who are already trying to bring control back to this uncontrollable situation. She can hear her colleagues blowing whistles, screaming orders on radios, struggling against fists and feet, struggling to even be heard. She watches hopelessly as two men crash onto Officer Dalbiac pulling him down with more and more bodies falling on top of them all. Then two more men push through, pulling apart the writhing knots of people. As a blow to her stomach wallops the breath out of her mouth more hands grip her shoulders tight, propelling her away. *"No no, not me"*, she tries to scream, tries to struggle, as hands continue to pull her forward. It's him, he did this on purpose. Followed her here because it's a perfect opportunity to kill her whilst everyone watches but no one sees.

"And you are fine with that? You are going to go down without a fight?" She's not sure if that thought is really a question or just a statement. No, she finally decides, she is not fine with that. Finally her fists respond the way she wants them too and she raises one as high as the pain will allow, ready to turn and punch.

"Easy Sam! I've got you!" She tries to focus her eyes, blinking through blood, sweat and tears. She knows that voice. "I've got you." Juda tries to reassure her, tries to help her stand steady. Robert Leona joins them, dragging Dalbiac along with him. More reinforcements are arriving, forcibly separating the crowds, pulling apart the worst of the fights.

"You alright?" Something is pressed against her head, sending more flashes of pain through her mind.

"Sam?"

The yelling and screaming grows loud again with a new anger. The crowd, those stupid enough to stay, are starting all over again. She looks up to see Robert Leona being relieved of Dalbiac by a paramedic, he is also staring at the crowd with pure horror as his own personal history begins to repeat itself again for the fourth time.

"Wait here Sam." Juda calmly shouts, motioning at Leona to follow him as he walks back into the worst of it. Colvin looks around again and can see the paramedic coming back to take her out of this deafening hell. She would have gone as well if she hadn't taken that extra moment, that last look and spotted him dodging a fist then jumping over something before jumping up at the locked cemetery gates. But she *has* seen him now and she has to do something. If Juda and Leona can redeem themselves then so can she. She waves off the paramedic, redirecting her to another more critical case. Then Colvin takes a deep breath and tries to casually walk towards the cemetery gates. *"Keep calm, take it slow",* she tells herself, *"and for fucks sake don't redirect the crowds attention over here".* She tries to nonchalantly jump the gate, moving as quickly as her bruised stomach and aching head will allow, trying not to cry out as her body doesn't quite make the leap as easily as he did, finally pulling herself up and over, dropping down and moving away from the gates and out of sight. She waits a few anxious moments worrying that someone might follow her. No one seems have noticed her little jump in the chaos. Shakily she pulls out her phone. She can't risk talking over the radio, can't risk someone not so friendly overhearing. She just hopes someone will see her text and that someone still has her back. Stiffly, she begins to move. Someone else could already be in here. They could have already gotten too close. She needs to find him.

"And then what?" That annoying inner voice chimes in

again, *"what can you do? You can barely walk."* Her hands twitch and she realises she has lost her torch. There is a nasty looking scrape on her hand and something else on her legs feels like it's bleeding. *"Enough, wait!"*, she decides but then continues to walk deeper into the graveyard.

The scream gives her a vital clue about directions. There is no such thing as a nice scream but this one is particularly bad. It is a long scream, a scream from someone who has repressed themselves for far too long and, in doing so, has forgotten how to express themselves, how to let loose their anger, which now has become radiation, glowing dangerously inside in their body, bringing a slow rotting decay to everything they touch. Within minutes she is there staring at the back of him, watching as he punches and punches away, pounding his fists against the granite of a gravestone.

Her mind forms a new plan; stay absolutely still, let Caleb tire himself out with his punching and his emotional breakdown then wait for reinforcements to arrive, get him into protective custody and, hopefully, also get him some kind of help. On no account should she approach him alone, especially not in this state, knowing how he feels about her. The others will be here soon, just keep an eye on him until... oh fuck.

Caleb has seen her. She wasn't expecting him to just suddenly turn around. Now they are just staring at each other, his anger burning through her. She is a visual representation of everything he hates; authority, the professional replacement of his mother. Does she even try to run? Fight? Reason with him? Then she notices the knife and freezes. She feels too tired, too dizzy to even try fighting. *"Stupid, stupid Sam, you have walked right into their trap. Remember what the website said, they are a father/ son killing team. One lures, the other attacks."* She has been so easily lured in her desire to help and now, any moment now, comes the attack.

As if on cue she turns to see Barry Bulrush moving towards them, closely followed by Morkam. She swallows hard, feeling very cold and dizzy. Is this how it ends? An unfair fight with no chances or fucks given? Just pain and suffering? Living on only as a memory in her colleagues stories just like the woman lying in the grave beneath Caleb's feet? They won't even be complimentary stories either, that's what is bothering her the most. She worked so hard yet she will only be remembered in such a negative way. Does she even try to fight? She tenses as Barry takes another step forward, not even looking at her, his eyes are focused on Caleb. It's probably Caleb's turn to have the honour, this last step in making him a man.

"Put the knife down!" Those are not the words she was expecting to hear, unless he is about to add "I have a better weapon right here." *"Don't let your guard down"*, she cautions herself. She doesn't even know how much longer she can stay conscious but she is determined not to close her eyes just yet.

"Put down the knife, Son." Five years ago Barry never thought he would have to say those words. Never thought he would be here, in a cold graveyard, begging his second son to put a knife down. His eyes drift back to the woman who is swaying slightly, smears of blood drying on the side of her face. Did his son do that? He wants to believe that his son wouldn't do such a thing, wouldn't be capable of doing such a thing. He wants to believe that just like he wants to believe that everything is going to be ok. But...

It has been one hell of a night so far, really it has been one hell of a year. He has spent weeks defending himself, his wife and his sons on the phone to random strangers. Strangers who just won't stop calling, won't stop making weird accusations. He thought they had finally stopped a week or so ago but then it turned out that someone had just unplugged the phone. Then there was the countless text messages and various pictures, mostly of Caleb but some of Adrian too, taken unaware, sent to god only knows who with vile messages and "tips." Concerned friends and family have been forwarding them to him with messages like 'I think you should know what is going on.' Or 'What the fuck is going on?' The braver of their remaining family members even offered to take in the boys for 'their own safety.' Barry doesn't know what has caused all of this or why they are targeting his sons and he sure as hell doesn't know how to make it stop. He has given DNA samples, fingerprints, alibis, consent for a DNA sample to be taken from his son. He did all this months ago hoping to make it all go away and yet it only seems to have made things worse.

"I am sorry." Barry still thinks he can reach his son. He has to. He isn't even sure what he is apologising for, that Caleb didn't get to be the teenager he was meant to be? That he's suffocating in the shadows of his mother's death? That he should have spent more time with his son

"I hate her." Caleb screams in response. "I hate her! I hate her! I hate her!" Colvin tenses up even tighter. She should have stayed back, stayed out of sight. As if shocked by his own outburst Caleb drops his head back down, closing his eyes tight. No one else knows what to do or what to say and no one dares to make the next move.

"Caleb, put the knife down." Morkam's voice is stern, finely edged by over twenty years of giving orders. There is a clang of metal as Caleb's hand obeys automatically without his mind even realising. Then Morkam is there next to Caleb, taking charge of the situation, leading Caleb calmly away, talking to him quietly. Morkam motions quickly to Colvin to pick up the knife and follow, expecting Barry to follow without question. In the distance she can hear the clamour of more people arriving and finally notices she can no longer hear those faint screams and yells of the rioting mobs just sirens now. Lots and lots of sirens. She shuffles her way to the cracked grave pulling a bag out of her pocket to bag the knife with, ignoring fireworks of pain within her. Barry is staring sadly at the gravestone. Colvin reads the lines 'Victoria Bulrush. Dedicated wife and mother.' From what she has seen and heard it really should read 'Dedicated police officer who tried to be a loving mother.' But there are probably rules about those things. Someone else has vandalised the grave and spray painted it with 'Fuck You!' and 'Bullface the

Bitch.'

"I tried to make him understand she didn't have any choice. She knew no one was coming to save her. The problem with stories, films etc. is that they always have someone sweeping in at the last moment to save the intended victim reinforcing the message that help is coming, if you can just hold on." They are not completely to blame but they are the easiest things for him to blame right now. No matter what he said to his son, he couldn't shake the belief that his wife could have had a happy ending if she had just done something differently.

When they told him how his wife died he was so angry at first, hearing how she killed some random guy and herself at the same time. He tried so hard to protect his sons from a lot of evil whispers. Knowing that they still heard. Then after a few days they told him the truth about who he was and why she did it and finally there was a sense of sadness. It hurt but there was a feeling of a good ending. That finally she was at peace. He knows his wife had no other way of fighting back, that despite her training she was overpowered and she knew that. He is proud of her, despite everything. But tonight, after seeing his son crying through tortured eyes, being hunted by random strangers, being led away by the police, he feels angry all over again. Angry and utterly heartbroken.

But all that matters now is being with his son... sons. He doesn't wait for any sympathetic words from Colvin, doesn't think to offer her a hand, he just follows after the retreating back of his son.

Colvin had been about to follow, anxious for the knife to be in someone else's hands and in dire need of an aspirin or perhaps something stronger. She had turned, moved about four steps in the right direction but then stopped.

The flowers seem to shine in the moonlight, ghostly shimmers of pink and white, with dark little spots. Someone must have really loved whoever is in that grave to leave them such a big bouquet of flowers. Colvin moves one more step towards them. It feels strange to be pausing here to look at flowers but, after the night she has had, it is a relief to spend five seconds focusing on something else. It also feels strange to be envious of flowers belonging to a dead person ~~but still~~. She can't remember the last time anyone brought her flowers. So fresh too, they must have been left here at some point today.

She notices the date on the gravestone first, "Died 19th January", three years ago. That's probably why they are here, an anniversary goodbye, left for the person who died on the same day as Victoria Bulrush... Colvin's mouth goes dry as she reads the name on the grave. Walker. Then she reaches out a hand to touch the dark spots on the flowers.

CHAPTER SEVENTEEN

You don't know this yet, but you are dead. D E A D. Not yet, but soon, sooner than you think. You made this mistake of telling me your password, not that you even realised that you were telling me. J3nna'sUP! It's a good password, has lower and uppercase, special characters just like it is meant to. It's such a good password you didn't just use it once, but for many different sites. You gave me access to your emails, those emails that tell me where you live, the emails that confirm certain activities that mean you are not home. Like this email, that cinema confirmation email, tells me that you are not home right now, you are enjoying the last few days of your life watching some stupid romantic comedy. I hate those. But still I know when you will leaving the cinema, I could even follow you home. A little fun before the main event.

You made it so unbelievably easy and I can't wait to thank you. I could thank you by giving you a lesson in internet safety but I think we can both agree that it's much too late for that.

I can't wait to see you. J-Girl-Down

According to Officer Tichan the flowers are 'Pink Spray Carnations and Alstroemeria (whatever that is) with white Gypsophila.' It doesn't mean much to Grimm apart from the revelation that Tichan is either a bit of a botanist or he gets in a lot of trouble with his wife. The flowers were sent with an "I am thinking of you" message, delivery note and address still attached. The flowers had not been sent to Walker but to someone named

Ella Tupper. Presumably it is her blood splattered across those fragile pink petals. Grimm is part of the team who have been sent to find out. He is hoping that when they arrive at the house he will be able to apologise to Ms Tupper for waking her, be given a perfectly reasonable explanation about why her flowers had been left on a serial killer's grave, even an explanation of why they appear to be splattered with blood and then be able to call it a night. Leave a few good officers there to guard the house, just in case. By that time Colvin should be going home too, he will be able to text her an all clear message and stop her worrying her bloody little head about Ella. She had been so insistent about joining Grimm in going to the house and Morkam had been equally insistent about her going elsewhere with that nice paramedic. Colvin really only relented when it was pointed out to her that, with that bleeding head wound, she was more than likely to contaminate a potential crime scene. Bless her, Grimm grudgingly gives her a little credit. He wouldn't have followed the boy into a graveyard and he wouldn't have looked twice at those flowers.

Grimm hopes he is getting the easy job tonight. Several other teams of officers have been sent to various street disturbances, putting out the last of the public fires of rage and another team has been sent to the Bulrush's house after reports of more disturbances there. In the car the conversation is all about what could have triggered the crowd tonight and the latest 'tips' concerning Marika Martin. None of them want to talk about what possible hell they might be walking into.

The lights are off in Ella's small house but the curtains are not drawn. Grimm and Seasons are considered to be the most seasoned officers and are 'volunteered' to be the first to go and ring the doorbell (there's no point in scaring the poor girl with a legion of officers only to find out that this is a prank). It would mean less officers contaminating the scene if it's not.

It's the smear of blood on the front door handle that gives them a big clue. The door itself is still slightly ajar, reminding Grimm of how Sarah Grieg had been found. He gently pushes the door open expecting to see her sat there, waiting with dead eyes. He is instead met with an embrace of freezing cold air. It's even colder in here than it is outside. Where is she? He flicks his torch on, shining the light around without stepping further into the room.

"Hello?" He calls out, knowing that there won't be an answer. Seasions is carefully staying behind him. They both know something is wrong. It could be because of the unlocked door, the silence or that coppery smell lingering in the air. Or perhaps it's the feeling that they are playing a very dangerous game, one that they know they are losing. Grimm takes one step into the living room and takes another glance around. This girl must have really liked the colours pink and bright pink. She must have really loved those flowers...

Another blood smear, very noticeable across the pink sofa. Grimm keeps moving forward towards the kitchen, drawn in by his own sense of dread.

The kitchen is a very vibrant red; a metallic red kettle shines in the torch light, red oven, red microwave, red chairs, red blinds, red blood splatters across the window, red puddle drying on a white floor.

"Get the forensics." Grimm tries to keep his voice calm, tries not to look directly at what once was Ella Tupper, no longer recognisable as such.

Colvin doesn't know why she feels like she should have been there, it's not like she really wants to see another dead body, she has seen far too many of those now. They told her that this one had been as badly beaten as some of the earlier victims, almost to the point of being unrecognisable. There's still no sign of Marika Martin. It was probably too late for her now. Colvin clenches her hand painfully in anger. She tries desperately to think about what they could be missing. It just wasn't fair, to be thrown through hell and still have nothing!

Grimm had told her that Ella had a deep number 11 cut

into her left hand and that they estimate she had died in the same time frame that Marika Martin had been taken. Those flowers, according to the delivery man, had been delivered around ten that morning but they had no way of estimating when the flowers had been relocated to the cemetery. Colvin can't help but wonder had they been led to the cemetery on purpose or was it just a nasty coincidence that they were both there at the same time? Did someone like Morkam or Barry Bulrush plant them knowing all eyes would be on Caleb? Did Caleb lead her purposely there to find them? Had the killer been in the graveyard the same time as them? Watching them, amused at how close they had been without even noticing until it was too late? Maybe that's why she wanted to be at the house so badly. She needs to see for her own eyes that there isn't another stupidly obvious taunt.

Instead it was "Go home Sam, you have a head wound." She is feeling fine now, a little numb more than anything. There is an angry bruise on her stomach, her hand is bandaged and she has four plasters on her legs but that head wound, for the record, wasn't as bad as it looked. It just stunned her that's all. She is still in better shape than Dalbiac, who people are already signing a 'Get Well Soon' card for. It will be a while before his bone fully heals.

She's fine, they would have kept her in the hospital longer if she wasn't. She is definitely better now she has had a nap, a snack and a pint of coffee. Home is too quiet, too peaceful and she's jumping with every loud noise whilst waiting for updates from Grimm who, for reference, isn't being as helpful as she would like. Se spent all day yesterday resting and now she really should be back at work doing everything she can to revisit Ella Tupper's last movements or trailing through the life of Marika Martin. If Amy Brown's death is an indicator then there is a suggestion that these kills are getting more personal. If this is the case there has to be something small to link them. Maybe the victims used the same dating website, frequented the same bar or the same gym for example? How can she rest when there is so much to do, so much that could be overlooked in those little details?

A memory tugs in her mind. There was a card, a business card. The one she found pinned to Aaron Fletcher's noticeboard and hasn't got round to following up on. Too many distractions recently. This could be a good time to have a little off the record, informal chat with the owner of that business card.

"This is a waste of time."

"You don't need to come in with me."

"That's good, because I have no intention to." As far as Grimm is concerned Colvin has until he finishes checking his emails and, if she is not back by then, he is driving off without her. He only called her to stop her whining texts and somehow that turned into agreeing to take her to see Ella Tupper's house and taking a quick detour to Manor Road first. It's not like he was getting anywhere today, so far all he has done is interview people who wanted to know more than they were willing to tell. He pulls out his phone as Colvin exits the car.

Colvin is inclined to agree with Grimm that this is a little stupid but then he has not seen some of the things she has seen lately. She shivers as she walks past a dilapidated house and checks the card again for the right address, worried for a moment that it might be this one. It is with a sigh of relief that she crosses the road and rings the doorbell of a more normal looking home.

The owner is a little surprised to see her and she wonders if maybe she should have called first but this is really just a last minute quick detour. Colvin introduces herself and asks if he is David Perron. When he nods a yes, she asks if she can have a quick chat with him. She is met with an eager smile and a "Of course. Come in! Come on in. Please call me Dave".

The first thing that Colvin notices is the sheer amount of books in Dave's living room. Everywhere she looks are books on serial killers, true crime, forensics, criminal profiling, criminal psychology and piles of papers everywhere. She is not surprised, Dave is trying to write a book about a serial killer after all. Colvin idly wonders what his other rooms are like.

"So," Dave rubs his hands together with an enthusiasm that Colvin hasn't seen in years. "How can I help?"

What Colvin really wants to do is censor him. Not in a dramatic way but he needs to tone things down and understand the damage he is causing to people like Caleb Bulrush, and how he is hindering their investigation. However she is also aware that this is a delicate request, one that needs to be handled very carefully (which is one of the reasons why she was pleased Grimm stayed in the car as diplomacy wasn't one of his strongest points.) She needs to lead into this gently, talk for a few minutes first and try to understand him as a person, maybe disarm any defences he has ready.

"I understand you are writing a book about the Numbers Killer."

He smiles, gesturing towards some chairs. "Come to ask me a few questions about your serial killer have you?" Colvin gingerly sits down thinking that this is probably a mistake and how she's almost certainly going to see an article about this later, gloating about how the police came to him pleading for help. Best to ask some really basic questions then make excuses and leave. She needs to be careful, she recognises this kind of keenness as an 'I will scratch your back if you scratch mine' situation. Chances are he will pry for 'off the record' information. She has already noticed him checking out her empty hands, disappointed she didn't bring him any crime scene photos to ponder over.

"And you are the creator of a website dedicated to talking about serial killers called ItCouldHaveBeenMe.co.uk?"

"Oh yes, are you on our forums?" Dave asks eagerly. Colvin settles for a brief nod as if to indicate she has merely glanced at it infrequently from time to time.

"A few months ago you received a letter from someone

216

signed BTY? You posted it on your site."

"Yes, it's upstairs, would you like to see it? I have been waiting for someone to ask about it." He pauses, cocking his head to one side. "I'm really interested in knowing what BTY could stand for."

"We think it could be initials."

"You don't think it might be an acronym?" Well yes, they do think that but she isn't going to tell him, playing dumb might hurt her pride but it is the safest option.

"You've heard of the BTK killer haven't you?" He doesn't even pause for a confirmation. "He was a serial killer active in Kansas from '74 to '91. The BTK stands for Bind, Torture, Kill. I have a few thoughts about what BTY could stand for." He quickly grabs a piece of paper off a pile without slowing down. Colvin is getting the feeling that Dave doesn't get the chance to talk to people offline very often and is eager to show off what he knows.

"Here's my suggestions." He takes a deep breath for dramatic emphasis. "Blind, Torture, Youth." He pauses as if expecting applause or perhaps even a hug and her eternal gratitude. Colvin doesn't want to point out that there is no evidence that any victim has been blinded, even temporarily.

"Bloody Tough Yielding." He must have hit the dictionary for that one.

"Bout To Yelp." It's possible but Colvin is not convinced.

"Blame the Y-chromosome." He is really scraping the barrel here.

"All good suggestions." She says carefully. "I will bear those in mind. Can I see the letter please?"

"Of course! I'll just be a few minutes." He darts out the room, Colvin hears him thundering up the stairs. She stands up and walks to the window, mostly to check that Grimm is still waiting for her and also to prove to him that she is still alive, not that he is even looking in her direction. Colvin isn't even sure that he saw which house she went into. Not that it matters, all she has to do is ask if she can have the letter and, more importantly, ask how he received it. Well it would have been important if she remembered to do this a few months back but there might be a few clues still there. She can send a team to talk to him about the website, one with more legal "cease and desist" warnings. She watches as a young girl runs past the dilapidated house, as if her life depends on it. Colvin can see the sheer fear in her eyes.

"That's Alexandra." A voice in her ear chuckles, surprising her, she didn't hear him thunder back down the stairs. "She thinks a monster lives in that house." Dave is standing a little too close for comfort, so close Colvin can see the tiny specks of blood on his glasses. Before she can react he hits her hard in her bruised stomach, knocking her down to the floor. Firm hands grip hers, pinning her down. "Do you know what's amazing about the internet? It can be used to connect like-minded gentlemen of shared interests, help them to find naughty young girls in need of a dire lesson from Daddy. Barry is a big believer in spare the rod, spoil the child as you may have already guessed. We have a little contest going on to see how many lessons we can teach. Currently Barry is winning but I reckon it would count for more if I killed a police officer. He will be so annoyed I got there before he did." He giggles as Colvin processes the words in her head, finally grasping his meaning. Then he hits her hard, banging her head back down to the floor, reopening her head wound.

"BTY stands for Better Than You, Bitch!"

His hands press tightly against her throat. Colvin's hands refuse to obey her, they struggle against the impossibly heavy weight, overloading with pain. She hears the front door bursting open and the heavy weight lifts itself in surprise.

"Sam?" A voice yells.

"Officer Grimm, how nice of you to join us." Dave's almost lovable dorkish manner has completely transformed now into something much more sinister. He waves a knife in the air in a welcome gesture. "I was just telling your colleague here about our little game. I think you will be interested in joining us. You will be able to get revenge against all these little bitches who have wronged you and we both know how those bitches have wronged you."

Dave watches as realisation spreads down Grimm's face, nodding with approval. Colvin shivers with terror. She can't form a sentence, she couldn't even fight one of them let alone two, especially not Grimm. Warm blood keeps trickling down her face, mixing with her tears. She cries with disbelief as Grimm motions for the knife and takes one step towards her.

CHAPTER EIGHTEEN

Fight or flight.
It all boils down to two types of people, the fighters and the cowards.
The powerful and the pleaders.
The rulers and the peasants.
Us and them.
Rule number one: Never be a pleader or a peasant.
Rule number two: Get them, don't let them get you.
Rule number three: Don't get sloppy.
Mostly importantly of all, if you get caught, don't even think about mentioning me. None of this plea-bargaining bullshit because I will make you regret the day you were born. What I did to them will be a mercy compared with what I will do to you. And you know no one will be there to protect you.

Donna trudges down her gravel driveway, her shopping heavy in her hands. She is tired and dying for a cup of tea. She jabs her key at the door, over and over, too anxious to get in and put her shopping down to pay attention. Something isn't right, her key is jamming against something. Annoyed she puts her bags down to look properly. Sellotape! Someone has covered her keyhole with Sellotape. Why would anyone do that? Of all the childish pranks... warning bells begin to ring in the dark depths of her memory and she fumbles at the keyhole in a panic. She needs to get inside fast, someone must be watching the house. No, she needs to get out of here and get help. Which bag had her phone in it? She is too busy searching to hear the second pair of feet crunching down her drive way, she is too bent over to see the shadow. She turns just in time to see the fist seconds before it connects against her head.

I smell the coconut in her hair and inhale deeply, savouring the scent. She doesn't notice, she is too busy crying and pleading, desperately trying to believe that I am capable of mercy.

Dave smiles, relishing the memory. He can't remember which woman that one was but what did it matter? There are ones he remembers more clearly like the girl who sneered at him, the girl who rejected him. Then that one who didn't trust him, but then made the mistake of panicking when he told her there was a spider in her hair, she lost all composure then, flailing, begging him to get it off, please, PLEASE! Giving him that perfect opportunity to grab and cut. She had been so wary yet so easy. They were all so easy.

And this is going to be easy as well. He has nothing to worry about it.

Grimm doesn't notice the small spot of dried blood on his wrist for hours. When he finally does he regards both with nonchalant curiosity and moves towards the bathroom. He scrubs his hands in the sink, checking his watch, shirt sleeves and fingernails very carefully for any other little spots. Eventually he turns off the tap, slowly drying his hands. He is just killing time now, waiting. Everything is being done for him and he has nothing else to do.

He didn't have the time to do the things he really wanted to do to Donna. She died too quickly but it was worth it. She had still recognised him, pleaded with him, bled for him. He had his revenge and she learnt a very valuable lesson. Dave had told him to choose someone today, told him where to take her, how to leave her, all nice and arranged. He doesn't like Dave telling him what to do but it had sounded like fun so he had agreed. He had even smiled at the joke as he carefully carved a 12 in Donna's hand, already looking forward to the next step of the plan. Dave was right about one thing, this game is ready to be taken up another notch. More teachers will be joining them. Each with their own particular skill set.

He can see police cars patrolling his special drop off spot. He frowns, pulling his van into a nearby road. He can drop off a less special delivery now and come back. He will bring Donna back here later or perhaps just dump her elsewhere. He isn't that worried; he won't get stopped, he never gets stopped, they all know who he is. Just an honest widower trying to make a living during some really trying times.

Adrian hasn't said anything for days. His father has been too exhausted too noticed, too preoccupied with Caleb and struggling with too many issues and not enough hours. Adrian spends most of his day just watching. Watching the world watching him, continuously running his hand over the bandage and the wound that is supposed to be healing but feels like it is growing. The reminder that the world hates him, wants to hurt him, the cut caused by the exploding glass. The Doctors said it would heal, that it would become a barely noticeable scar hidden under his hairline and that he won't notice it. But Adrian knows he will always remember. It burns just like his mother's last kiss, a constant reminder for what has been lost.

What happens now? He can't just forget what they did and they won't forget those lies, those that they still believe to be true. Sooner or later someone is going to throw another physical or metaphorical brick at him so he needs to be ready to throw one back. Until then, all he can do is watch and wait and inwardly burn.

Dave is tired of waiting, tired of remembering the good times. He is still angry but is trying to appear calm. It has been hours since that Colvin bitch turned up at his door. He hadn't expected her this early, another week or so, then he would have been ready, would have lured her like he lured that Drake bitch. The bitches are only supposed to move at his command, the pawns die quickly and quietly, the rooks and the bishops require more time and most importantly of all, no one touches the King! Just who the fuck do they think they are?

Initially he'd been impressed, wondering why she had come, what she knew about his website, thinking perhaps she might just be another one of his 'groupies.' He had thought she was stupid enough to come alone and that was his mistake. He had her all ready for a little game, then everything changed. He didn't expect Grimm to come barging in. He should have locked the door, he should have checked the area more carefully before inviting the bitch in. He should have probed her carefully, made sure she was alone, stupid fucking rookie error. He of all people should not have made such a stupid mistake.

Grimm should have accepted his offer too. All that work destroying his reputation online and for what? The stupid git to refuse him? Him? No one refuses him. All his other recruits had accepted, some more than eagerly. Grimm had been tempted, you could see he was, that's why he'd handed over the knife. He should have kept it, should have tested the little shit more carefully but no, he was caught up too much in what he was going to do to that little bitch, what fun he was going to have, he didn't stop to think and that's what got him arrested. Grimm should have realised what a good offer it was. Grimm would regret it later when those bitches were whining at him again. Eventually Grimm will crack. Maybe he'll even beg Dave for a second chance, a chance to do what is right, then Dave will smile and repay him in full for that painful arrest. He doesn't give anyone a second chance.

Dave leans back in his chair trying to calm himself by thinking more good thoughts, remembering those good times, those little looks of fear, those last chokes of breath. This isn't going to be the last of him. He knows he can talk his way out of this just like he knows the police ARE that stupid and can be manipulated just as easily as his victims. All he needs is a half decent explanation for why Marika was in his car. That's presuming that they bother to search his car. Maybe they won't search that hard, it all depends on what they think they have on him and why that bitch turned up at his door in the first place. She had wanted the letter, that's all. He can still control this situation, everything still has a plausible explanation. He didn't attack that bitch. She'd tripped herself on purpose to incriminate him for no good reason. Yes, that's a good one, she did it on purpose to set up him and draw the attention away from her partner. No, better yet, they incriminated him to protect their boss. Dave is just an innocent victim in all of this, they planted all that evidence at his house. He was brutally attacked by two officers in his own home! For no good reason. He sits back, mentally writing out a very carefully worded article. He will write an article detailing his poor treatment, his wrongful arrest and how he is being attacked because he dared criticised the police. He has thousands of followers now on his website who will help him spread the outrage.

There will be a huge campaign! More angry letters will be written, emails angrily typed with one finger by his followers, his recruits who will not stand for this indecency towards such a hardworking man. By the time he has finished no one will believe he even thought about killing one woman and he is certainly not capable of personally torturing and killing ten women. Not him.

It will be over as soon as he gets a television interview. One chance to talk in a friendly and approachable way and, with some practice, he might be able to come over as vulnerable, respectful and shy without laughing. He will have them all believing his innocence, then one little rousing speech and they will be protesting for him, demanding his freedom. People always trust him, always believe him. No one will even believe that someone called Dave could be a serial killer. It is one of those sacred names, like Bob or Andy, a name that promotes trust. No one called Dave could possibly be dangerous.

Just get him to a computer or just one reporter and he will

be out of here before the police knew what hit them.

Fried. That's the best way to describe Grimm's brain right now, fried and extra crispy. These last few days… how can he even begin to describe them? First, starting a few days ago with the graveyard, fuck knows what happened there. How did his partner always manage to get caught up in the most random of occurrences? He had warned her to stay away from that kid but no, she had to follow him, alone. Somehow that led to him having to go to another house of hell, find another … destroyed victim and whilst he was still trying to process that, Colvin somehow, despite looking like a walking corpse, managed to get herself discharged from the hospital and also convinced him to do her one tiny little favour. Whilst he was waiting in the car the news came in that another woman had been abducted and he had gone inside the house to tell Colvin they had to go, only to find her bleeding on the floor with a guy he has never seen before towering over her with a knife and offering him the chance to really make his partner bleed.

No, thank you. Despite what they say, Grimm is not that kind of person.

That look Colvin gave him before she passed out, that hurt. That look that guy gave him when he gestured for the knife, so sure that Grimm was about to join him, that really sickened him. It had felt so good to grab that knife, that wrist and arrest him. At that point Grimm didn't even know why he was arresting him, he just grabbed and let his training take over. Assault on a fellow officer, that would do, enough to hold him, give Grimm enough time to find out what the fuck was going on. Then all that time, waiting for back up, for an ambulance, torn between restraining that guy and helping Colvin. All the while the twat was struggling and screaming 'You will regret this' like a demented movie villain.

He had wanted to leave the house after that, they had no reason to stay, but Colvin just wouldn't go. She wouldn't even let the paramedics touch her until she spoke to him, trembling, blood pouring down her face, looking like she was barely clinging on. She told him that there were two of them.

Two of them? Two of what? Two knife wielding maniacs in the house? He, like an idiot, told her he would search the property. She was unconscious again before he had even finished speaking. He should have just ignored Colvin and joined the hunt for the missing woman instead of staying to search.

The missing woman, Donna Stewart, had gone missing at around 9:30am. Neighbours had reported hearing muffled shrieks and had rushed out to help just in time to see a white van driving rapidly driving away and Donna's shopping strewn on her driveway. In the last six hours they have stopped and searched over thirty white vans but there has been no sign of Donna.

As Donna had gone missing before David Perron attacked Colvin, no one thought Perron was anything more than an aggressive idiot. Colvin didn't tell him why she wanted to go to that house, she'd just muttered something about a website and asking a few questions. They thought they were searching his house for another attacker and so Grimm had idly stepped into the garage, not expecting to see someone sitting in the front passenger seat of the car. A woman, patiently waiting to be taken on one last ride, destination unknown.

He tapped on the window without thinking, preparing himself for a confrontation but she didn't move. He tapped again louder, verbally identifying himself as the police, attracting the attention of another police officer, but she still didn't move. He knelt down to take a good look through the window, taking note of the passenger's purple hair, purple lipstick, purple bow tied around her neck, closed eyes, defeated slump in posture. It didn't take a genius to figure out something wasn't right. He tried the car door, locked. He stepped back to meet the horrified gaze of the other officer.

"Isn't that Marika Martin?"

One small search of the house later and they found David Perron's car keys. One longer search of the house later and they found photos, Amy Brown's hair-slide and other mementos, things they didn't even know where missing, displayed proudly on the walls like hunting trophies. Dave never suspected anyone would ever have reason to enter certain rooms and never saw any point in hiding what he had done. Even his knifes are here, all clean and freshly sharpened. As one Forensic team worked to slowly extract Marika Martin from David Perron's car, another worked to slowly extract Cathy Clark from his freezer.

Police are still moving around the house with stunned expressions, searching through his numerous books, writings and, most importantly of all, his computer. They keep talking excitedly about some website that David created. Grimm didn't really understand what they are on about and made his excuses to retreat back to the station. He spent six hours in David Perron's house and he had seen enough.

It was six hours then before he noticed that speck of blood on his wrist. He washed it off without thinking, preoccupied with other things, then immediately regretted it. In a weird way it felt like Colvin was still with him, still helping to oversee everything.

"Fuck that stupid twat and fuck his stupid plans!" He thought as he pushed Donna out of the van and on to some random street, driving off before she had even bounced off the ground. Bitch had caused him more trouble than she was even worth. He is in a foul mood now, a dangerous mood. He heard about an arrest on the radio so he drove past Dave's street, just to be sure. Even though he couldn't actually turn into the street he saw enough, enough to confirm that the stupid bastard had been caught. Now he is thinking he never should have trusted that little shit, never should have allowed Dave to join him. Should have gone with his first instinct and just killed the bastard when he had the chance. Did the little shit try to set him up earlier? Is that why the police

were waiting in his planned spot?

What had he told the little shit before? *"If you get caught, don't even think about mentioning me. None of this plea-bargaining bullshit, because I will make you regret the day you were born."* What an empty threat that was if the little shit was hiding behind walls of police. Maybe he is over-reacting though? Maybe Dave will talk his way out of this? He clutches the steering wheel in frustration, trying to think. The only link between them that he can think of is his mobile phone. Digging it from his pocket he throws it out of the window and proceeds to drive over it back and forth, crunching it out of existence.

What else? If they go to his home what will they find? Nothing and he left nothing in the van either, it's all in his car now ready to be dumped and replaced. Even if Dave dared to give them his name they won't find anything else, they might not even believe him for that matter. But they will probably be watching him, just in case and that means, although he might be free, he won't be able to have any more fun.

And he really likes having fun.

He has money, he has his car and he has his knife. He can still go on. Go on for a few more months even, maybe a year. He can still settle a few last scores and have some fun on the way. It is not over yet.

Colvin doesn't know what their problem is. She spent last night in hospital, the doctors have given her the all clear again and she has rested so what exactly are they wanting from her?? Yes, privately she will admit that her head is still banging but it is a steady beat of pain, she has ignored worse. There is no need for them to keep attempting to send her home, certainly no need for Juda's comment that she should have never gone to David Perron's house in the first place as she was supposed to be recuperating. That led to a very tense stand-off for a few awkward moments, neither of them willing to stand down. The more they try to push her to leave, the more she wants to stay. Colvin knows that she owes Juda one but, at the same time, it is none of his damn business. He got to be the hero already, now it's her turn.

She wonders how differently things might have gone if she had followed up that business card weeks ago? How many women might have survived and how differently things might be now, if she hadn't of glanced at Fletcher's notice board, hadn't had noticed the distinctive logo for ItCouldHaveBeenMe.co.uk? She wouldn't have even recognised it if she had never looked at the stupid website in the first place. And that stupid domain name, itcouldhaveme.co.uk, how long has David had that one registered? How long has he been planning this for? He must have been laughing for weeks over it.

It amazes her sometimes how the most unlikely things can lead to someone's downfall, like noticing a sleeve, visiting a website, stopping the wrong car or just not ducking in time. The tiniest detail can end everything.

The others can deal with David Perron now, she is still grimacing at the thought of his twisted smile and swinging fist. She has heard about Marika Martin, found in his car with a bow around her neck and a 10 in her right hand. She doesn't feel a glimmer of satisfaction knowing that she was right about the numbers or that Cathy Clark had been found with a 5 in her right hand. She can't feel anything, not one bit of pride, until the person responsible for the left hand numbers is caught. The more violent, aggressive of the two. "Barry"

What was said before? "Barry is a big believer in spare the rod, spoil the child as you may have already guessed." That unguarded sentence is haunting her, that little slip of a name. David Perron had slipped up there, gloating to someone he didn't expect to survive. She has to find Barry and she can do that without even leaving her desk. Soon she will have a list of every Barry who lives in the city and a second list of everyone with Barry as a middle name. Unless she misheard and he actually said Larry or Gary. Maybe he did say Gary? Oh damn it!

Jenna's hands shake spilling driblets of coffee on her desk. She tuts with irritation, wiping up the spillage with her sleeve. Doesn't matter, no one is going to see her today anyway. She is annoyed as it has been nearly a day and ItCouldHaveBeen-Me.co.uk STILL hasn't been updated! What are they playing at? She needs to know what's going on! What were all those sirens yesterday? Have they found Marika yet? Are the rumours true, has another woman gone missing??? Has anyone replied to any of her comments? She needs to know! Why have there been no updates??

She hits the refresh button again only to find the site is now completely down! Can this day get any worse? Well, she can't spend all day just sitting here. Maybe she should go to the gym, work off some of this nervous energy? Maybe someone there will be able to give her an update, there is always someone there who knows something new.

She changes into some slightly less stained gym clothes, pulling a hoodie on top. She is about to leave as someone knocks on her door. That's odd, she isn't expecting anyone. It's probably a charity collector or doors sales, someone she doesn't want to interact with. If she waits, they'll probably go away. She pauses and can hear someone talking into a radio. Then the knocking starts again with more urgency this time. Startled, she opens the door without thinking, forgetting to check the spyhole.

Oh fuck.

She recognises one of the men instantly, his photos have been posted so many times on ItCouldHaveBeenMe.co.uk and always with a warning. Not a man that should ever be let inside your home. What does she do now? It's too late to pretend she is not home. She can't slam the door in their faces and she can't call the police because they are the fucking police. Oh fuc...

No one was really congratulating Colvin, Grimm has been trying not to take any credit, but still, the congratulations were only begrudgingly offered. There are mutterings too, ones that abruptly stop when he is in earshot. No one thinks Colvin should be sat at her desk right now and Grimm does agree with that but he knows that the only reason Morkam isn't sending Colvin home is because Morkam has seen some of the rambling notes on David Perrons computer and knows for certain that Perron was not working alone. They also know that he was planning something big with someone, someone they are now expecting to panic and do something stupid. Time is not on their side.

They found Donna Stewart soon after she was dumped, one team is already out interviewing, searching for eyewitnesses and CCTV, every white van is to be stopped today, every single one.

It had been a night of revelations and they are not completely in the dark anymore. They know now that David Perron was a part time taxi driver, they had even interviewed him as he was the one who drove Natalie Ivanovich home. However, given that his car tracker showed him immediately leaving after dropping her off, to respond to another call, they never considered him to be a suspect.

They know Mary Angus, Priya Smythe and Kate Drake were all once active members on ItCouldHaveBeenMe.co.uk. That David Perron somehow was able to find out their contact information and use it to stalk them. They are still going through his "observation" notes but they suspect that certain victims may have been chosen purely because they lived near certain 'suspects' or males who could be easily manipulated to look like suspects. People like Aaron Fletcher and Caleb Bulrush. They have seen the notes observing "J-Girl-Down" or Jenna Dow and, as a precaution, Juda has been sent to offer her protective custody and the strong advice to change her passwords immediately.

They know that David had several different aliases on ItCouldHaveBeenMe.co.uk which he used to support certain arguments, to post incriminating testimonies and to implicate the previously mentioned "suspects". For example he had been the one who took the photo of Caleb Bulrush 'following' Marika Martin. He even used some of the aliases to contact various victims' families, to pump them for information and to point them in wrong directions. They don't know for certain as they are still going through the website but Grimm strongly suspects that the other killer might also be an active user. Grimm has also seen the content posted about himself and is seriously not impressed. Finally though, he has an answer for why certain "friends" suddenly became so cold to him.

All of this because of one business card! Grimm wonders if Fletcher had looked at the website, had seen the content posted about himself? Whether he too was 'approached' to join Dave? Grimm tries to remember, did Fletcher give up that business card without hesitation? Or with a knowing smirk? Perhaps it is a double bluff, perhaps he is the second killer? Colvin is insisting that Dave said the other killer is called Barry, but Colvin also has a pretty bad head injury...

"Tell me about Barry."

Finally they are talking to him. They are not asking the questions he wants them to ask but he can work with this, oh yes, he can work with this. Dave leans back in his chair with a big grin.

"Barry Bulrush? What do you want to know?"

He never should have said Barry's name out loud before, he knows that now. He should have waited until he had the bitch down in the cellar, waited until she was at the point she was about to pass out from the pain. She was supposed to be alone, she acted like she was alone, it wasn't fair!

"Is he the one you have been working with?"

"Yes." They don't believe him at first but he can see the doubt already creeping in. Maybe he is telling them the truth. It's just amazing the people you can find online, what you can find out about their children and just where that can lead. He stares hard at the officers but he doesn't recognise them. He is annoyed

232

he doesn't have someone more important interviewing him. He hasn't waited around all night just for nobodies! He is also annoyed that Grimm hasn't made another appearance. He knows he can still get into Grimm's head, knows he can still cause doubts, he smiles again knowingly.

Maybe he should give Barry up. It would be a kindness to him. Barry will be so lost without him, Dave had to teach him about the importance of wearing gloves for starters. Barry doesn't quite understand how to be discreet either. Dave is the one who comes up with the ideas, like carving the numbers on the hands. It was such a great idea too, a homage to their inspiration and a way of wasting precious police time, such a classic misdirection and it's one he can continue to exploit. He bets no one has even figured out its meaning yet.

When the time is right he won't hesitate to let it be known that he is willing to be helpful in return for a more lenient sentence. If he waits a little while, Barry is certain to do something stupid and they might become desperate, more open to certain demands. He can still say that he was only an observer, it was Barry who went too far. Yes, he likes that, he can definitely say that it was Barry who killed all those poor girls, he was coerced, too afraid to stop him. These idiots won't know any better, they will believe him. People always trust him.

CHAPTER NINETEEN

I had to teach my daughter a lesson, spare the rod, spoil the child and she was a very spoilt child. It is my duty to teach other spoilt little girls the same lesson.

Many years ago, Nic's father told her to always walk with her head held high. At the time, she had dismissed her father's advice, seriously what did he know? He died before she understood what he had been trying to teach her, victims walk with their heads down, easy prey walk with a little sheepish shuffle. If you stride, head held high, refusing to move off course and don't smile, not only will you see what's really going on, but also people will know not to fuck with you.

She noticed him within seconds. Even recognised him from the news. She can remember thinking that he looked just like the kind of man, who would purposely frequent a store, waiting for that moment when the youngest member of staff was there, working alone. Just so he could intimidate that staff member into giving them a refund or spend twenty minutes loudly complaining about things that staff member had nothing to do with, just to see them squirm uncomfortably and simper apologies. She really really hates that kind of man. She also remembers thinking, she wouldn't want to meet him alone on a dark night and here they are, it might not be dark yet but it's getting there. It is in her best interests not to make eye contact and to move away as quickly as she can, because whilst this man is not a murderer, he looks like he is looking for one.

Ruby William's father walks purposely down the deserted street, head held high, eyes constantly searching, crunching discarded drink cans down hard as he walks over them, not noticing what lies beneath his feet, striding towards the darkness of Kings Park, unaware that he is being followed.

He is thinking, as usual, of the day after his daughter died. Fourteen times he tried calling her mobile, waiting impatiently, first angrily, but as the morning went on, becoming more frantic, waiting for a voice to answer, waiting to hear why she didn't come home last night, waiting for something but getting nothing. Finally, swallowing his pride and calling the police, finally admitting to someone that his daughter had fallen in with a bad crowd, that she was going through a phrase, working through those issues brought on by her mother's abandonment and he was concerned, could they please help?

He walks deeper into the park, somewhere around here, about here.

Nic lost sight of Mr Williams somewhere in the trees, she is not great at following people and had been somewhat slowed down by the realisation that she was standing close to where at least three victims had died. She shouldn't have anything to fear, she had heard on the news that they had apprehended the bastard and she doesn't believe in ghosts.

But, as a gust of winds rattles a few more empty crisp packets, as the coldness creeps in, she convinces herself that she can feel their sad eyes watching her, silently pleading with her to be put to rest, pleading with her to run before it's too late. Spooked, she turns around, intending to leave as warm fingers press hard into her neck.

Nic struggles against the tight grip, flailing wildly, her hands scratching against those that held her tight, trying to draw the breath to scream but only managing a choke. In response the hands pull tighter, with a chuckle, then loosen. She tries to react as a strong fist connects hard against a face.

Colvin didn't expect there to be so many Barrys in the city, so many men with Barry as a first name, others with Barry as a middle name. Then there were surnames and their variations, Barry, Barries, etc. So many Larrys and Garys too.

So many names she already recognises, like Barry Jones and Craig Barrie, Cathy Clark's ex-boyfriends. Micheal Barry, a suspect from the original Numbers cases, oh please don't be him, please don't let the other officers be right. Her head is aching badly now, she wants to go home but she doesn't want to. She won't admit this to anyone else but she is afraid too. She is the one responsible for the arrest of David Perron, and even though David Perron hasn't been given a chance to communicate with anyone except a lawyer, she wouldn't put it past him to get revenge of some kind, she is not safe to go home until the partner is arrested. But maybe, she will have to watch her back for years to come now, he will find a way to manipulate someone... No, concentrate on the task at hand, comparing her Barry lists with the lists of those registered as an owner of a white van. Which list had those names on? She knocks over another pile of paperwork, eyewitness testimonies from those who last saw Ella Tupper alive. She needs to put these back, someone was looking for these earlier and she had sworn she hadn't seen them. She glances at them, she needs to put them back into order first, the testimony from the flowers delivery driver should be on the bottom of the pile not the top, she freezes, recognising the name of the driver, Barry W- oh shit.

Fourteen times he called, in the beginning he was angry, so angry, his own daughter a shameless whore. He soon taught her that the world has no place for whores.

Fourteen times he called, slowly calming down, even feeling tinges of excitement knowing that she wouldn't answer. She will never disgrace him again. Neither will her stupid friend. Neither would his wife. No more would he be held back by those disgraces, not by people like Donna Stewart either. Not this little girl, why was she following him? What does she know? All he needs to do is apply the right amount of pressure, in the right place and she will tell him everything. He smiles, everything he wants to hear.

Barry Williams recoils as a different fist slams hard into his face, catching him off guard. He lets the girl drop down to the floor, to be dealt with later, turning his attention to this new challenger. Another fucking woman, all these little bitches are just falling at his feet today. He draws back his fist, readying for his next important lesson, as a burning pain erupts in his lower body, as her next kick connects hard against his testicles, knocking the breath right out of him. Then comes another kick, as someone behind him kicks him hard into the back of his knee, a scream chokes in his throat, tears burn in his eyes.

"Stay down." A female voice orders. No, it doesn't end like this. He is not going to let a fucking woman end him. He struggles against the pain, to rise back up, his hand moving to his waist for his knife. Fuck it, he can take them all on, he thinks, as another blow connects against his head.

CHAPTER TWENTY

Do you think you are safe now?
Some of us, as you will know, we like to take our time, we don't rush. We like to enjoy the moment. We don't make stupid mistakes, we take things nice and slow. And you know what? Walker, Perron, Williams, they may have brought us together but they are nothing compared to us. We really are Better Than You.

Alexandra doesn't know what kind of monster a Colvine is, but it doesn't really matter, because her Daddy is going to get it. Erase it from this earth for what it did. She doesn't know what Colvine did or who Barry is, but she knows he is an idiot. Her daddy has said so, in angry muffled tones, so many times over. Bit it didn't matter, it is not going to stop them from continuing the good work.

Alexandra hopes they are going to do something nice. Maybe she can help them with their good work.

AFTERWORD

At the time of writing, ItCouldHaveBeenMe.co.uk was not a real website.

Let's leave it that way.

Printed in Great Britain
by Amazon